T0159046

BETTERTON

JOSEPH JOHN SZYMANSKI

iUniverse, Inc.
New York Bloomington

BETTERTON

iUniverse books may be ordered through booksellers or by contacting:

iUniverse
1663 Liberty Drive
Bloomington, IN 47403
www.iuniverse.com
1-800-Authors (1-800-288-4677)

ISBN: 978-1-4401-7771-2 (sc)
ISBN: 978-1-4401-7772-9 (ebk)

Printed in the United States of America

iUniverse rev. date: 9/29/2009

PREFACE

"Betterton" starts out as a story of a small town on the upper Chesapeake Bay at the mouth of the Sassafras River in Kent County, Maryland. From a historical standpoint, around 1850 Richard Turner, a Quaker, moved his family from Baltimore and purchased a parcel of land from Edward Crew, including a wharf called Crew's Landing. In 1860 Turner named the Bay side hamlet after the maiden name of his wife Elizabeth. His family eventually built a mill and warehouse for shipping products, mostly seafood and produce such as corn, soybean and peaches harvested locally via steamboat ferry to Baltimore, Philadelphia, and Wilmington. When incorporated in 1906, Betterton supposedly prospered with dozens of restaurants, hotels, amusement arcades, a gambling hall, shops, and a sandy beach for tourists who wanted to escape the summer heat and humidity of big cities, especially Baltimore. A ferry service between Baltimore and Betterton thrived until the Chesapeake Bay Bridge was completed in 1952, and afterwards, people traveled by car everywhere and made Ocean City their primary beach resort destination.

The ferry is long gone, and Betterton has slipped gradually into a sleepy hamlet spread over about one square mile. It appears that the townsfolk have little interest in commercial or residential development. The town has no hotels, motels, restaurants, grocery stores, nor filling stations. There's not even a cafe where anyone can meet for a beer, cup of coffee or ice cream sundae. Less than 10 percent of members of its 100 families living there have college degrees. But Betterton's beach, a 300-foot long sandy playpen on the Chesapeake Bay, is generally free of sea nettles, and remains the main attraction.

Today information over the Internet includes statements about a renaissance occurring in Betterton, which is wishful thinking. From the author's viewpoint Betterton is still a town unchanged, and everyone likes it that way. The sleepy hamlet has remained almost as it has existed for a couple of generations, and the few families living there all year round refuse to waiver despite the needs of future generations.

But change is coming. It's just around the corner, unexpected and significant, because, blowing in from Baltimore, is a rich, handsome, talented, and ambitious 26-year old former Navy SEAL Lieutenant. Could he be the unknowing instigator of a renaissance there?

While this novel is essentially a tale of two towns, Betterton and its neighbor Rock Hall, the author has altered the names of real people, locations, and events. Any resemblance of characters in this story to persons living or dead is entirely coincidental.

One final comment here: As you probe deeper into this book, you will eventually discover that "Betterton" is more than a story about one or two towns and the people currently living there. Betterton is a way of life or state of mind or psychological complex, something like an itch that suddenly makes you want to scratch it, or a sick feeling in your stomach from something bad that you've experienced, or better yet, a moment when you see a sign flash across your mind that says, "YOU CAN BE SOMETHING BETTER THAN YOU ARE."

ACKNOWLEDGEMENT

This book is published with contributions from the following friends: The first is Paul Gregory, legendary agent and producer, who managed, in his own words, "to plow through" one of the early revisions, gave it a "Heads Up," and suggested the possibility of transforming it into a television series. ...The second is Dr. Ellsworth Boyd, a colleague at Washington College, who was a steady wind behind my sails, helping to reset my compass, and guiding me with advice and encouragement... The third is the late Gordon Beard, whom I've never met but used words from his humorous pronunciation guide "Basic Baltimorese," to give certain persons in this book a colorful Damon Runyonesque speech. Finally and most importantly are Stanley and Elle Piotrowski, Rudolf Veltman, Joseph Buron, Richard Parlow, and Mike McGrath who provided valuable regenerative feedback designed to make this novel something special...Oh, I almost forgot to thank Andy Musser for being Andy Musser, the best friend God ever put on this earth. And I would be remiss if I failed to acknowledge the inspiration from my late wife Renate and support from my brothers Tom and Frank and their spouses. My sincere gratitude is extended to everyone specified above, with the hope that "BETTERTON" will meet their expectations. Joseph J. Szymanski.

CHAPTER 1

It's the dawn of a new day, the first Monday in September, as the early morning sun glitters off the foamy waves of the Chesapeake Bay. The waves slap one another and roll inward towards each shore. The turbo-shaft engine of a Black Hawk helicopter roars like a Boeing 747 warming up on a runway. The blades of its rotors whip the air above the Bay and give the copter plenty of lift and thrust to propel it anywhere at speeds up to 200 miles per hour. The identification "BLUE ANGEL 329" is stenciled on both sides of the exterior frame in glossy black paint over a base layer of camouflage. The pilot is outfitted in a bright orange aviator's suit with shiny silver captain bars on his lapel and wears an unusually large helmet with electronic mics extending to his mouth like two straws bent in a cup. Tinted goggles, the kind skiers wear on snowy ski slopes, completely cover his eyes until he moves them to his forehead and blares out in a southern accent, "Captain Grant calling Flight Control." He pauses and lowers his voice, "Blue Angel three-two-niner approaching eastern shore of Murlin and entering the Chesspeek Bay…finally."

A female voice behind him says with a chuckle, "Would I be out of line if I said you're talking through your hat, Captain? I mean, with all that audio gear attached to your helmet. Aren't you feeling a little heavy headed?"

The pilot laughs as his body shakes a little inside his loose fitting suit, and acknowledges, "Heavy headed or hatted? No, I'm feeling like a million dollars after taxes. What a gorgeous day to be over the Chesspeek Bay, Major."

The rays of the sun reflect off his captain bars again onto the instrument console with all its electronic dials, meters, gauges and switches, only two feet from his face. He glances towards the middle of the console at the gas gauge that indicates full capacity and the altimeter with its white arrow twitching at 1,000 feet. Within the next 10 seconds the copter moves steadily inward across Maryland's eastern seaboard, as Captain Grant accelerates his copter upward. He talks into his helmet mic, "Blue Angel three-two-niner… elevating from 1,000 to 2,000 feet, approaching the Chesspeek Bay Bridge and hurtling over the double spans."

As the copter crosses over the second span, its silver-colored girders begin to shimmer in the direct sunlight. Sitting behind and to the right of the pilot is a stunning dark-haired 27 year old woman dressed in a light blue two piece business suit. A small gold-plated oak leaf is pinned to one lapel and a badge pinned to her upper pocket identifies her as "Major Liz Carter, Pentagon Special Forces." Because of her small aluminum-framed seat wrapped with canvas, something resembling a beach chair, her tight fitting skirt seems to have a mind all its own, and with each bounce of the copter, the hemline crawls slowly upward, exposing more of her thighs than she would like.

She looks repeatedly at her Rolex, calculating the time and location of the flight. From her purse she removes a small mirror and lipstick, and attempts to apply a touch to her lips just as unexpected gusts lift the copter upward. Her hand holding the lipstick is swept halfway up the side of one cheek. She bellows out, "It would be nice if you'd give me some warning of upcoming turbulence."

"Major, you should've taken a cab from Dover to Wilmington and caught the Metroliner heading north to New York."

"That was my original plan, Captain, but when I heard you're flying to Bawlmer, I decided to hitch a ride with you. I was raised in Bawlmer, and this is the first time I've ever seen the Chesspeek Bay from the air. I'm in no hurry to get to New York as long as I get there by 10 pm."

"Do you know what's aboard besides you?"

"Yes, I met the Honor Guard, Captain Kasoff, who was transferring a coffin from the cargo plane at Dover Air Force Base to the rear compartment of this Black Hawk."

"This operation is called Angel Flight. We're bringing home a fallen warrior, a comrade who was killed in Iraq. His family will meet us at the Inner Harbor. From there, they'll take him on a ferry for his last ride across the Chesspeek Bay for burial in Betterton."

Liz declares, "The road to victory is paved with men and women who gave their lives for our country." She pauses to look again at her watch, and continues, "I don't mean to be callous, Captain, just grateful that you gave me permission after clearance from Colonel J.R. Spencer, my boss at the Pentagon. If I don't catch the Metroliner at Penn Station in Bawlmer, I can easily take the intercity train. It runs every hour on the hour. No big deal."

Captain Grant turns around to get a better look at Liz. "It's nice to have you on board this morning, Major," he says in a baritone voice.

"It's a pleasure to hitch a ride with you this morning, Captain."

He asks, "Are you involved in Iraq?"

"As a matter of fact, I'm on my way to New York to interview some applicants for surveillance work over there."

Grant lowers the altitude of the copter to 1,000 feet again, and the turbulent winds calm considerably. The copter proceeds on a course that the compass registers North by Northwest as Liz glances out her side window to see the shoreline of the Bay. He gazes at the compass and says to no one in particular, "North by Northwest…Wish I could've taken Hitchcock on a helicopter ride to Mt. Rushmore."

"You must be a movie buff, Captain…to remember that Hitchcock thriller."

No. I just like Hitchcock and the suspense and thrills he injects into his films."

She says, "Well, I'm delighted that the flight is steady again. Thank you, Captain, That's more like it. My name is Liz Carter." She brags facetiously and continues, "At the Pentagon, they call me Liz, the Biz Wiz. I don't know whether or not that's a compliment."

Captain Grant continues, "Well, Major, I promised to get you to Bawlmer, alive and all in one piece, didn't I?"

"That's precisely what you promised me, Captain, but promises are one thing, control is another, and sometimes, control is uncontrollable."

She pauses and stretches her head towards the window, and says, "I see the Eastern Neck Wildlife Refuge and Rock Hall coming up on our right side...and farther up is Betterton, but you can't see it from here. It's probably another 24 miles."

He smiles and says, "We're turning leftward now and the Patapsico River's coming up on our left side."

Captain Grant lowers the copter to 500 feet, where both occupants can see the entrance to the Potapsco River. With relative ease he steers his copter leftward and moves to the center of the river, and close enough to see almost every detail of the gold and red colored autumn leaves and white shingles on the porch-front houses lining the shore.

He turns partly around in his seat again and tells her, "It won't be long now. We're passing Bethum Steel at Sparis Point on your right. See those giant towers belching a few puffs of smoke from the steel mills. That's Sparis Point all right. My father often told me stories about those Bessemer furnaces in war time, in the 1940's. He said you could see from 20 miles away the nighttime glow and blow of those hot exhaust gases coming out of those smokestacks. A lot of steel went into those Liberty ships, and most of it came from Bethum Steel." He pauses to gaze again at the speed indicator on the copter console.

"I'm enjoying every word, Captain. Like I said before, I was born and raised in Bawlmer, and never grow tired of hearing 'bout its history."

"On the left, we're approaching Locuss Point, with the historic Fort McHenry, the massive Domino sugar refinery and sign, and two marine terminals for giant cargo ships."

Within seven minutes Captain Grant maneuvers his copter over the target pad of the Inner Harbor heliport, where water ends and concrete begins. When the wheels of Blue Angel three-two-niner touch down, Captain Grant turns off the engine and walks around the copter to open the door for Liz, and asks, "Did you say your name was Major Liz Carter? I didn't even have time to log you in this morning."

She answers, "That's right. You sure kept your word about getting me here safe and sound." With a touch of levity, she taps the top of his aviator's helmet like a Queen knighting a subject, and says, "Captain Grant. I appoint you "Tops of Props!" A second later Liz turns, stands at attention, and holds her salute as the pilot takes a few steps and reaches for the rear door of the Black Hawk helicopter.

Four middle age men, from a local mortuary, dressed in black suits, rush and stand by the helicopter as Captain Grant opens the rear door. First stepping out of the helicopter is Army Captain Harvey Kasoff, senior ranking officer of the deceased soldier's service branch. Kasoff gives the four men permission to remove the coffin, draped with the American Flag.

Following Kasoff, they walk with precision, slowly and solemnly, to a ferry moored nearby where a special ramp has been lowered for them to carry the coffin onto the ferry for placement in a private compartment concealed from the public. The ferry's ultimate destination is the small town of Betterton, a two hour trip down the Potapsco River and across the Chesapeake Bay.

After the coffin reaches the bottom deck of the ferry, Liz sighs and lowers her salute. She quickly surveys the area and locates the taxi stand about 100 feet away from the helipad. She walks hurriedly past tug boats and fishing trawlers tied up to piers.

A fisherman stands in front of his trawler, points to a display of fresh fish evenly spaced on a bed of ice, all resting on a wheel barrel, and hollers over to her, "Hey little lady, how 'bout some fresh fish for lunch today?"

Liz waves him off with a smile, then hears the captain standing in front of his tug boat holler, "How 'bout a cruise this afternoon or evening to Paradise?"

Shaking her head from side to side and wagging her index finger out like a teacher scolding a student, Liz continues to walk briskly towards the taxi stand just as a bright yellow one screeches to the curb and out jumps a family with some kids.

The father confronts Liz, and asks her where to find the charter boats. She listens, but the sudden blare of automobile horns forces her to spin his body a quarter turn, point out the direction, and gently nudge him along to charters moored at the piers. She runs a few steps and jumps in the back seat of the waiting taxi. She bounces about a foot into the air.

She laughs and utters, "What's your name, driver?"

"You can call me Harry," he tells her while looking in his rear view mirror.

"Well Harry, get me to Penn Station as fast as you can, and I'll make it worth your while."

Harry quickly drives away from the curb and moves his taxi onto Pratt Street going south, and tells her without any prompting, "The old central fish market used to be on our left side, where watermen brought everything they caught in the Chesspeak Bay and all the rivers in Murlin. One whole city block of wholesalers who shipped seafood everywhere until Mayor Schaefer and contractors teamed up to develop the Inner Harbor." Two blocks later, he makes a sharp left turn onto Charles Street, and says, "That's a Pittsburgh turn, you know, not from the end lane where I should've been, but too busy watching you through my rear view mirror. You've got to be the prettiest lady I've ever had in my cab!"

"Compliments are always welcome, Harry. I'll have to increase your tip!"

"Luckily, there's not much traffic this early in the day, but I'll make it a horse race to Penn Station like Storm Cat in the Preakness at Pimlico. I've got 250 hosspowair under the hood now, and this baby is running like a Timex this morning…you know, takes a licking but keeps on ticking."

He pauses to gaze again in his overhead mirror to see if Liz reacts to his last remarks, then shrugs his shoulders and continues, "In the old days they called me Harry One Hoss Power, just my hoss and carriage, hauling seafood all over Bawlmer, me and Betsy. You should've seen me rolling those big barrels of raw urshters into Mueller's Restaurant on Bond Street in Fells Point."

Liz says, "I remember Haussner's on Eastern Avenue that served those fabulous dinners, but I never heard anything about Mueller's on Bond Street."

Harry continues, "That's 'cause they closed in the 60's, long before you were even born. It's true. Eastern Avenue had Haussner's, known for fine food and beautiful art, but Bawlmer, in the good ol' days, had Mueller's of Bond Street, the best crab cakes, steamed crabs and fried urshter patties, handmade by Mom Mueller and her friend Alice Gerstung, These were two Irish women who married German immigrants in Bawlmer."

"Was Alice the wife of Harry Gerstung of Gerstung's Bakery on Fayette Street?"

"That's right. Harry Gerstung was a master baker, trained in Germany and baked the best bread, buns, and muffins in the city.

When the wind was blowing in your direction, you could smell all that baking from a mile away."

"Tell me more about those urshter paddies. I heard that urshters are loaded with iron, good for …" She pauses and blushes a little.

"I know the word you're thinking here. But the secret was the vegetable oil that turned almost brownish-black when those urshter paddies in strainers were dropped into the boiling oil. That was BC."

Liz is curious and asks, "What precisely is BC?"

Harry continues, "Before Cholesterol!" He begins to laugh and continues, "Yes, those were the days before anyone knew about cholesterol! Even Governor Gerald McKeldin and Mayor Tommy D'Aliceandro, father of Nancy Pelosi, ate those urshter paddies along with Chesapeake Bay blue crabs, steamed with black pepper. Mueller's was *the* place for the best seafood in the city and the pride of Bawlmer. Furthermore, they had something that Haussner's never had."

"And what was that?"

"Shorty, one of the best piano players who could play and sing almost anything ever written or published in Tin Pan Alley. He was a wonderful black man, in his 40's, who reminded me of Eddie playing the piano at Rick's Place in '*Casablanca*'. Shorty worked during the days at Sigh-a-neye Hospital, and played on Friday and Saturday nights for tips. He always had a smile on his face, and was one of the best liked men God ever put on this earth, believe me."

"I believe you, Harry." She leans back in her seat and says, "Harry, I think you're a one-man Wikipedia on the history of Bawlmer. I'm enjoying every syllable that you utter. You love the city and your work, which makes the trip much more enjoyable this morning. Helps me to relax too" She unexpectedly sneezes.

"God Bless You."

"Thank you, Harry." She pauses and asks, "Do you remember their prices?"

"Well, you won't believe it, but at Muller's Restaurant, the crabs were fifty cents each, and six of those large urshter paddies plus a small cup of Cole slaw and crackers cost thirty-eight cents! And I bet you won't believe it, but customers still complained that the price was high."

"You're right, Harry. I don't believe you."

"If you look straight ahead, you'll see we're coming up to Mount Vernon Place with George Washington standing on top of the tower. It's not really George Washington in person, just a statue of him, standing 178 feet above the ground."

"How's it possible that you remember that number, Harry?"

"I play it every day in the Maryland lottery." He laughs and continues, "And on the right side is the United Methodist Church with its incredible Gothic design and spires."

"I know this area well, Harry. I used to study piano at the Peabody Institute on the right side, across from the church, and loved to visit the Walters Art Gallery that we just passed on our left."

A minute later the taxi pulls up in front of Penn Station where Liz thrusts a handful of cash into Harry's hands. He says, "Let me get the door for you," and rushes around to open the rear door, where he gives her a tip of his cap, a big smile, and says, "Hope to see you again."

As Liz steps away from the taxi and heads across the short concrete plaza, he blabbers to himself, "Did that little vision of beauty just come out of my cab? What a figure." He plumps down in the driver's seat, adjusts his rear view mirror so that he can see his face, and says, "Oh, if only I were thirty years younger and a million dollars richer, what I could do with her on a Caribbean Cruise."

Liz walks within 25 feet of the front brassy doors of Penn Station just as a young handsome Navy SEAL officer, in his well tailored white uniform, emerges. He takes a few steps away from the doorway area and drops his duffel bag, then pauses momentarily to take a deep breath and survey the area. He removes his officer's cap and combs his wavy dark hair with his fingers and rotates his head to get the kinks out of his stiff neck.

His body and duffel bag block the doorway area just as Liz approaches the front door. Instead of walking around him, she marches up to him, notices his rank, and asserts, "Would you mind stepping aside, Lieutenant!"

He asks, "Are you talking to me?"

Liz looks up slowly and savors all six feet, four inches of his muscular frame, stares into his bright brown eyes that look like Aunt Jemima's syrup and just as sweet. His movie star caliber face reminds her of Burt Lancaster, and almost takes her breath away as she begins to laugh and says, "Well, you're the only one blocking my path to the door, Lieutenant, aren't you?"

He looks down at her five foot six inch body and leans his body sideways. He surveys her figure, starting with her feet in blue leather pointed shoes with the miniature Ferragamo brass logo on the instep. His eyes move slowly up until they eventually settle on her baby-blue eyes for a moment, and then descend slightly to the gold oak leaf pined to her lapel pocket and the Pentagon badge attached to her upper pocket. He rocks his head backward in surprise when he realizes that she's a Major at the Pentagon.

"I like the color blue," he says with a hardly noticeable flirt. "Blue shoes, blue suit, blue eyes. Were you trying to pull rank on me, Major? That Pentagon badge on your lapel doesn't carry any weight or give you any authority here this morning, Major, Sir." He senses that she's in a hurry and speaks rapidly, "I'd like to introduce myself and I'll make it quick. My name is Mark Hopkins, back from Iraq, finished with military duty, and home again in Baltimore. It's a pleasure to bump into you this morning, Major."

She laughs and answers with an even quicker tempo, "I'm Liz Carter. Pleased to meet you, Lieutenant. I'd like to hear all about your experiences in Iraq. Your military life there as a Navy SEAL interests me more than you realize. Here's my card. Give me a call when you have the time."

"How do you know I am or was a Navy SEAL?"

"Telepathy."

He smiles and steps away to allow Liz to enter the front door. His eyes follow her body until the front door closes behind her He glances at her name card and mutters to himself, "I'll have to file Liz in a high priority category, something for a rainy day in October, if not sooner."

Just then a newsboy standing nearby shouts, "Read all about it! September and Oryuls in first place!"

Mark looks down at his duffel bag, pulls his cap tightly down on his forehead, and says to the newsboy, "September...Oryuls ... first place. Impossible!"

The newsboy bellows back, "If you don't believe me, check your TV or your cell phone or call the sports desk of the Sun papers." He pauses to survey the area for customers, then shouts out, "Last to first... Oryuls in First Place...Read all about it in the Sun."

Mark says to the newsboy, "I believe you, but still impossible."

"Impossible? Where have you been, Sir? In Bawlmer, nothing is impossible."

"Yes, in Baltimore. I guess everything is possible. What's your name?"

He answers, "My father named me "Little Mac" Bride. He's "Big Mac" and bigger than you, sir!"

Mark looks down at his five foot two inch body topped with a battered Orioles baseball cap, and orders him, "Give me the Sun. I want to frame the sports page for posterity."

Little Mac asks, "What's posterity?"

"That's when you have success and good fortune."

"You can't fool me. That's 'prosperity', not 'posterity', and if you don't believe me, look it up in the dictionary."

Mark doubles over in laughter as he hands the boy a five dollar bill and tells him, "Keep the change. You deserve it."

Little Mac stares up at him and bellows out loud, "Wow. You mean it? I can keep the change?" Mark nods his head in agreement, as Little Mac releases a giant smile that fully exposes his shinny white teeth, and hollers, "Never underestimate the power of the Schwartz!"

Mark pauses to study this youngster and watch how he blares out the news headlines. When no customers buy his paper, he says to him, "I don't remember seeing a newsboy selling Sun papers outside Penn Station before. They have a news stand inside the train terminal. What's going on here?"

"I'm in a summer apprentice program at the Sun, training to be a line reporter. They send me out to look for interesting people to write about. This is a good spot to catch somebody going or coming, but most of the time they brush me off."

Mark asks him "How old are you?"

"Seventeen, sir."

Mark takes a twenty dollar bill out of his wallet and hands it to him, explains, "You remind me of myself. I used to sell the Sun between school semesters when I was about seventeen too. Here's a deposit on our next story and my card. How do I get in touch with you? I think we're both going up in this world. Maybe we can help each other out someday."

Little Mac tells him how to reach him at the Sun and says, "I'd like to do a story on military life. I've always been curious about the difference between an officer and an enlisted man. My grandfather was in the service and had it rough because of the color of his skin. He was a private in the army."

"I'll help you to write his story and my story, but later. You've got to make a little money, at least for lunch, don't you? Get busy, hustle those papers, and find your next story. It's out there somewhere, waiting for someone like you to write about it."

Mark folds the paper in half, tucks it under one arm, and twists his head to get some more kinks out of his neck. He releases a wide smile as he watches Little Mac race across the plaza to a business man calling to him. His eyes eventually look leftward where he spots a taxi stand with a long row of taxis waiting for customers.

Within a few seconds he casually walks over to the curb, picks the next vacant taxi, and tosses his bag in the backseat. He jumps in the back, bounces about a foot high off the rear seat and hollers to the taxi driver, "Take me to Homewood."

The driver asks, "Where in Homewood, sir?"

He sighs, "4915 Greenspring Avenue."

The driver moves his taxi slowly away from the curb and, after fifty feet, makes a sharp right turn, and heads north on Charles Street at 40 mph. Immediately the driver sees two black teenagers darting across the street without looking at oncoming traffic. The driver swerves his vehicle to his left. Both wheels and tires on the right side of the taxi lift off the ground as the driver frantically continues to turn the steering wheel counter-clockwise to avoid hitting them and a row of cars parked along the right curb.

Mark asks, "Hey driver, what's your name?"

The driver answers, "You can call me, Mel."

Mark says, "Well, Mel, that was close. You sure know how to handle your cab. We could've used you in Iraq, believe me. You have good instincts, good reactions. I still see some litter on the streets and sidewalks, and teenagers engaged in what looks like money being exchanged for drugs, all out in the open. It's clear to me that these few blocks are still a high crime area. This is one place where Baltimore hasn't changed."

"Lieutenant, you're right. There's always something going on around here, and usually bad. We can't take any chances on speeding over here either."

"Mel. I'm in no hurry. Take your time."

"We have to keep our eyes open for the unexpected."

"You know Mel, I'd never thought of telling anyone that I missed the smell of exhaust fumes trapped between these row houses or the sounds of screeching brakes and blaring horns reverberating up the sides of three story houses in these blocks, but I do. No comparison to Iraq."

Soon these blocks of row houses around the railroad station give way to individual homes with well manicured lawns and trees growing everywhere. Sunlight brightens this stretch of Charles Street because its not shielded by three story homes built side by side with a common wall. Even the air begins to smell fresher, perhaps because trees are growing every 100 feet along this increasingly prosperous section of Homewood. The taxi passes Johns Hopkins University on the left side, and historic stone mansions on the right. Each mansion has its own individual architecture. No two houses are the same, with their complex, gabled rooflines with prominent stone and brick chimneys, wraparound porches and bay windows, and overall rich character and charm.

The taxi makes a quick right at Greenspring and a quicker left, passes the numbers 4915 on the brass plate of the mail box, and pulls up sharply into the circular driveway.

Mark grabs his duffel bag and drops it beside the taxi as he pays the driver and watches his yellow cab slowly leave the driveway. He turns and inhales a deep breath that fills his lungs and seemingly lifts his body an extra inch off the ground. He pauses to let his eyes skim the front of his two-story mansion built in a simplified Second Empire style. His eyes move slowly to the upstairs windows to see if anyone is gazing down on him, like so many times before when his mother seemed to know when he was coming home again. Although he was born in this house and has seen it a thousand times before, looking again at the exterior seems to carry a special meaning today.

From the large stone blocks of the foundation to the arched stained glass windows and slate roof, the quality of construction cannot be duplicated today, regardless of how much money is spent. It's simply a fact that the old time craftsmen are no longer around and did not pass on their craftsmanship to succeeding generations. He says to himself, "Grandfather said these green-gray stones for the foundation were selected because they reminded him of the waters of the Patapsico River where he built Bethlehem Steel. He boasted that he had the fairest wife, the fastest horses, and one of the finest houses in Baltimore."

Mark cups his hands, blows into them, and rubs the palms together like he was washing them. It's a habit from his childhood days when he used this little quirk to keep his hands warm on a wintry day. The habit of blowing into his cupped hands now is something that he does instinctively when he's embarking on something new or special. He stretches his fingers, grabs his duffel bag, walks a few steps to the front door, and rings the bell.

A maid answers the door and lets him inside, then offers to take his duffel bag. He drops it as his mother, Sara Hopkins, rushes down a stairway leading from the second floor into the front foyer. Within seconds they embrace. The embrace says it all. Eventually she whispers in his ear, "Thank God, Mark. You're back home and safe at last. Oh, how I've missed you."

Mark looks into his mother's eyes and immediately sees a moment of happiness coupled with worry as if she might be trying to hide something. One of his best assets has always been his ability to size up people and situations quickly, and this characteristic goes double when he is involved with his family. But now is not the time to express his suspicions. He pulls his mother closer to his body, so close that it almost takes her breath away.

As he slowly releases her, he gazes over her shoulder into a long and wide hall leading away from the foyer. His eyes settle on a large portrait that dominates a far wall. It's a sporting painting by the British painter Alfred Munnings of Mark's grandfather. Munnings was at his best when he painted the family patriarch in the early 1930's, dressed in a red fox hunting outfit and astride his favorite grey hunter named Alert, surrounded by bloodhounds. The current value of the painting is over one million dollars.

Mark's father, William Hopkins, suddenly comes out of the library at the far end of the hall, near the portrait. He is dressed in the same hunting outfit with red wool jacket and high black leather riding boots, except his father carries a leather riding whip in one hand. He strikes it against his leather boots as a sound of happiness, and the smack of leather striking leather echoes in the hallway.

He says boastfully, "Well, my boy, should I address you as Lieutenant Hopkins? Are you here to stay this time or just stopping over? I hope you're ready to drop anchor here or at least permit us to show you how happy we are to have you back home, safe and sound."

Mark answers, "I'm mustered out of the Navy and finished with military duty, but I left some good buddies behind."

He grabs his pint-sized father by his elbows and practically lifts him a foot off the floor. It's a habit he acquired during his SEAL training days when he wanted to show off his newly acquired physical strength. His father begins laughing since it brings him pleasure to see his son so well fit and as someone who still remembers the importance of a family embrace. But his father's laughter is curtailed as he continues but in a slow and deliberate manner, "Either you are getting much stronger or I'm getting smaller and lighter. I hope you don't drop me like a hot potato...But seriously, son, those experiences and memories will never be forgotten. And frankly, they should never be forgotten because of the sacrifice made by our military men and women who did their part in helping to keep America safer."

Mark tells them, "I'm still a little dizzy or perhaps woozy from that taxi ride. We almost hit two kids who darted out into Charles Street. Then the driver almost collided with cars parked on both sides of the street. How he managed to control his taxi was brilliant. It's almost as bad as Baghdad!" He grabs his duffel bag and tells them, "If you don't mind, I'd like to freshen up and get into something more comfortable, like civilian clothes if they still fit."

Mark climbs the stairs and quickly enters his bedroom at the end of the balcony. He unpacks his duffel and places all his military clothes in a cedar chest at the foot of his bed. He removes his officer's uniform and folds it carefully as the last layer in the chest. He leaves his under shirt and shorts on, and makes his way across the large bedroom towards the bathroom. On the way to the bathroom he stops to admire another painting, three feet high by two feet wide, of a well endowed female nude leaning over to bathe herself by a pool of water. Framed in an elaborate hand-carved wood frame, gilded in gold leaf, the oil painting is striking in its brushstrokes and dazzling burnt sienna colors by the great French impressionist, Pierre-Auguste Renoir.

On one side of the Renoir hangs a Martin acoustic guitar. He removes it from the wall, cradles it in his arms, and begins singing and strumming the opening bars of the song "Crazy" by Patsy Cline. He stops in the middle of the song and says, "Still in tune. Martin really knows how to make a great acoustic guitar."

He quickly showers, changes into his dark blue Navy SEAL fatigues with the insignia woven in the upper left-hand chest area, and removes Liz's name card from his wallet. He opens his cell phone and inserts her telephone number into the address book. A light-weight belt is strapped around his waist and pulled tightly until the Velcro end is closed. A dagger is removed from the sheath attached to the waist belt, and his fingers move carefully over the handle encrusted with jewels and Arabic writing.

Mark closes his eyes, and his mind dissolves into a flashback of him standing outside a Quonset hut in Baghdad. He adjusts his helmet as someone taps his shoulder from behind him. He turns quickly and his knees buckle as he reaches for a pistol. "Hold off, Lieutenant," bellows a female Lieutenant half his size. "No need to reach for your pistol here. This is a safe zone."

"There's no such thing as a safe zone in Iraq…and the way you creped up on me was like a SEAL ready to strike."

"I apologize, Lieutenant," she says timidly while handing him a sheet of paper. "Orders just came down for you to take your squad up the road where there's been some gunfire in Quadrant Four."

"Don't squib me, Lieutenant. You know I only have two weeks left on my tour here…Why in the hell do they always call this a "tour"? It's far from it, isn't it?"

"I just follow orders just like you, Lieutenant. You better gather up your squad, get that area cleared, and come back to us as soon as possible, all in one piece. I know flirting is not permitted, but I've watched you the past few months and I'd like to see you one of these days back in the states, if you get my drift."

Mark smiles broadly, salutes the Lieutenant, and hollers out for his squad to gather up. He tells them of his orders to check out Quadrant

Four, and leads them into an armored car. The roar of the motor makes it almost impossible to hear anyone talking inside. "I don't know what's worse, hearing that damn motor when you can hardly hear yourself think, or bouncing around inside this tin can on these Godforsaken roads," he screams out. All the members of his squad nod their heads in agreement.

A few minutes later Mark spots a suspicious truck bearing down the road towards them. Gripping binoculars tightly against his eyes, he sees a suicide bomber holding a grenade launcher on the hood of the truck. He shouts to his driver and team, "Enemy at 11 o'clock! Listen up! Remember: Expect the unexpected."

Within seconds both sides exchange mortar fire, but the missile-grenade launched from the oncoming truck explodes in the road directly in front of their craft. The impact lifts and cartwheels their vehicle 90 degrees, tossing everyone through an open door and into a huge crater directly in front of them. Mark is the last one that is thrust through the door. He rolls over the limp body of one of his team. His helmet is missing from his head, and Mark remembers that they called him by his nickname, Carrot Top, because of his flaming red hair. He checks the carotid artery in his throat to see if there's a pulse, then Mark drops his head to his chest and curses the ground. The impact must have snapped his neck.

A few seconds later he looks around the cavity of dirt and notices the shiny blade of a dagger partially embedded in the dirt between him and the limp soldier. He picks it up and instinctively shoves it in a pocket-pouch of his jacket. The loud sounds of mortars and rockets exploding slowly fade away as Mark's mind returns to reality.

He hears a loud knocking at his bedroom door as the dagger is carefully placed in its sheath and his fatigues are pulled over the waist belt. He glances towards the door as his mother enters his room. He places his wallet in one back pocket and his cell phone in the other pocket, then picks up a small brush and begins brushing his hair in front of a mirror.

She tries to engage him in an effort to get him to slow down and at least give his father a long-awaited moment to welcome him back home. She takes his arm and tells him, "I'd like to see you both riding together at the next fox hunt."

Mark puts his arm completely around her waist as they walk slowly down the staircase to the foyer. She tells him, "Son, I can see everything in you that I first saw in your father 30 years ago when I married him. He had dreams and ambitions, just like you. Dreams are good. I want you to put your dreams into reality, pursue and fulfill all of them, but keep an open mind, especially with your father. You're all he has. You're his future!"

Seconds later both are taking the final steps down the staircase where Mark's father is patiently pacing the floor, waiting to continue his conversation. His father turns in the direction of the Munnings painting, then swirls back to meet Mark, face to face. He puts one hand on Mark's shoulder and tells him, "While you were away, almost all of my thoughts were concentrated on one thing and only one thing. I've prepared myself and the execs around me that you would be coming into the firm and helping me to run things at the mill. The doctor has repeatedly said that I have to slow down and there must be a change in my routine, and that means a change in leadership, where I hand off the reins to you. It's time for you to begin running Bethlehem Steel."

"Father, it's a great opportunity. Don't think for a moment that your offer is not appreciated. But if you gave me an executive job to start my career, what would your line workers and other execs say? Can you imagine the resentment? But don't think I'm callous or insensitive to your offer. I just want a chance to make my own mark in life. You'll just have to pass that red jacket to someone else or put it in mothballs for now." He pauses to watch the reaction in his father's face, and continues, "Can we both have some time to think this over? Right now I'd like to dig into a nice crab cake at G and M in Linthicum or Faidley's Stand in Lexington Market."

"It must be telepathy," says his mother with a broad smile on her face. "I've prepared a light lunch for us on the verandah, and guess what's being served? Crab cakes from G and M."

"We certainly are operating on the same wavelength," he replies while placing a chair for her mother to sit in. "Tell me, what's going on at the mill, father?"

"The same problems with the unions but double the pressure now since our labor contracts are up for renewal, and as usual they want an increase in everything...wages, benefits, paid vacations...despite lower sales because those foreigners in Japan and India have government subsidies so they can sell their steel at lower prices than us," he sighs and pushes his crab cake aside. He reaches for a glass of wine, raises it but doesn't drink it, and utters, "The forecast doesn't look good and the doctor has told me to slow down…or else."

His mother joins in, "Or else you're headed for a heart attack." She turns to her husband and continues, "Those trinitroglycerin pills you've been popping behind my back are only temporary relief. No wonder my hair is turning gray. I have two men in my life to worry about…Sometimes I feel so helpless…like being a spectator instead of a participant and taking some action…but what action…what can I do?"

There is a long pause as Mark eats only half of his crab cake and pushes his dish away from his place setting.. All three rise from their seats and join in a huddle. Mark puts one arm around his mother and the other around his father, looks down at their bodies, and says, "I love you both very much. You are very important to me, more than you will ever know. But I can't be of much help to you right now. Give me a little time to digest everything you've said. Don't think for a moment that I'm being selfish if I tell you that you have your life and I have mine. And right now, despite your worries about the firm, I need some time alone to clear my head and decide the next setting of my compass."

"Finally, something just crossed my mind that you might not like to hear me say it," he voices strongly in his father's direction. "You are and have always been a hands-on manager. Everything must go through you. Well, whether or not you like it, you're going to have to release the reins a little. With your permission, I'd like to make a personnel search for a good manager to take some of the burden off your shoulders. In Iraq I met one of the contractors from Germany that is building a new factory with tons of steel from Germany. He mentioned that his firm is threatened with laying off some highly-skilled managers, in an effort to cut costs and raise profits so that the stock will look good to potential investors. I could contact him to get a resume of someone that might be the right person for the right time to help you."

"Permission granted," echoes his father, "with my blessing."

His mother nods her head approvingly and begins to shed a tear.

Mark inhales a deep breath, gives each of them a gentle kiss, and continues, "I'm going to take a long walk down to the Inner Harbor, and see what new buildings have been added to former Mayor Donald Shaefer's original layout, perhaps even take a ferry ride across the Chesapeake Bay, maybe get away for a day or two. I've got to see the sky when I look up. It's therapeutic. I'll call you later to let you know where I've settled. Don't worry too much. I can take care of myself. I've got your genes and enough iron in my blood."

He looks around at the splendor of antiques decorating the hall, and says, "I know that you're carrying the firm on your shoulders, the firm that grandfather created when he split up with Carnegie and Mellon. You're 'Mr. Steel' in Baltimore. But I want something else. I don't know what it is yet. I'll have to find it out for myself. It won't be easy, but please give me a chance, like the chance grandfather gave you, to make your own mark in life."

His father asks him, "You will let us know where you are, won't you? I have to say, I think that we deserve more time together. After all, we're a family, aren't we?"

His father manages to emit a half-hearted smile as Mark gives him another kiss. He turns to his mother, hugs her more strongly, and gives her a parting kiss too. "Don't worry too much about me," he tells them as he walks towards the front door. "Try not to worry too much about me. I can take care of myself," he says with complete assurance as he checks his back pockets to see if he's forgotten anything, and exits through the front door.

Once outside in the fresh morning air, he takes a deep breath and walks through the courtyard of the family mansion, crosses the street, and heads in a southerly direction down Charles Street. As he takes each step along the sidewalk, he begins to feel somewhat energized. After all, he's alive and back home with his family, and with much to be grateful for.

Mark casually looks to his right at a bronze statue of two students, a boy and girl holding their books and standing on a pedestal at an entrance to Johns Hopkins. He almost collides with a short thin elderly lady with a leash attached to her pet poodle. She drops the leash and hollers out in the nick of time, "Hey, watch out where you're going! You're going to hurt somebody, and I don't want it to be me, you big ox!"

Mark abruptly sidesteps her at the last second and gently twirls her around in a circle, never letting go of her arms. He tells her, "Close call. I hope you'll forgive me." He quickly picks up the dog's leash and hands it to her with a second apology. "I'm sorry. Did I frighten you? I should've been paying more attention. Many a day I passed through that entrance on my way to classes. My coach used to call me a 'big ox' too."

His eyes look down at his size 12 Under Armour pro-trainer shoes that remind him of his practices at Hopkins and bumping into his track coach on graduation day. His mind drifts into a flashback of his coach telling him, "Well, Mark, you've come a long way, just like your father. Thirty years ago your father and I graduated from Hopkins. He was a wiz in metallurgy, and I was a medalist on the track team. When I first saw you trying out for the team, you reminded me immediately of your father, a serious, dedicated, and hard worker. In my thirty-year coaching career, I never saw anyone work harder than you. When you won the long distance race against Washington College, we, especially your father, were very proud."

His coach's words linger and echo as his mind returns to reality. He grabs the neck of his sweatshirt to wipe the perspiration from his forehead. He resumes walking again down Charles Street, talking to himself all along the way, "Perhaps this is the day I have been waiting for all my life. I survived Iraq, four years on and off of kill or be killed, never knowing if I would come out alive or in one piece. One thing is certain. I will put my trust in God. I guess the Good Lord wants me here yet. I wonder what he has in store for me."

CHAPTER 2

Mark glances at his watch and realizes he's walked the four miles that takes him to a pier at the Inner Harbor in about an hour. He hears a loud succession of boat whistles, and notices a ferry pulling away from its mooring. As the gangplank is being raised, he dashes over, leaps with both feet and lands in the middle of the plank, then takes a giant step to make it safely on board, just in the nick of time. An attendant hands him a ticket and takes his money for passage from Baltimore down the Patapsco River and across the Chesapeake Bay to the quiet hamlet of Betterton.

After a stroll around the crowded bottom deck, Mark finds a quiet private corner where he takes out his cell phone and calls Liz. "This is Mark. Do you remember me? Where are you right now?"

"I'm on the Metroliner, just crossing over the Susquehanna River, on my way to New York," she answers. "Where are you?"

"On the bottom deck of a ferry on my way to Betterton. I haven't a clue where I'm going or what I'm going to do next." He pauses to switch from his plans to hers, and asks, "When will you be back to the DC area?"

"I'll be in New York for a few days, depending on the interviews with applicants." She hesitates and whispers, "I have to be cautious with you over the telephone since this is not a secure line. I'm on a recruiting mission. We're looking for several men and women for undercover surveillance work in Iraq. Maybe you'd like to reconsider a return to military service, with a jump in rank?"

"Are you kidding? The only combat I want right now is to dig into a Maryland crab cake." He laughs and in a more serious vein, says, "Your work seems very demanding. You never know what a person does under combat or critical situations. I hope you find the right people." After a pause, he continues, "As they say in Hollywood, let's do lunch. Until then, order a Navy grog with extra Jamaica rum and put it on my tab. When you settle down in the Big Apple, behave yourself."

Mark puts his cell phone in the back pocket of his fatigues and buys a Coke from the canteen nearby. He moves to the stern of the ferry and looks out at the foamy wake in the Bay, then turns and notices an attractive middle-aged woman, unescorted, standing beside him. He says, "Isn't it interesting to people-watch from the stern, and wonder what they have on their minds today?"

She gives him the brush-off and walks away.

Mark says to himself, "I take rejection well but better when I know the basis for the rejection…Hey, her loss. Not even a 'hello' or 'how are you'." He dumps the remains of the Coke in a litter container, then crushes the cup with one hand to show a slight touch of anger, and throws it in the container like a slam dunk.

He notices a stairway to the upper deck and double-times the steps upward. A minute later he leans against the port side railing and admires the beauty of the trees lining the shore. He turns around to resume his people-watching just as several husky skinheads, wearing leather vests with tattoos exposed, begin to harass three teenagers nearby. He's tempted to get involved, but realizes it's just teenagers flexing their muscles and showing off.

Finally Mark's eyes settle on a young attractive brunette with long hair flowing over her shoulders, in a simple black dress, leaning against a vertical support pole about 10 feet away. She stares back at him, and slowly wraps her hands around the pole as if trying to hide behind it.

He makes his way over until he stands a few feet beside her. "Now, why do I get the idea in my head that you'd like to talk to me?" he asks.

"Are you a mind reader or do you ask that question to all the girls you meet for the first time?" she inquires.

"No, I'm not a mind reader. It's probably telepathy or magnetism that draws me over to you. It's the start of a beautiful day and a beautiful trip to Betterton."

She smiles but is reluctant to say anything. She studies his physique, then his face.

Gaining confidence, he can't resist the urge to size her up and inquires, "Five feet, eight inches, 145 pounds, and fancy free at 21?"

She raises her eyebrows and declares, "If you're referring to me, you're right on the mark. But isn't it better to know something about what's inside a person?"

"True, but you never know what's inside a person because they're constantly changing, aren't they?" he answers. "And I've only got two hours to find out something about you, with your permission, of course."

"I'm guessing that you get a great deal of fun and satisfaction in sizing up people and situations, don't you?"

"Well, one of these days, I might get my face slapped if I size something up the wrong way."

"Or punched in the nose by her husband or boyfriend," she tells him and begins to laugh. She extends her hand, "I'm Sandy."

He grasps her outstretched hand with both of his hands, and releases a giant smile, "I'm Mark Hopkins. It's a pleasure to meet you, Sandy."

She turns to her left and says, "Mark, I'd like you to meet my mother, Annette."

"Like Mother, like daughter, in almost identical and beautiful charcoal colored outfits. Ladies, you look MAUVE-A-LOUS," he says in his best imitation of Billy Crystal.

"Are you thinking the same thing I'm thinking?" Annette asks Sandy.

They both recognize his muscular build, and Sandy confesses, "You know, Mark, now that I take a good look at you up close, I see that you're wearing Navy SEAL fatigues. You remind me of Tommy."

Mark asks quickly, "And who's Tommy? Is he a SEAL?"

Sandy confesses, "Tommy's my brother and he's not a SEAL. He's coming home today from Iraq."

He sighs and admits, "Well, Sandy, we have something in common after all. I'm coming home from Iraq too."

Changing from a happy smile to a solemn look, Sandy whispers in a quieter voice, "Yes, but you're not coming home like Tommy's coming home to Betterton. Below deck."

Waiting for more words from Sandy, he reluctantly asks, "And?"

Sandy manages to gather some strength and whispers, "In a private compartment of this ferry, with an honor guard, watching over his coffin."

Mark's smile and enthusiasm is tempered by immediate pain and grief at this shocking news. He instantly reacts and manages to whisper, "Oh God, have mercy on his soul and these good people."

Annette droops her shoulders and bows her head sadly, and confesses, "He was killed about a week ago by a suicide bomber." She pauses and turns to look upward and directly into Mark's face, and continues, "He was only 24, about your size, and always had a smile on his face. I still can't believe that he's gone from us, taken away so suddenly, without any..."

She hesitates for a moment, trying to find the right words as her chin sinks into her chest. She gathers her strength and continues, "There are so many questions bouncing around in my mind, about the war, about our president and the military rushing to call up his reserve unit, giving them only three months of training, and finally thrusting them into Iraq."

Marks pauses to weigh the gravity of her words, gathers them both in a huddle in front of him, and whispers, "I hope you won't take it the wrong way here, but I felt an attraction when I first caught sight of Sandy leaning against that pole. A SEAL has to know what's around him at all times. It can mean the difference between life and death. You might call it a mental awareness, an aura. I felt it the first moment I caught sight of Sandy and can still feel it about both of you now. It drew me to you like a magnet."

He hesitates to gather his thoughts and continues, "It doesn't take a rocket scientist to size up the situation here. For all intents and purposes, I don't want to probe into your personal grief. For the rest of this trip, at least for starters, my time is your time. Let me know if there's anything I can do to ease your pain, any questions or concerns. I'd like to help in any way possible."

All three slowly bow their heads in a long moment of silence to digest Mark's remarks. Without realizing it, the threesome moves to a railing near the back of the ferry. Annette gazes in the direction of the Bay Bridge. "Tommy loved the water and the Bay from the moment he took his first plunge off the pier at Betterton Beach," she discloses slowly and in a soft voice. "Eventually he became a waterman like most of the kids around Betterton and Rock Hall. They couldn't wait to get out of school and work for themselves, earning just enough money by fishing and crabbing. I still own his work boat."

Annette puts her arms around Sandy and Mark and brings them into a closer huddle. Together they are pleased and impressed by Mark's sincerity and directness. There are no pretenses with him. What you see is what you get.

Sandy tells him, "Under military protocol, the War Department normally would have a military escort from Dover Air Force Base all the way to his gravesite in Betterton, but my mother and I decided on something different, something that Tommy would have liked on his last journey across the Chesapeake Bay."

Mark inquires, "And so you both decided on one last trip for Tommy on this ferry?"

"That's beautiful, Mark," answers Annette. "Sandy and I tossed around the notion of doing something different, something that Tommy enjoyed, and that was this ferry ride to and from Betterton to Baltimore. I remember the first trips, and the way they gripped the railing so tightly with their little hands that I essentially had to pry away their hands finger by finger. Their eyes were glued to the water, and the action of the waves and foam hypnotized them. Today this trip will be remembered forever and cherished in our hearts."

There is a long pause until Sandy boldly asks, "We've told you about ourselves, Mark. Would you mind telling us what lead you to board this ferry from Baltimore to Betterton, and something of your life in Charm City?"

"I thought it was time for me to be completely on my own. I've finished with military service, and I'm looking for new opportunities. No strings attached to anyone. Now the pleasure of meeting you, and the chance to help out leaves me with a good feeling." He pauses and looks upward at the sky, and continues, "As an officer, I know firsthand about the life of a soldier fighting in Iraq. I was stationed there for four years. In the military, we're all brothers, and I think Tommy would want me to bring you some comfort, even though I never knew him."

With 10 miles remaining on the trip, Mark offers to get them some refreshments from the lower deck canteen. While he's below deck, those same husky skinheads eventually converge on Sandy and

Annette who are backed gradually and rigidly against the rear corner of the stern railing.

Within a few moments two skinheads turn their attention towards Sandy who is separated from her mother. When one of them approaches too closely, Sandy accidentally loses her balance and trips backward against the railing. She tries to grab hold of the railing and screams as she begins to fall overboard.

As Mark carries the tray of refreshments and reaches the top deck, he catches a glimpse of Sandy falling backward over the railing. Her screams along with those of her mother are followed by the crash of the tray of refreshments hitting the top deck.

He races through the crowd, dodging and pushing people out of the way, and plunges overboard. Annette looks out in horror, but realizes that she is helpless and can only watch and contemplate what tragedy is rapidly unfolding before her eyes. The thought of losing her daughter crosses her mind. She begins to pray for help by pleading, "Dear Lord. You've taken my son. Please spare me my daughter."

Her eyes never leave the spot where Sandy splashed into the Bay. She watches every stroke as Mark swims partly on the surface and partly underwater. In less than a minute later she sees Mark lift Sandy out of the water, then tears blur her eyes, and the distance is too great to see what happens next.

As the ferry continues on its journey to Betterton, an older couple comfort Annette and stay with her for the duration of the trip.

At the helm of the ferry, the captain tells his first mate, "Don't sound the alarm. I'll contact the Coast Guard and advise them that I see a yacht following us in pursuit of the two passengers overboard. I trust that they'll be rescued momentarily."

Through the wake of the ferry, Mark continues to hold Sandy's head above water and spots a yacht about 100 meters away that suddenly turns and moves towards them.

The throttle of the 30-foot yacht *BETTERTON-WISHBONE* is thrust all the way forward by the skipper to accelerate as quickly as possible in the direction of the two bodies floundering in and out of the water. At the controls is a slender, six foot six inch, 30 year old man with his yachting cap slanted to one side, sporting a smile that is contagious and self-effacing.

As the yacht draws closer, he pulls the engine throttle backward into idle, and tosses them a life preserver. He attaches the end of the line from the preserver to an anchor fitting at the stern of the yacht, and lowers a ladder for them to climb aboard.

Once they're all safe on deck, he retrieves some large Turkish towels so they can begin to dry themselves. He tells them, "I was trailing along in the wake of the ferry, on my way back home when I heard a scream, possibly two screams, and just caught sight of someone falling backward over the railing and seconds later another figure diving off the top deck of the ferry. I realized that's not the way to do a back flip or swan dive. Within seconds I heard an alert broadcasted on the VHF radio. But you're in safe hands now, thank God. I'll get you a stiff drink to get your blood back in circulation."

"How did you manage to fall off the top deck?" Mark asks Sandy.

"I didn't fall off. Those muscle guys scared the life out of me. I was forced backward and tripped over the railing."

"I didn't fall off either," admits Mark. "I heard you scream and dove off the top deck. That could have been a disaster since I never took the time to look and see where or what I was diving into. Suppose there was a boat close by. They'd be scrapping my body off the deck."

"What a morbid thought," she utters nervously. "You did the right thing, Mark. It was reaction and action."

Reggie interrupts, "After you dry yourselves, I want to hear every disgusting detail of your plunge into the Bay. I might write a symphonic piece and record it for posterity."

Mark says, "That's the exact word I used this morning when I was talking to a newsboy outside Penn Station."

Sandy is obviously weakened, and her knees begin to buckle and sag. Mark grabs hold of her body from behind to keep her from falling to the deck. He rapidly dries her hair and somewhat frantically begins to massage her back, all steps to get some circulation back into her limp body.

Within minutes Reggie hands them a shot of whiskey and tells them, "This may help you to gather all your senses. You'll want to get out of those wet clothes too, so follow me, please." He takes them below deck into a luxurious stateroom, walks over, and opens a woman's wardrobe closet, and tells Sandy, "My mother shops at Bloomingdales and Nieman Marcus. Don't be bashful here. Take whatever you want.

I know she would want you to have it, under the circumstances." He walks over to opposite side of the stateroom, opens a man's wardrobe closet, and tells Mark, "The same applies to you. Help yourself. My folks won't miss it."

Sandy's limpid body collapses on a corner of the bed as Mark continues to dry her hair and massage her back. Eventually they begin to chatter and talk over each other's words. No one bothers to wait for an answer or reply. Words and expressions just sprout out spontaneously. The rambling goes on for a minute before they all stop talking and begin laughing. Each one has questions and answers about what happened aboard the ship and the aftermath.

"The important thing here is that you did the right thing at the right time. You saved my life. I was going under for the third time. I saw my life passing right before my eyes. You may not believe it, but I saw your face, before my eyes." Sandy begins to sob until Mark puts his arms around her, and the two of them thank Reggie for rescuing them.

Reggie tells them, "I was just out on the Bay this morning, trying to relax before heading up to New York for a recording session. You're on you own now. I'll get us back on course to Betterton. That's where I live. That's where we moor this beautiful plaything." He nods his head and releases a big smile of accomplishment for a safe rescue. "If you would like another drink, help yourself. As I said before, take whatever you want. I'll be topside at the helm if you need me. By the way, I'll notify the Coast Guard and the ferry that you're aboard my boat." He pauses to collect another thought and says, "Did I mention that I heard about you on a broadcast from the ferry on the VHF channel? I advised them that I had you in my sights and was in rapid pursuit."

Sandy and Mark suddenly take a closer look at Reggie. Mark asks, "What kind of music do you play?"

He says, "Everything from the classics to jazz to hip-hop. Everything up to and including the Funk Brothers."

Sandy mentions, "I think I've heard your name bantered about, around Betterton, as a genius on the guitar."

He says, "Far from it. I'm just a jack of all trades, master of one, the guitar, but no genius, but enough about me. I'll be top side if you need me."

Sandy is still shivering a little and turns to Mark with a request for her another shot of whiskey. As he hands it to her, she looks right into his eyes and asks, "Am I the first, first one you ever rescued in the water?

"You're not the first rescued but the first woman I've rescued and the prettiest too."

She yearns to hear more about his first rescue and asks, "Can you tell me about your very first rescue or is that confidential information?"

"Since you've asked and I'm no longer in the Navy, I see no reason for secrecy anymore. It was last September in Iraq. Six of us were stationed in the city of Babylon when orders came through to move quickly to the Euphrates River where a small freighter was tied up to a pier. Terrorists on board the freighter were holding the captain for ransom.

Intelligence sources never gave us the exact number of terrorists involved. All we knew was that everyone was somewhere on the top deck. It was close to midnight and we were in the water about two hours, hidden below the sight line of the railing, waiting for the signal to board the ship."

"How long did you say you were waiting in the water?"

"About two hours. I could feel my muscles tense up. There was no light from the dock, pitch black everywhere. I could hardly see anything beyond 20 feet in front of me, which helped to conceal our position too. I don't even remember seeing any moon that night either."

Interrupting, Sandy asks, "Mark, you have me in suspense. What happened next?"

"Suddenly out of the blue, there was a big splash right before my eyes. It was a small body tied with rope. I managed to pull it close to me and out of sight, and within a few seconds, I cut the rope to free his hands. . It turned out to be the captain, very weak from starvation and a brutal beating. I guess the terrorists panicked or didn't need him anymore and tossed him overboard. I gave him some oxygen from my tank and handed him over to our crew chief."

Sandy says, "I've heard or read that SEALS are trained for almost every possible incident, isn't that right?"

"Training is one thing, but until the real thing stares you right in the face, you have little time to think. You mostly react on impulse, just like when I saw you falling overboard on the ferry."

By now Sandy pulls his body closer and plants a kiss on his cheek. She confesses, "Mark, I guess I'm reacting on impulse too. Thank you for saving my life."

He says, "Maybe we should go up on deck and check with Reggie to see where we are right now. We should be approaching Betterton soon, don't you think?"

"Perhaps Reggie will loan me his cell phone so I can telephone my mother. She's probably scared to death by now, and I'd like to tell her we're both safe and sound."

They climb the stairs to the top deck and find Reggie at the controls and humming to himself. He looks them over from head to foot, doffs his cap with a big smile, and declares "Quite a transformation. It's amazing and true that the right clothes on the right person can produce astonishing results. You both look mavveeelllooouuussss! I can see both of you have good taste in clothes. They look better on you than on my parents."

Sandy points to his cell phone, attached to his waist, and says, "I'd like to call my mother. I know you have a VHF radio on board, but the cell phone is a little more direct."

Before she can finish her last word, Reggie hands her the phone and tells her, "Let her know that we're about 10 minutes behind the Betterton ferry and not to worry too much."

While Sandy calls her mother, Mark hovers over the console of the yacht and asks Reggie, "What's our heading?"

Reggie answers, "For Betterton, the longitude is 39 minutes, 23 seconds North, and the latitude is 76 minutes, 4 seconds West. We've got radar and depth finders on this console, but I still have to be on the lookout of debris floating in the Bay. Last year we hit a float tied to crab pots entangled with a submerged trunk of a tree. Now, that was a mess, believe me!"

After Sandy finishes her conversation with her mother, she hands Reggie his cell phone and says, "I can see the Betterton pier ahead. I can't wait to get back on land. It's funny and strange. My brother loved the water and I love the beach. I guess that's because of our genes. We had different fathers."

By the time that Reggie maneuvers his yacht into a dock space near the ferry, all the passengers on board the ferry have already dispersed from the landing area. The only people waiting for Sandy and Mark are Annette and the Honor Guard of Captain Kasoff, who stands at attention beside the coffin draped with the American Flag.

Annette runs over to the yacht and begins sobbing as she huddles in a reunion with her daughter and their new friend Mark. Moments later, after Reggie secures his yacht at a mooring, he joins the reunion. Sandy introduces Reggie to her mother and excitedly tells her about the rescue. Annette is overcome with emotions that shake the living daylights out of her body. She whispers to Reggie, "One tragedy in our family is enough for a lifetime. I can't figure it out. Thank God, you returned my daughter to me again. When I saw her go overboard, my heart almost exploded. How can I ever thank you both?"

Reggie says, "It was Mark who rescued Sandy just in time. All I did was to be in a position to fish them out of the Bay."

After a pause, all eyes gaze at Tommy's coffin when Mark raises a question: "What's happening here? Just listen! No traffic. No motors, only seagulls flying overhead. It's so quiet!"

Annette admits, "At last Tommy is home again, but not as we expected. I can't tell you how many times I traveled away from Betterton to Annapolis or to Baltimore on this ferry, and how I always felt so happy to come back home again to Betterton. It was always so comforting to stand on this exact spot, full of joy watching Tommy unload his catch. Today Tommy is home but the feelings are just not the same. Maybe it will never be the same again."

Sandy tells them, "Nothing will be the same again here without Tommy. It's noon and about this time Tommy would be returning with his catch of crabs or rock fish from the Bay. His demeanor was always the same, whether he caught one crab or 10 bushels, whether he caught one rock fish or a quarter ton. He really liked the water and the Bay. He always talked about the treasures of the Chesapeake like it was something magical."

There's another long pause. Mark slowly surveys the area all around them, perhaps looking or listening for something to bring relief and consolation here. Reggie pulls out a pack of cigarettes and offers one to Mark, who tells him. "Not for me anymore. I used to smoke always before combat, just to steady my nerves. Finally I quit."

Reggie takes the pack of cigarettes and stuffs them into a back pocket of his trousers, and says, "Well, I'll give it a try too. No time like the present to turn over a new leaf in life."

Annette nods her head to Captain Kasoff, who then relays the signal to four mortuary men waiting beside a hearse. The men walk solemnly to the coffin and transfer it to the hearse. As the shiny black vehicle moves slowly up a slight incline, the mortuary men walk in pairs behind it, in slow-step, followed by Captain Kasoff.

Sandy takes her mother's arm and the two of them follow closely behind him. Reggie and Mark join in the procession at a reasonable distance behind Sandy and Annette.

Along the way Mark surveys the homes on both sides of the street. He first notices on the left side a one-story home with a sign with peeling paint that says "Annette's Antiques." Then on the adjacent house is a sign of equal vintage saying "Boyd's B&B" On the opposite side of the street is a one-bay fire house, a small country post office, a few more clap-board or vinyl-siding framed houses with peeling paint that resemble nothing like the stone mansions of Homewood in Baltimore.

Reggie whispers to Mark, "My father's poultry farm is just down the road about a mile on the left, and there's a horse breeding farm about two miles out of town on the right. Most of the time visitors here just catch their breath long enough to meet family and friends, and move inland to slightly larger towns like Rock Hall and Chestertown. There are no bars or restaurants or motels here. No police. The fire house is all volunteers, good people ready to risk their lives. That's the way the town likes it. They don't like change."

Along Main Street on the way to the cemetery, neighbors join the procession behind Mark and Reggie. One neighbor folds her hands in prayer. She is Nellie Fox Boyd, a spinster who owns and runs the B&B next door to Annette's Antiques. Sandy lingers in her walk, then in a quiet voice, tells Mark, "She's two-faced, says one thing to your face, and another thing behind your back. She's also the town's gossip who enjoys spreading rumors everywhere about us 'chicken-neckers'. She has no conscience."

Annette puts her arm around Sandy and pulls her closer to her body and whispers, "Careful, Sandy. This is not the time or place for such words."

Sandy says, "Considering what's happened today, it's probably an over-reaction on my part, but sooner or later, I'd really like to tell her a thing or two, and get it off my chest. She never liked us 'chicken-neckers' anyway."

Annette says, "But not today, Sandy. There'll be another time, a better time later."

Eventually they reach the top of the inclined road where Mark notices a Catholic church on the left side of Main Street. It's a typical rural country church, with white vinyl siding on its front face and a small steeple above the front door. Along each side wall, about 50 feet long, are large gray colored stone blocks that rise all the way up to the roof line. Three large stained glass leaded windows with an ecclesiastical arch at the very top spring up along the wall like flowers rising in bloom in spring time. On the lawn on one side of the front of the church is a two-by-three foot case or message board enclosed in glass. Inside the case the following words appear: 'God Is Watching You'. But someone has inserted an arrow between the words 'Watching' and 'You' and above the arrow added the word 'Over'.

Mark turns to Reggie, points at the case, and says, "Reggie, have a close look at the showcase over there. That's an example where one word can change the entire meaning."

Reggie asks, "What do you mean?"

He answers, "Without the addition of the word 'Over', it means simply that God sees you and is watching you, your every movement, so to speak. But with the added word 'Over', the meaning changes into something much more important. God is watching OVER you, caring for you like the good Shepard that he is."

Reggie says, "Very astute, Mark. I knew there was something special about you that appeals to me, something that seems to grow on me. It's your sensitivity, clear and simple."

The procession now takes a left turn towards the cemetery located behind the church proper. A minute later all are standing at the gravesite, surrounded by neighbors and friends.

Standing in a row directly behind Sandy and Annette is a lanky blond haired 27 year old man, Bud Wayne. From the look of his rumpled clothes and blank stare, it's obvious that his mind is elsewhere. "A cemetery is the last place I'd like to be today, and surely not standing next to my wife at a funeral," he mumbles to himself. His face is swollen and tense. He looks over at the coffin and continues to talk to himself. "I should be working at my marina. I don't know why I agreed to come today simply because Vera said it was compulsory. I never met this guy before. I know that Vera met him and had some dealings with him in the crab business, but what else was going on between them? I wonder if she slept with him too?" He pauses to look down at Vera, his shorter wife beside him, and continues talking to himself with increasing fury, "I wish you were in that coffin instead of Tommy. One of these days, if you don't stop chasing military men, I'll be putting a rose on your coffin."

Vera, five foot eight inches and very attractive at 30, three years older than her husband, stands in a casual posture, and is well-endowed physically after giving birth to a baby one year ago, a baby whose birth-father is still undetermined. Their marriage is just a little over one year old, and might be considered the definitive 'shotgun marriage'.

She senses his silence and immobility, looks up at him suspiciously, and says to herself, "He's as quiet as a clam. He's got that look of jealousy and rage again, but what can I do about it?" She continues to face him, smiles facetiously in a weak attempt to put him at ease, and continues talking to herself, "When I married him, I guess I dug my own grave and have to live with it." She takes one hand to her forehead to adjust her hair that has fallen out of place, and cautiously whispers, "Lighten up, Bud. I can see what you're thinking here. Tommy was a nice guy that sold me his crabs, that's all. Relax. I didn't sleep with him."

There's a pause in which everyone is frozen somewhat in their places around the coffin, except for Vera who suddenly, and perhaps with good intent and certainly without following protocol, takes a step towards Annette and Sandy to extend her condolences.

Finally a young handsome priest, standing only about five feet and weighing less than 150 pounds, adjusts his collar and steps forward until he stands at the head of the coffin and says, "My name is Father Timothy O'Malley, newly ordained and representing the diocese of Murlin and Delaware, under the auspices of Bishop Winterhalter. On behalf of the Sacred Heart Church of Betterton, I welcome all of you this afternoon. Bow your heads and let us begin by reciting together the Lords Prayer.

In unison Reggie and Mark lower their heads, then halfway through the prayer slowly raise their eyes to study the faces of Sandy and Annette standing beside each other on one side of the coffin. On the opposite side, standing at attention, is Captain Kasoff.

They periodically hold their breath as Father O'Malley ends the Lord's Prayer and closes his prayer book. He bows his head and takes a deep breath and says, "Today, we are celebrating a life, not dwelling on the death, of one of our young people of Betterton. His name is Thomas Joseph Wells who lived on earth 24 years. For eighteen years he lived with his family here in Betterton and worked the last four years as a commercial waterman. A year ago his reserve unit was called up, given basic training, and sent to Iraq. He gave up his life one week ago when a suicide bomber killed him and four of his comrades. When he was called into action in Iraq, he performed his duties with no complaints or regrets."

The priest pauses to gaze at the American flag draped over his coffin, and continues, "I think it is safe to say that he accepted what God had in store for him. He loved his life on the water almost as much as he loved his family. His love for both was strong and unconditional. These military men and women who surrender their lives in wartime, so that we all have a better life here, are special and should never be forgotten. Each of them makes the ultimate sacrifice. I know that you all may not believe it, but time will heal your pain. I want all of you to remember one thing here today." He pauses for about 10 seconds and continues, "Today Tommy is the blessed one. Tommy is with God."

The priest turns towards Annette and nods his head as a sign for her to step forward and offer her comments.

Annette steps closer to the coffin and struggles with her words, "The two happiest days of my life were when Tommy and Sandy were born. The saddest day of my life was the day that I got the telegram from the War Department. It took my breath away. After the shock passed through my body, I visualized in my mind the reality of never seeing him again." She begins sobbing but manages to continue, "Never being able to kiss him goodnight, never being able to tell him how much we all loved him, never…"

Her sobbing increases until she regains her composure. "He always told me to take care of the Bay and the Bay will take care of you, be good to the Bay and the Bay will be good to you. We could have buried Tommy in Arlington National Cemetery, but we chose this resting place, in Betterton near the Bay. I know Tommy will like it here, by the Bay."

Then Sandy steps forward beside her mother, takes her arm, but cannot offer any words immediately. She looks upward towards the sky as if God will send her the right words to offer here. When her eyes focus on the American flag draped over his coffin, she gathers some strength and says, "No one has ever seen a broken heart, have they? Well, my heart is broken." She begins to sob but continues, "As Tommy's younger sister, my broken heart is not important, is it? I know it doesn't make much sense here for me to talk about a broken heart, but it doesn't make much sense either to lose my brother under these circumstances in Iraq. Why? Why Tommy? He was so young, so good-hearted and innocent. Why did God take him away from us? Lot's of questions remain, but no answers yet." She pauses momentarily to catch her breath.

"I've always believed that God put every person here on earth for a purpose," she cries out as she looks upward to the sky. "Tommy's life on earth was short, but he made the most of it every day. He made me proud to be his little sister. I looked up to him and admired his work ethic…up before dawn, work until you are completely satisfied with the effort and results. He set a good example. It doesn't get any better or simpler than that."

The priest closes the service by saying, "I will now read from the Book of Common Prayer. In sure and certain hope of the resurrection to eternal life through our Lord Jesus Christ, we commend to Almighty God our brother Thomas Joseph Wells, and we commit his body to the ground, earth to earth, ashes to ashes, dust to dust. The Lord bless him and keep him, the Lord make his face to shine upon him and be gracious unto him and give him peace. Amen."

The entire ceremony closes with Captain Kasoff removing the American flag from the coffin and folding it according to protocol. He walks slowly to Annette, hands her the flag, whispers something about condolences that only she can hear, and concludes with the words that everyone can hear, "…on behalf of a grateful nation."

Then each person takes a flower from a bouquet beside the coffin and gently places it on top of the coffin. An older gentleman, wearing a VFW medal on his lapel, plays Taps on his trumpet. The four mortuary men then lower the coffin into the graveside, which concludes the ceremony.

Mark approaches Father O'Malley and thanks him for his sensitive comments. Mark feels rejuvenated by Father O'Malley's words and expresses it in the clenched fish and more erect posture. It's almost like his muscles are beginning to bulge out of his clothes. He asks him, "You look to me like someone who is barely eligible to vote. Are you over 21, Father? Where did you acquire this sensitivity?"

Father O'Malley says, "When you're a black man growing up in a predominately white country like Ireland, you learn a lot about sensitivity very quickly, otherwise you won't survive in life, will you?"

Mark says, "I didn't know that you were black. I just looked upon you as one of God's servants. Frankly speaking, the war in Iraq made me color-blind!"

Once outside the cemetery gate, Annette lingers long enough to join a group of neighbors and explains, "I want to thank you all for coming. Your presence here is gratefully acknowledged. It's been a long day, and now Sandy and I need some peace of mind, for reflection and contemplation. There'll be a formal church service later."

Church bells ring out, somewhat off-key as Annette takes Sandy's arm, and together walk back down Main Street. The clock on the old firehouse registers 2 pm. Annette turns to Mark and Reggie, and invites them to their home for a mid-afternoon respite. Annette's house is a stone's throw away from the church, less than two blocks on the right side of Main Street.

CHAPTER 3

Within a few minutes everyone is inside the white shingled house with the sign hanging on the front porch that reads "Annette's Antiques." Reggie looks around the front room crowded with antiques. While the other three are preparing food and setting the table in a small dinning room at the back of the house, Reggie finds a guitar hanging on a wall. He begins to play and sing a ballad. Everyone stops in their tracks as Reggie begins playing "I'll Be Seeing You In All The Old Familiar Places." The words and music bring tears to their eyes. Reggie's words are almost spoken rather than sung. His voice is secondary only to his skills as a guitarist.

Sandy whispers to Mark, "He's supposed to be one of the top guitarists in the record business…the favorite guitarist of Johnny Mathis and Natalie Cole. I can't believe he's here with us. We always heard about him through the local newspapers. We never knew where he lived."

Annette says, "I hope you will like our Murlin crab cakes. The recipe is handed down from one of our neighbors whose husband was a waterman on the Bay. But like all good cooks, I add some parsley for vitamin C and some sprinkles of Lea and Perrins and Ol'Bay seasoning salt plus a touch of lemon, all blended together to bring out the sweet natural flavor of fresh Murlin crab meat. You know, there's nothing better than a homemade Murlin crab cake."

It's not easy, but everyone makes the best of the situation. Words are hard to come by, but expressions in their faces tell you everything you want to know about what is stirring inside their minds and hearts. Annette says, "It is good to be alive. Thank God for our family and our new friends, Mark and Reggie."

Afterwards, while Sandy and Annette clean up the dishes, Reggie takes Mark off to a corner of the front showroom and tells him, "It seems very clear to me that they could use your presence here a bit longer, mostly because you have the experience of having been in the military. You can't leave them this way. They're hearts are not just broken, they're ripped apart!

I've always heard about the brotherhood among military men, sharing, caring for each other, right? Here's your chance to be a brother and son to them. So many things still need to be resolved in their minds and hearts. You can see that, can't you? You know, Mark, I really don't know you at all but so far, I like what I see in you, and believe me, I've seen good and bad people in my short life, especially in the music business. The bad ones come and go, almost through revolving doors, but I get the feeling you are something special, something different, a force for good. I urge you to think about staying awhile longer in Betterton. In fact, if you need a good job, executive or administrative work, I can speak to my father who's always looking for talented, creative people."

But Mark tells Reggie in clear and finite words, "Don't think that I'm ungrateful for your overtures here but I have to be on my own. It's my goal now to take the helm, be my own pilot, navigate, and discover new territories, a fresh start. Be my own boss for the first time in my life."

Reggie tells him, "I think you have too many 'be's' in your head, too many 'me's' too. This is the time now to think of others. Your time will come soon enough, and you'll have new friends to help you along the way."

Eventually Annette finds Mark and escorts him around the front showroom, slightly cluttered with everything from vintage clothes, chinaware, showcases with costume jewelry, and colorful Victorian prints from an age no longer popular. The overall look is one of clutter instead of class, with no visible theme or specialty. She asks him if he knows anything about antiques.

Mark confesses, "As a matter of fact, I do. I loved to go to auctions in and around Baltimore, almost twice a month, when my mom and dad were furnishing our house in Homewood. I made several good discoveries that we still cherish in our collection of furniture and paintings. If you'll forgive my boasting her as a feeble attempt to impress you, I even know what it's like to bid on a painting for $100,000 like the Renoir nude that now hangs in my bedroom in Baltimore."

Annette says, "Good for you. Now I'd like you to think hard about working for me in my shop! And to start things off, what would you say to your relocating to Betterton and living in Tommy's apartment over the garage out back behind the house? It's private and no one will be using it now, so why not you? I think the Good Lord brought us together and maybe the Good Lord intends to keep us together a while longer. After all, you did save my daughter's life, didn't you? I think you owe it to us to stay a while longer, starting this very moment." She looks right into his big brown eyes and takes his hands into hers just as she completes her offer.

He sighs and answers, "I really don't follow your logic, Annette. I think you twisted something around here, but it's getting late and decisions have to be made now about where I'm going to spend the night, so let me check out the apartment over the garage. It has to be better than those Quonset huts we were living in Baghdad a few days ago.

"Come to think about it, I just never planned on spending the night here in Betterton, but my intuition tells me to drop anchor and settle down here for awhile. I wonder and hope Sandy feels the same about my staying with you. She's a beautiful girl, and I wouldn't want to create a scandal in a little town like Betterton. You know, a Navy SEAL living above the garage with a beautiful girl living close by."

Soon all four walk to the garage behind the main house and climb the steps to the apartment overhead. Once inside, all four seem to bump into each other because of the cramped quarters. Mark notices immediately that the walls are not wallpapered but painted a drab gray, with waterman's clothing hanging on hooks everywhere. There are three rooms comprising a small bedroom next to a bathroom with a shower tub, and one room that serves as a living room with a battered sofa that should be tossed into the junk heap.

On the whole, the overall look is a little depressing. Austere is the word that comes to Mark's mind, but that would be an understatement. It was obviously and previously occupied by someone who didn't care one iota about nice furnishings and just plopped down in front of an old black and white Admiral television with rabbit ears stretching awkwardly to the ceiling.

Annette asks Mark, "Well, what do you think? It's not the Plaza Hotel in New York, but it's home."

Mark smiles and answers, "To tell the truth, it's a little breathtaking. It really takes my breath away, way away. It reminds me of a scene from Steinbeck's "Grapes of Wrath." I'm trying to imagine myself living here, living in Betterton. It's so far from reality really. I might be getting in over my head here. If I were a waterman, I could literally fall out of bed, roll down a short hill, and land directly on Betterton beach, couldn't I? However, I like a challenge now and then…Let me take a deep breath of fresh air outside if you don't mind and ponder exactly what I might be getting myself into."

Reggie suggests "Wouldn't this be a good time for all of us to take a short walk to Betterton beach and digest those delicious crab cakes? Along the way maybe we can all try to convince Mark to stay awhile longer in Betterton, at least tonight for starters. If we can get him to drop anchor for only one night, I feel certain that the peace and quiet of Betterton is just the right thing for a Navy SEAL about to embark on a new course and maybe carve out a new career in the antiques business."

As they walk from the garage back to the main house, Annette takes hold of Reggie's arm and tells him, "Whether you like it or not, you're now part of our family too. I just love your phrasing, and those dominant 7th chords strike the center of my heart. Would you mind playing for us down on the beach? I know a quiet spot where we can stretch out some towels and let the bay breeze take over. I think you get the picture here, don't you? When we have some privacy, I'll tell you about how you remind me of my first real love, Sandy's father, who was a music teacher in Baltimore and handled the electric steel guitar almost as good as you play the acoustic one."

It's now close to 5 when everyone is settled in a secluded cove on Betterton Beach. Reggie starts to improvise on the guitar his rendition of the song "September" but speaks the words, "For it's a long long time from May to December, when the autumn leaves change in September." His eyes eventually settle on Sandy.

Mark notices Reggie's interest in Sandy and tells her, "Reggie's eyes are roving tonight just like his fingers on the guitar. Make sure, Sandy, his fingers never leave the strings and hold the fort while I have a private talk with Annette, O.K?"

Sandy responds, "This cove is normally used for private sunbathing, sometimes topless too, where men can flex their muscles and girls can flex, well, they're free to flex whatever they want to here."

Reggie counters, "I like flex. I minored in flex in college. I think they called it flexibility."

Then Mark asks Annette to take a short walk with him to another quiet area where they can talk. He tells her, "You really don't know much about me. In fact, I don't know much about myself either, but I will tell you one thing. I have seen the way my father operates his business at the steel mill and I won't have a life like that, ruling with a iron fist, 'my way or no way'.

It might sound naïve but now I want to be my own boss, but also a boss or leader that is part of a team, where everyone is treated fairly and equally, where everyone works for one common goal, where everyone benefits. I don't have all the answers, but I can tell you after serving in combat in Iraq, teamwork will work. I am standing here only because of teamwork, where everyone in my squad looks out for the other member of the team. Do you follow me, Annette?"

"So far, so good."

"I've given serious thought about what you said back there and want you to know that I'll try to help you and Sandy with your life and your business here in Betterton, up to a point. I would not be here if it were not for my ambition to be finally on my own, to be my own boss. I'm willing to work with you, but not for you, in the antiques business. What would you say to a partnership for a three-month trial period?"

"That's fine with me. I have a feeling that we are going to be good friends and successful in the long run. I don't need much in my life to be happy. I'm very lucky to have Sandy and you too. We will be equal partners for 90 days, split everything right down the middle, and take each day as it comes along. I won't expect you to make a big impact on me or Betterton, but whatever you do from this moment in time, it'll be for everyone's benefit."

"My father liked to use the expression 'we will forge a bond' when talking with his workers at the mill. I think that you and I will forge a bond now in the antiques business."

They give each other a big long hug. Mark mentions that he must telephone his parents in Baltimore tonight. He confesses, "I'm still their juvenile always jumping ship. I certainly don't want them to worry about me, especially since I left them abruptly earlier this morning!"

Annette tells him, "There's a telephone in your flat. Make all the calls you need to let everyone know you're in Betterton now."

"I have my own cell phone, and I'll arrange to get some of my clothes shipped here. Plus I have to buy a new computer, install a satellite system with Wildblue dot com, and acquire some wheels. I was thinking about a Camaro, or maybe a hybrid BMW convertible."

Annette raises her eyebrows and asks, "A convertible, in Betterton? The town will throw a parade for you."

Then both walk back towards the sounds of music to watch Reggie serenading Sandy, whose gaze towards the Chesapeake Bay turns into tears. She thinks of Tommy, and how lucky she is to have her mother and two new friends nearby, beautiful music in the background, the tide rushing in with waves splashing on the shore, and geese flying overhead in the direction of the fading sunset. On the horizon is another spectacular blend of blue and white swirls intermingled with blazing red and orange. It's a magnificent scene when Reggie says, "The sunset tonight reminds me of the skies in those magnificent landscape paintings by the great American painter Thomas Moran."

The sun falls below the horizon, and the evening sky dissolves slowly into a harvest moon.

The next morning, during breakfast in the main house, Annette asks Mark, "Well, how did you spend your first night sleeping in Betterton?"

Mark tells them, "It was the quietest night that I can remember. Not a sound, except for a horned owl in a tree near my window. It was quite a nice picture with the owl perched on a limb and a full moon overhead. I watched him in that moonlight for five minutes. The way he moved his eyes and head…he looked like he was trying to tell me something."

Annette says, "Perhaps he was trying to welcome you to Betterton. At any rate we'll need your help this morning because, on Tuesday mornings like today, we usually start to load the truck with things to take to a big country auction in Crumpton on Wednesdays. We take things that don't sell quickly or purchases made mistakenly in the first place. As you know already, when you buy something at auction as a dealer, it's no guarantee that you will sell it.

"There's always a risk in business. The secret is to minimize the risk. Splurge when you find something very special that you can turn into big bucks. We also like to turn over our inventory, keep things fresh for our customers. Normally we expect to take a small loss on returning merchandise, but if we're lucky, we can buy other things to bring back on the return trip. So, partner, I was thinking that this morning we'll start to clear out everything that you and I don't need or want from your new apartment over the garage."

While all three are moving things out of the apartment and down the steps, they chatter back and forth about what things are worth keeping and what they should sell at the auction or at a garage sale later. Mark probes for more details about this auction in Crumpton, and Annette explains the procedure and process involved.

"For your first plunge into Dixon's Auction, we'll try to keep things simple, but I guarantee you that it'll be a different auction than the auctions you've probably attended at Cooper's or Opfer's in Baltimore. You may even see some dealers that you recognize, too. They all come here to buy something for their clientele. After all, it's only a two hour drive each way from Baltimore over the Bay Bridge or up the 95 expressway towards Elkton."

In the next hour Mark strips down to his bear chest and carries a large TV on his shoulders down the stairs and over to the truck.

Sandy's eyes pop widely as she tells her mother, "Look at that physique. Lean and mean I would say, wouldn't you?"

Annette says, "There's no fat on that body, at least as far as I can see."

Sandy continues, "He's too good to be true. In the sunshine he looks more like the God Mercury, moving swiftly with wings on his feet. Look at the way he flies up and down that staircase!"

Mark transports boxes of clothing, an old mattress, a pair of end tables stained with water marks from wet beer bottles, an old trunk, and a rusty file cabinet from the apartment to the truck. Then in the garage below the apartment, Annette asks Mark to remove some old boat motors that are rusty and broken. She tells him, "At Crumpton, someone might buy them for junk metal if they're not working. There are always salvage dealers looking for these motors because of the copper and other metals that are still worth money at the salvage yards."

Annette asks Sandy, "Do you see the way he has stacked everything in the truck, with the heavy stuff on top so that nothing will fall off or blow away? That's military training and experience. But we'll still have to tie everything down. We don't want anything falling off on our ride to Crumpton."

Soon all three return to the antiques store where Annette asks Sandy, "Would you mind coming with me this morning to shop for groceries in Chestertown?"

Sandy agrees, and Annette advises Mark, "This would be a good opportunity for you to take a closer look at everything and get familiar with the store. And please don't hesitate to give us your ideas or suggestions to make it better. You won't offend us with your criticism, believe me. We'd rather hear it from you than from a customer."

Annette and Sandy exit by a back door leaving Mark to roam around privately. He begins by picking up an ornate vase to feel the weight and study the details of flowers hand-painted all around it. He examines the underside to see if it might be the cross-swords mark of the Meissen factory in Germany. He says to himself, "Not Meissen. No quality, no money here. I guess it's simply something for the tourist trade and not a collector. It won't be easy but things will have to change here. I don't want to waste my time in the nickel and dime business with stuff like this. I hope Annette will go along with me and try to upgrade her inventory."

As Mark walks past the front window and peers out, he notices a short old man, wearing what looks like a tug boat captain's cap and coat, pacing up and down the sidewalk in front of the store. He blurts out through the open door, "What's going on out there?" When there is no response, he walks down the porch steps and short path to the sidewalk. Soon he stands in front of him. Mark repeats loudly, as if the man might be hard of hearing, "What's going on here?"

The old man says, "Well, I got a problem."

"A problem? Maybe I can help you, but first, would you mind telling me your name?"

"I'm Knute Runagrund. That's pronounced "Ka-noot" like in 'cute'. You can also call me "Cap" or "Cappy" but don't ever call me "Pop." He makes fist and jabs it comically in front of Mark's nose, and continues, "I might just pop you right on the nose like Rocky Balboa." He begins laughing and watches Mark's reaction, "I used to be a tug boat captain in these here parts, for over 30 years in the Chesapeake Bay, been everywhere, seen everything, used to think I knew everything too."

Mark puts his hand to his chin and grins, "Hmmm. Runaground sounds Norwegian, close to Runaground."

"You heard of me?" bellows Knute in a high pitched voice.

Mark scratches his head and says, "It's a hellava name for a tug boat captain, I mean, Runaground?"

"It's Runagrun, mate. You know, according to Norwegian legend, the Vikings ranaground in America long before Columbus, but now I have a problem."

Increasingly intrigued, Mark asks again, "As I said before, maybe I can help you."

"Well, you see, I have this bird. When I first got him many years ago, I had to promise that I would care for him the rest of my life. Now I have to go into a senior home up the street, and they don't allow no birds, no pets whatsoever. I saw your sign about antiques and thought you might like to have some company when things are slow, maybe keep him for me in your store so I can come by every morning to see him.

"He's very smart and you can teach him plenty too, like when someone picks up an object in your store, he could say "That's beautiful. Why don't you buy it and take it home. I tell you, he really likes people, especially kids, but hates cats. I could come by in the morning when you open up to see him, maybe even help you out in the store too. I see you have that model ship in your front window. Believe me, young fella, I know a lot about ships ever since I was eight years old in Norway and a stowaway cabin boy on a ship that went around the horn. I know what responsibility means too. I take responsibility serious-ous-ous. That's a hard word to pronounce in English by a Norwegian like me."

Mark asks, "Do you mean to say, 'seriously'?"

Knute says, "Yes. You get my drift. Look at this coat, 30 years old, like an old friend, and still looking like new. Every thing that I've ever owned, I've always taken good care of it. You wouldn't even have to pay me if you don't want to. Aw shucks, you must think I'm a little touched in the head. You know, when you get as old as I am, you'd still like to be useful and productive in life. Whataya think?"

Mark listens carefully and digests every word. He immediately likes the old man and relates to him almost like a son to a grandfather. He begins to smile, then bursts out laughing while scratching his head, then slowly nods his head approvingly.

He explains, "I'll have to talk to Annette, my new partner in this crazy antiques business, but I think I can persuade her to take you on, part time, for a few hours in the morning, if that's all right with you, say for a three month trial period? We can always use good people, especially those who like people and animals"

They shake hands on it, but Mark issues a condition: "As long as you or the bird is alive, right?. Oh, by the way, what's the bird's name?"

"Gertrude, but I call her 'Gertie' for short."

"I thought you told me the bird was a he, not a she?"

"Well, honestly, I haven't figured that out yet" He pauses to scratch his head and continues, "But I know several women who are called men's names, like a doll I once knew named 'Sam' in Saskatchewan up in Canada way, so maybe the previous owner of this bird just reversed the name-calling process. I just don't know, but I think you'll have fun with Gertie. Trust me here."

"Well, Knute, let's meet Gertie."

Knute walks over to a tree nearby and brings a covered bird cage over to Mark who carries it up the porch and into the store. He clears a table and puts the cage on it, then gradually lifts the cover like a curtain going up on opening night at the Hippodrome Theatre in Baltimore. Lo and behold, there is the world's most beautiful talking bird.

Gertie squawks out loud, "Hello cutie, hello Doll, what's up, Doll?" The bird continues squawking: "Let's Sing a Song…Ho hum and a bottle of rum. Hi Doll. *Want'a* dance? *Want'a* go to my place? Make yourself at home, Doll."

Mark has a bellyache from laughing so much and tells Knute, "I think this is going to work out great. What do you feed her?"

"It a secret, my boy, just like the secret recipe of Bush's Baked Beans," he answers. "Normal birdseed is fine, but I also feed her one new word a week, kindah like 'food for thought'."

"You lost me, pal."

"I cut a word out of the newspaper or magazine and put it on the bottom of her cage, so she can look down and read it. Then I pronounce it for her, and by the end of the week, she's learned a new word. I know it's hard to believe, but it really works."

Mark almost falls to the floor as he doubles over again in laughter. He waves good bye to Knute as he heads out the front door of the shop and walks down the steps to the sidewalk. Along the way, he gives a slight hop, skip, and jump and happily heads back up Main Street towards the senior home.

Mark recovers from his laughing spell and looks around the antique shop, trying to find a quiet spot for Gertie, somewhere in a corner, out of the way. Mark says, "Just tell me if you're comfortable here, Gertie, because you and I are going to be good friends, right? How about singing a song for me?"

Gertie begins singing an old ballad "Roamin' in the Gloamin' With My Best Girl Pearl," a little catchy tune with some provocative rhymes thrown in for good measure. Gertie continues, "Roll me over in the clover, lay me down, and roll me again and again."

Mark soon realizes that Gertie is a poet that might even make Sir Walter Scott blush. After Gertie finishes her tune, Mark declares, "You know, Gertie, I might even make you a star and put you on the stage at the Hippodrome Theatre over in Baltimore. How would you like that? I'll get a professional photographer to take a picture of you in the store, perhaps even a reporter to write a feature story for publication in the Kent News or Baltimore Sun, give you a moniker, something like 'Bewitching Bird of Betterton'. Make you famous in the antiques world."

Mark slaps his face and says, "Hey, wait a minute. What am I doing? I have Little Mac at the Sun, looking for a story, and Gertie my girl, you're just the type of story for Little Mac, If I handle this situation correctly, with the right promotion, tourists will flock to see you and hear you singing a 'Song for Six Pence'. Nothing wrong in thinking big, is there, Gertie girl?"

Mark puts the cover over the bird cage and locks up the front door of the store. He exits by way of the back door and walks towards his apartment, and says to himself, "Tomorrow will be a long and challenging day, and I'll need a lot of rest tonight. It's time to catch some Z's upstairs at last!" He climbs the stairs to his apartment and collapses on his bed.

CHAPTER 4

Early the next morning, before dawn, Annette and Mark are full of energy as they grab a cup of coffee percolating in the kitchenette. When they finish the last sip, Mark says, "Good to the last drop! Now where did Maxwell House get that wonderful slogan? That's what we'll need too, a slogan that will attract tourists to our store."

Annette laughs and locks up the rear door. They climb gingerly into their pick-up truck parked along the side of the house for the 40 minute drive from Betterton to Crumpton. She looks at her watch as she drives up Main Street, then begins singing the opening words of a song from the movie 'The Wizard of Oz'.

In a good voice, but much softer than Judy Garland's, she sings somewhat rapidly, "We're off to see the Wizard, the wonderful Wizard of Oz, we're off, we're off, we're off, we're off , we're off to see the Oz." She laughs a little and turns to Mark and confesses, "I just love that movie with Judy Garland, don't you?"

He says, "It's one of my favorites too, but don't expect me to start singing 'Somewhere Over the Rainbow' like Judy, especially at 6 in the morning."

"No, I don't expect you to sing, but I hope you and I can find that rainbow over Crumpton this morning. By the way, Mark, I heard the strangest sound this morning coming from one of the corners of the shop. It sounded like a parrot squawking."

Shaking his head and laughing again, he confesses, "I forgot to tell you. I met a wonderful gentleman named Knute, a retired tug boat captain. He's living at the senior home up the street and offered to help us out in the shop, for a few hours each day, just so he could come by and see his pet parrot, Gertie. They're really quite a pair of characters, and together it'll give our shop a boost in good humor, if nothing else. I told him to leave the bird with me while I talk it over with you, and hopefully get your approval."

"Well Mark, I can't wait to see our new friend in residency. As far as I'm concerned, change is good. I like to stir things up, even if it upsets the locals."

"They're not paying our bills, we are, so we should forget about what they think. We have to use our brains and do what we think is best for the store."

"Mark, you're a breath of fresh air. The shop could use a changeover too, something to spruce up the old place, something to give our returning customers the impression of freshness. And the best way to achieve that change is for us to buy new inventory."

She glances quickly over to look at Mark's face and continues, "But let's talk about what's ahead this morning. Perhaps I should give you a picture of the layout at the auction site along with some pointers of what to buy for inventory this morning. It will take some time for you to get a feeling of what things are risky to buy, what's in demand, and what sells to tourists. You can forget about selling anything to the local residents of Betterton. They're not interested in art and antiques. So my advice is to keep your eyes open for something special, out of the ordinary, that we might buy today and sell to a tourist or special client with deep pockets.

Our goal each week is to buy something that we can turn into a profit of, say $2,000. That figure should not put you under any stress. It will at least cover all our expenses, such as insurance, utilities and occasionally give us the pleasure of buying some fresh crab for our crab cakes."

You can tell by the smile crossing his face that Annette's coaching is beginning to register. She concludes, "One thing that you want to remember here is this: When you're thinking about buying something, stay right with the auctioneer, and if we're successful, give him my ID account number 233, and be sure that whatever he is pointing to or his helper is holding up in his hands is the exact item you are bidding on.

After he says 'sold', you own it and someone, usually a Dixon helper near the auctioneer, will hand the item to you. At that point, you cannot take it back, so try to take it directly from the auctioneer or his aide. It's always best to stand as close as possible to the auctioneer.

If items are passed through a crowd to you, you can expect damage because they just pass things around without thinking about how fragile they are. Do you get the picture here?"

Mark shakes his head and mumbles, "This is suddenly beginning to seem complicated, at least at first, but I'll get the hang of it. I have confidence in my ability to size up situations quickly."

Annette looks at her watch as darkness still covers the two lane road. She asks Mark, "What time do you have? I can't read my watch. We have another 10 miles to go to Crumpton. If you look in the easterly direction, you'll see the first traces of the sun breaking through the trees. But in this particular heavily wooded area, I have to be very careful 'cause this is where deer are known to jump or spring out of the woods and cornfields, dashing directly across the road. It can scare the daylights out of you."

Mark laughs, "In the military, we use a different word."

Finally it's dawn as they see an 8 foot high chain-link fence surrounding a farm with a giant hangar in the center. At the main entrance, Mark notices a big billboard with lettering 'DIXON'S AUCTION - CRUMPTON MD'. Annette drives her truck slowly along the dirt road and directly into a long line of vehicles waiting in line to register and eventually unload their consignment junk in the outside field. Within 15 minutes they are greeted by a Dixon employee who hands them a ticket with their consignor name and pile number clearly indicated. He looks at their load, does a quick estimation of the space that they will need, and points to a location where they'll find another employee ready to tell them exactly where to drop their consignment for auction this morning.

About 10 minutes later everything is unloaded from the bed of the truck directly on the dirt and gravel of the Field #1. Some things are piled on top of others as space is limited. Together they jump into the truck again and find a parking space on the periphery of the outside auction field. Annette grabs Mark's arm and leads him through the maze of junk that will be auctioned off precisely at 9.

She tells him, "We'll concentrate on trying to find better quality things for our shop from the consignments inside the hangar, but it doesn't hurt to scan these rows just in case you might spot something that jumps out at you. You never know when someone has put something rare outside without knowing how valuable it is."

As they walk, arm in arm, in the direction of the main hangar, they continue to glance downward at rows cluttered with furniture, boxes of dishes silverware, rugs, even sporting equipment, ranging from golf clubs to baseball bats and gloves.

Annette whispers to Mark, "It's equally important to watch people too, not just the things coming up for sale. You can always learn something by watching others, especially how they are looking or handling something that they picked up for a closer look. A special joy will come when you outsmart somebody by recognizing the value and knowing or guessing how much to pay for it. It might be your day to discover a small treasure buried here among this clutter.

"But remember that at this auction, you don't have any time to think about a 'buy'. Either you know what you are doing or you lose out. There are thousands of things to sell in about 8 hours, with sometimes three auctions going on simultaneously, inside the hangar and outside in three different fields of this 20 acre site."

Suddenly Mark hollers out, "Holy Mackerel!"

Annette stops dead in her tracks and looks over at him, "What is it, son? Did you see a snake?"

"No, I didn't see a snake but this sight is really overpowering. I can't believe my eyes. There's everything from everyone's home, garage and business. Good God! We'll never get through the day, will we?"

"Well, Mark, you told me you were slightly familiar with auctions in Baltimore, didn't you? "

"Yes, I did, but I've never seen anything like this mess...and you want to convert something from trash to cash, right?"

"Well, it'll take all your talents, instincts and ingenuity, to find one jewel in this mess, to make all your work worthwhile. Remember Rome wasn't built in one day. Just take it easy, try to enjoy the hunt, have some fun. Don't make it seem like work. While you're searching along these rows of junk outside the hangar, remember that the good stuff, the better stuff, is inside on tables waiting for us. We've got about an hour before the auction starts inside at 8 am."

Mark shakes his head in disbelief, and without thinking, mumbles "Expect the unexpected."

Standing near Mark and observing him carefully is a distinctive chisel-faced, dark-skinned man in his early 30's, someone whose face reminds you of a painting, a portrait of a Taos Indian painted by Nicolai

Fechin. But this trim, five-foot tall figure wears a heavily-worn Levi's shirt and trousers with tattered holes that look like they're ready for the junk pile. Of course, these Levi's have the feel of velvet from years of wear, and are not easily discarded like parting with old friends.

He takes a few steps towards Mark, begins laughing, and tells him, "If you start mumbling or talking to yourself here at Dixon's, they'll call the paddy wagon, and haul you off to the funny farm up in Sykesville. So be careful about talking to yourself as you mosey along like one of those Ay-rabb men on their horse-drawn carts in back alleys of Bawlmer."

"You're from Baltimore? I mean, you know, you remember those Ay-rabb horse and carts going up and down back alleys in Baltimore, hauling away all that trash? How did you know I was from Baltimore?"

"I got my start by working on those carts, collecting trash from all over the city. I bet some of that trash was turned into treasures and ended up here in Crumpton. And as for how I knew you were from Baltimore, I really didn't know. I just noticed that you were letting your eyes do all the talking. You didn't bend over once to look inside a box or turn something over here and there. You won't get lucky here unless you dig like a farmer, plow through this junk, and turn things over, and that takes work and time, believe me." He pauses to look around at the rows of junk, scratches his chin, and exclaims, "This is like a Field of Dreams."

"A better name is "Field of Screams."

"You can call me Tony Wanderer, and starts to extend his hand in a handshake, then suddenly makes a wave sign like a Navajo Indian.

"Are you trying to fake me out? You're an American Indian?"

"Mostly Navajo, with some Apache, and a sprinkle of Nanticote Indian thrown in...The Navajos are hunters and gatherers. The Apache are plunderers, fierce fighters, and always at war. Somewhere along the line two souls must have mated, and I was the result. I have both in my blood, which is good when it comes to this hunt every Wednesday. Did you know that there were a number of tribes living along the Patuxent and Nanticote Rivers on the lower Bay?"

"No, I didn't know that. Tell me more about yourself."

Tony laughs and tells him, "I guess that makes me a fruit cake, with all those Indian tribes running through my blood."

Mark laughs and asks, "Where are you working nowadays?"

"When I'm working, it's part time with the Bureau of Indian Affairs in DC, but I'm studying architecture at night. I'd like to be an architect, build things for my people on our land in Arizona. You know, eco-friendly."

"Annette told me it's important to watch the people here too. She said you can learn from them."

"Who's Annette?"

"She's my new partner in this crazy business. She owns a shop in Betterton. Ever been to Betterton?"

"My ancestors have lived all over the Bay, from Betterton to Chincoteaque Island. In fact, I bet that you'll be surprised if I tell you that my people called it the Chesapiooc in the 1600's, long before the white man called it the Chesapeake."

"Very interesting, Tony."

" Mark, it might be fun and better if I teach you a few words in Navajo, like those Navajo Indians speaking in code during the war against Japan, then no one here would know what we're talking about, especially if we spot something valuable."

"Good thinking," says Mark. "We'll have to do some business together. I like the vibrations coming from you. So for now, give me your telephone number where I can get hold of you." They exchange telephone numbers and both promptly insert them into the address book of their cell phones. Mark closes with, "I wish you good hunting."

Tony gives him an open hand extended upward to the sky, the Indian sign for farewell.

Mark turns and walks down a narrow path between two rows of consignment and lets his eyes look for something special while Annette talks to two other dealers about 30 feet away. Within a minute Annette meets him and says, "Have you noticed the license plates and signs on the sides of those trucks parked around the perimeter. Dealers and collectors come from Massachusetts all the way down to North Carolina."

He pauses to watch men, women, and even teenagers unloading their junk from their vehicles right onto the dirt and gravel. He is temporarily hypnotized as he now realizes how the entire process outside really works, starting again with the registration by a Dixon rep holding his clip board and wire labels. Mark shakes his head and mumbles again as he continues to digest everything. He eventually finds Annette near the end of Field #1 and asks, "You mean to tell me that this action occurs every Wednesday, regardless of the weather, in rain, snow, and wind, every Wednesday?"

Annette tells him, "You're getting the picture. But here's another thing for you to keep in mind. After dealers drop off their junk, they try to buy other merchandise to take back home with them. No one wants to go back home with an empty truck. The expression floating around here is 'Make a Buck with Your Truck'. For us, the name of the game is upgrading inventory."

Mark shakes his head in puzzlement and sighs, "Isn't it strange and a little funny how antique collectors and dealers are always looking for something new but old? Is there a fallacy here?"

Mark and Annette walk away from the outside Field #1 and enter the main hangar. Once inside, Mark surveys the vast alignment of 40 wooden tables, each 3 x 6 feet, and piled high with everything from jewelry to sculpture, paintings, furniture, porcelain, fabrics, musical instruments, rugs, dolls, clocks, everything that was ever made in the world from around the world.

It's now exactly 8 am and the auctioneer, Albert Hobbs, and his female accountant step up onto a mobile elevated two seat podium and sit side by side in front of Table 1. Today's auction begins precisely on time, and you can feel the excitement oozing from Mark's skin. He wipes a slight layer of sweat from his forehead as he now listens to the auctioneer's opening remarks.

Dressed in a gray jumper with 'Dixon's Auction' woven on an upper pocket, Hobbs brings the flexible microphone close to his lips and adjusts his glasses so that they sit half way on his nose. This position enables him to look through the lens up close or over the lens to see farther away. He has the habit of twitching his nose when he moves his eyes through the glasses, and everyone who knows him, just smiles at his antics.

He takes a deep breath, pounds his wooden tabletop with a gavel, and begins, "Welcome to Dixon's and good luck in your bidding today. Remember there are no guarantees whatsoever, so think before you buy and everything is sold as is, where is. No returns. Once I say sold, you own it. Give your ID number to the accountant lady sitting next to me or a Dixon rep that might be roaming around the table. No cash please.

You have to register first at the office to bid here. And remember, if you snooze, you lose!"

Mark watches the action on Tables #1 and #2 and sees a dealer looking into a small price guide, checking out prices for some items on the table in front of him. Then he realizes that the auctioneer just sold over 100 items in only 20 minutes and that he has to bid quickly if he wants to buy anything in this rat race of competitive bidders.

Mark spies and picks up a nice guitar on Table 3 and gives it a cursory inspection, then puts it back on the top of the table. When the auctioneer moves his mobile podium in front of Table 3, the Dixon rep, Dave Bloom, takes the guitar, holds it high in the air, and shouts out, "Acoustic guitar!"

Mark takes the initiative and without consulting Annette, battles at least five bidders until his bid reaches $300. The auctioneer asks, "$320 anyone?"

Within seconds, the auctioneer points to Mark and says, "Nobody higher, so I guess it yours at 300. Sold to…?"

He hollers out "Annette's Antiques #233."

Dave Bloom, one of the main Dixon reps, is dressed as always in his red football jersey, which is easy to spot when he's hovering around the tables. He hands Mark the guitar with one hand and an 18" high wooden model ship, "*Gratitude*," with the other hand. Bloom, standing about 6 foot 2 inches and weighing about 250 pounds, looks more like a pro football offensive lineman without shoulder pads. He tells Mark, "I can see by the look on your face that you didn't hear the auctioneer tell me to combine that model ship with the guitar."

Mark glances over to his right and tells a lady standing next to him, "Is that the same as two for one? I thought I was buying just the guitar, but what the hell. I got the model ship as a throw-in."

Two attractive women, twins in their mid 30's and dressed in distinctive cowgirl outfits with the head of a Texas longhorn steer insignia woven into one pocket, are standing at one end of the table when one says to the other, "Do you see what I see?"

The other says, "You mean on Table 3?"

"I mean AROUND Table 3. That handsome dude that just bought the guitar. Isn't he hot? He looks as if he just stepped out of a Calvin Klein ad."

"I see what you mean. He could play his guitar under my window any night. How I'd like to take him back to Texas with me. Forget about buying anything for our store. Let's bundle him up before he gets away!"

"Too late, he's got his hands full, and I doubt if he's interested in starting a romance at 8 in the morning. Frankly, I can't blame him."

Mark turns away from Table 3 and tries to maneuver carefully through the maze of people crowded mostly around the front of the hangar. It's difficult for him to move his body because everyone is focused on the auctioneer or items on the tables, and not aware that he's trying to make his way through the crowd. His steps to move through the front of the hangar and advance into the middle section are more like a halfback dodging and evading tacklers and blockers in a football game. He protects both of his purchases by tucking them close to his waist and lowering his shoulders so that anyone in his path knows what his intent is. Good manners don't apply in these crowded conditions. He finally sees Annette talking to other people in the middle of the hangar.

He whistles to get her attention and tells her, "Well, I took my first plunge here with you - actually without you. I saw an interesting guitar that Reggie might like to play but needs some repair, and they also gave me this model ship of the *Gratitude*. I had no idea it was included in the lot, so it's a freebie, so to speak. I have a hunch we can make a little profit here after some minor repair. What do you think?"

Annette says, "You have me here. I know nothing about model ships, but as for guitars, I can tell you something about Hawaiian electric steel guitars later. All in all, I think it may be worth the gamble. I like the fact that you used your initiative and instincts too. Our main goal today was to introduce you to the Dixon auction and to clear out the clutter from the apartment and garage. Everything after that, is icing on the cake. But Mark, you really can't think about selling it to Reggie, can you? I mean, after he rescued you and Sandy in the Bay?" She pats his left cheek gently to take the edge off his remarks, and tells him, "I'll take your plunder to the truck while you get our invoice from the Dixon office. You might as well learn about the entire process this morning. I'll be waiting in the truck for you. No rush. Take your time."

Mark answers her, "How stupid of me to think of making a profit on Reggie after all he's done for us. If he's not interested in it, I might buy it for myself."

Annette counters quickly, "You don't want to fall in love with things that you buy here Mark, unless it's something so outstanding that you absolutely can't part with it. Remember, we're a business, and right now, our goal is to clear out things from our store and garage and buy new inventory for our customers."

While paying for his goods at the counter inside the hangar office, Mark stands in front of a distinguished looking, tall and slender, well dressed gentlemen with a slight touch of gray in his hair who says, "My name is Richard Honus Wagner. I see you bought that guitar on Table 3. I intended to bid but loss my concentration and train of thought. That happens when you get to be my age! Perhaps my 55 years is beginning to show on me."

"It's not the years that count. It's probably the stress that can change your hair from black to gray. I've seen it close up on my father's head after being away from him in Iraq while he runs his steel firm in Baltimore single-handedly."

"Since I retired from Washington College in Chestertown, 12 miles away, I like to come here to see what other collectors and aficionados are buying nowadays. It's fun to jump into this den of antiquity, and fish-out something, especially something acoustical that I can fiddle around with. You probably didn't realize it but I bought the amplifier for your guitar."

"You really can't hesitate or the auctioneer will yell 'Sold'!"

"My hands were holding the amplifier while my eyes were looking at the electrical hookups, and I suddenly lost my concentration of the auctioneer, and completely forgot about what was being sold!"

"You know the old axiom, 'He who hesitates is lost'. Well, your loss was my gain. But let's keep in touch. I'm thinking about a client who plays guitar that might want this one after I try to repair it. He's not a collector per se, but a professional guitarist."

Richard interrupts, "I must have overlooked something. Did you see some damage?"

"Not major but something that aroused my curiosity. When I looked inside the sound chamber, I suspect that the acoustics might need some repair or alteration. Maybe you have some ideas and would like to help me. Two minds are better than one, right?

"If my client doesn't want it, I'll sell it to you. I'm a dealer and must turn over my purchases and show a profit at the end of the month. Here's my telephone number in Betterton. Call me tomorrow. I'll buy the lunch."

Mark looks at his wristwatch and realizes it is almost 5 pm as he walks out of the hangar and jumps into the passenger seat of Annette's truck for the drive back to Betterton. Along the way he gushes like a little kid, and tells her, "That Crumpton auction is unbelievable, but like everything in life, it'll take hard work, ingenuity and perseverance to succeed. But I have a good feeling inside. The adrenaline from the action of finding and buying something gives me a slight high that no drug or alcohol can give me. But now, we have to think about turning the buy into a profit, don't we?"

Annette tells him, "From my observation of you today, Mark, I have to apologize and let you know that I feel a little guilty in throwing you into the battle. It must have appeared like your first day in basic training, with everything new, which is probably a stretch in words here. But I watched you carefully and am convinced that you will make a very good dealer, even better than me, which is not saying much. But you have the potential and all the ingredients to become something special in the antiques business."

Mark opens the top button of his cotton sport shirt and soaks in all of Annette's remarks. He's feeling good but used. After all, this is just his first skirmish in Dixon's. But good feelings are expressed and shared by both of them as they chatter back and forth during the 40 minute drive back to Betterton. It's a good time to review and report, just like a sports broadcaster giving the results of today's game. They also recognize that it takes teamwork to succeed in the antique business. By the time they arrive back at Annette's shop, both are exhausted and head for their respective bedrooms for a well-deserved sleep.

The next morning, a Thursday, after breakfast, Sandy asks Mark, "Would you mind helping me clear out more stuff in the garage, things that we no longer need? I could use the space for an art studio. I've been wanting to convert it into a studio for sculpture and painting for years. Maybe you could help out in the construction, too."

She walks with him to the side door of the garage behind and offset to the right of the main house and tells him, "This garage is about 14 feet across and 24 feet deep, but you wouldn't know it with all the clutter in here. It gives me claustrophobia." She walks to the main garage door that normally opens to park a vehicle and lifts the door manually to let in the early morning sun. She sighs, surveys the clutter again, and tells him, "Let's start by getting these old rusty iron pipes and old wood beams and other lumber out of here, so we can get a better perspective of the space that I'll need for my sculpture and painting work."

Within 15 minutes, the back half of the garage, about 14 feet across by 12 feet deep, is cleared and already looks spacious enough for a small artist studio. The remaining portion is still cluttered with furniture and cartons that the family has accumulated over the years.

Sandy indicates with her hands, "I would like a partition here to hang paintings, some shelves along the walls where I can stack canvases vertically, some track lighting, and a bathroom in one corner, please."

Mark tells her, "Naturally all the walls around the periphery of the garage will need insulation and drywall since you'll be spending time and working here all year round."

Sandy continues, "By the way, you might be surprised to know that I have some ideas for making wind chimes for tourists."

Mark confesses, "Sandy, in the brief time that I've known you, nothing you do surprises me. You're like a bottle of seltzer with your ideas and energy, and you need only a little coaxing to erupt."

Before he can finish the last word, she takes a set of 10-inch long tubular chimes out of a cardboard box hidden in a back corner of the garage. She hangs them on a nail protruding from an overhead rafter, pushes them into a cluster, and says, "These are for the outdoors and need only a little wind to cause them to collide and produce beautiful chimes." Then she hangs a set of 6-inch tubular chimes nearby and says, "These work on the principle of an electrostatic field. All you have to do is move your hands up and down and around them. Just listen to these delicate chimes. I learned the basic principles of an electrostatic field in my physics class in high school."

Mark says, "I'm surprised at your ingenuity and inventiveness. I'm also disappointed that you keep these things hidden in your garage instead of getting up the courage to follow through on your projects.

You know, Sandy, you could have the best ideas in the world, but sooner or later, you have to release them and let the world see the results of your creativity.

"As for the conversion of the garage from a parking and storage usage into a studio, off the top of my head, I must confess that I like your ideas. They're all doable, and for very little money. I'll be happy to draw up some plans for your review and approval later in the week. And I have another suggestion for you. After the garage is converted into a studio, how about opening your studio on Saturday mornings to teach a class in sculpture or painting? I have a feeling that you might generate some extra income when not occupied with your own private projects, maybe something like a morning class for anyone interested in learning a new trade or skill, that would benefit everyone, from kids to seniors."

Sandy says, "Teaching classes? I'll take it under consideration. Kids and seniors don't have much money to spend nowadays on art classes, and I can spend my time more efficiently on my sculpture and painting."

With a little hesitation, Mark reflects, "Obviously, I'll have to find a contractor or at least a carpenter to complete this construction project. I'll help out as much as I can but I'm no good with a hammer and saw, believe me. I prefer to work with my brains, whenever possible.

"I assume you have some money put aside for this conversion, for labor and materials. Since it's an interior remodel and we're not changing the original footprint of the property, I don't think you'll need a building permit, but maybe you can inquire with the county building inspector or permits office. Adding that bathroom in the rear won't be difficult either, since you already have water pipes going to the apartment upstairs."

As Sandy and Mark leave the garage, two young watermen in their work clothes and boots stroll slowly up the path to the garage and express their condolences awkwardly. They never introduce themselves and only one of them begins by saying, "We attended the ceremony for Tommy and wanted to tell you in person how much we regret his passing, and how much he will be missed by everyone who worked along with him in the Bay. We weren't close friends with Tommy in school, but knew him and shared his love for the Bay. We never talked much and never gave it a thought that he was a chicken-necker, like some of the others living around here. We were too busy trying to make a living and doing whatever it takes to make a living on the Bay."

With no introduction, the other waterman gains some confidence and says, "I believe that Tommy liked to do his thing on the water alone. He seemed to be happy just working on the Bay. We knew each other but really didn't know each other, if you understand me. We were raised on the Bay from the time we could walk or swim. Tommy was part of us. We just thought that you'd like to know that he will be missed."

Then they turn away from Sandy before she can offer any words, and walk together back down the sidewalk and climb in their pickup. In the driver's seat is the one who ended the conversation. He turns the ignition key and the engine, covered with a body badly needing a fresh coat of paint, barely starts turning over. Eventually, with a little coaxing from the driver, the engine produces a loud bang, along with a cloud of black smoke from the exhaust pipe, perhaps a back fire of combustion misfiring, but settles into a purring sound as the truck makes a U-turn and heads up Main Street out of town.

CHAPTER 5

Mark and Sandy return to the antiques store through the back door just in time for him to answer the telephone. On the line is Richard Wagner, the absent-minded professor. He asks, "Would you mind if I could have a look at the guitar? I have some ideas about possibly improving the acoustics if you can spare the time today."

Within the hour, Richard is inside Annette's Antiques and leaning his tall body against the open doorway of a back room that normally serves as an oversized walk-in closet. He is in rapture mode as he watches Mark as he inserts the sharp blade of his Baghdad dagger about 1/8 inch into the top lid of the guitar and carefully cut around the periphery of the top surface, thereby removing the top lid of the guitar. When he lifts the lid, the entire electronic guts of the acoustic chamber are exposed.

Richard admits, "Mark, you made that incision with the precision of a surgeon at Johns Hopkins Hospital."

Mark pauses to scratch his head in a puzzling gesture and confesses, "It seems to me that someone has already fooled around with this guitar. There's an electronic plug-in module missing from one cavity. What I would like to do next is use my dagger in a way that it was never intended, to clean away the old dried and brittle glue so that the replacement or substitute module will fit easily again in its cavity."

Suddenly and without warning, Richard asks him to stop his work and trade places with him. Richard takes the dagger in his right hand and unconsciously weighs it, then asks, "Where in the world did you get this dagger? It looks more like a precious jewel that a sultan would wear around his waist to give the impression of manliness and great wealth. I seem to recall reading about such a dagger in a reference book on strange historical music."

Mark asks, "Historical music?"

"Well, Mark, I was teaching a class at Washington College, and one lecture was devoted to historical music, its origins and usage. In my research I discovered something that will probably amuse you."

"Professor, please continue. I could use a laugh this morning."

"Well, according to this reference book, a dagger, something like this one, would whistle or zing, not sing, through the air when thrown at an enemy. Furthermore, a legend developed that the dagger had a mind all its own and would only harm someone deserving to be harmed."

Mark interrupts, "That's the strangest story I've ever heard, and certainly not amusing to me."

Richard continues, "Yes, I have to agree with you, but apparently the blade was made with special metals that could be forged in a foundry, hammered, shaped, and sharpened in a special way that gave each dagger its individual sound. I never will forget my reading about the power within the object itself. That theory makes sense to me.

"As I hold your dagger in my hands this very moment, it seems to want to guide me in removing a small chamber wall so that something much larger can fit there. Yes, one could say the blade has a mind all its own."

"I probably shouldn't be using it here but it's expedient," Mark confesses. "It does the job. I haven't owned it very long and never really studied it closely, except to admire the jewels blended into the enamelwork and Arabic writing. I call it my equalizer. I found it during combat in Iraq, unearthed by an explosion that overturned our armored vehicle."

"It must be older than Methuselah. But getting back to this cavity, I think a miniature transducer could fit nicely and improve the acoustics considerably. This solid state cube includes a pick-up that receives the sound waves. The transducer should embellish and perhaps even change the sound wave pattern by looping or double looping, to produce a slight echo that the amplifier will amplify into the speaker or your headset. The looping is what I've been searching for in my experiments in Chestertown.

"What do you think, Mark?" He turns to look at Mark leaning over one shoulder. When he doesn't answer and just scratches his head in puzzlement, Richard excitedly confesses, "I might have a transducer in my gizmo box in the trunk of my car."

Mark follows him and says, "You're free to try any of your ideas as far as I'm concerned. I was a psych major, not an electrical engineer, at Johns Hopkins, so give it a try, please."

When Richard returns from his car, he is carrying in one hand the amplifier that he bought at the Crumpton auction and in the other hand a miniature black cube with each side about the size of a nickel. He admits, "The idea of looping or double-looping of the acoustics is entirely possible. Les Paul experimented with this technology in the 50's when he did those fabulous recordings with Mary Ford, except he wired everything outside the guitar in his recording equipment. We're re-wiring everything inside the guitar."

Mark says, "I wasn't around then but I've certainly heard those recordings, especially 'How High The Moon', all my favorites, even to this day. In fact, Les Paul's improvisation probably inspired me to take a few lessons on the guitar."

Richard continues, "It's like recording the melody on one track of a two-track recorder at a millisecond slower than the other track containing the harmony. The delay creates a new synthesis of two sounds like an echo. Now, when that echo is fed into the pick-up and eventually magnified by the transducer, the resulting acoustics should be something special to hear.

"I'm amazed that I never thought of this before since I've been experimenting for over a year in my little workshop. When you removed that partition, you opened my eyes and mind to another possibility, another design modification that seems so simple. It was ingenious of you to remove that partition."

"Let's get one thing straight here. It wasn't me, pal. It was all you. I guess it's true what they say about four eyes being better than two, two brains better than one, especially when they are all working towards the same goal, right?"

They test the new design and both are shocked with the increased acoustics and resonance. Richard admits, "I think we just gave birth to the echo-acoustic guitar."

Mark asks, "Are you the mother or the father?"

"I wonder if the expression 'necessity is the mother of all inventions' applies here."

"You lost me there."

"It really doesn't make any difference. It's the end result that counts."

Mark concludes, "I think this baby is truly something special, perhaps exceptional, don't you agree?"

Mark hands the guitar to Richard and tells him, "I can't wait to call my friend, Reggie. He lives nearby and should be the first to play it and really bring it to life!"

A minute later Reggie is in a corner of the kitchenette, seated comfortably on a high stool. The acoustics in this small room are perfect. Reggie exercises every string, and plays several passages from three or four popular melodies like the virtuoso Tony Mottola and Frank Sinatra's favorite guitarist, Al Viola.

Sandy hears the music and quietly peers over and around everyone, almost out of sight.

Reggie ends his test of the guitar with a crescendo, and exclaims "Sold! I've got to have this baby, here and now!"

Mark says, "You didn't even ask the price."

"When you have an opportunity to buy something special and unique, I just have to trust the seller that the price will be a fair one.

"How's $3,000 sound to you?"

"I'm happy with that figure, if you are."

Mark looks at Richard who pats him on his back and whispers, "That's a nice profit, isn't it?"

Mark confesses, "Before we all get carried away here, I must confess that I can't sell it to you after all."

Reggie frowns and asks, "Why not? My money's as good as the next man, isn't it?"

Mark responds, "More so. But there's no value one can place on friendship, and with Sandy's permission, we'd like you to have it as a token of our appreciation." He turns to Richard and tells Reggie, "Here's my collaborator, the genius who deserves all the credit for the new acoustics. But he and I will share equally if we decide to file a patent for the innovative design."

Reggie is so impressed with the acoustics and reverberations that he can't wait to play it on his next recording date and tell all his musician friends in New York about it. He says, "Wait until Les Paul and Bucky Pizzarelli hear about this!"

Richard, growing in confidence, gets Reggie's attention and solicits, "When you have time, perhaps you'd like to read some of my original compositions, based on the heroic classical passages by Richard Wagner, but with my modern dominant 9ths, a blend of two composers, like Wagner meeting Lilo Schifrin, or in art, something like Rembrandt meeting Picasso."

Reggie tells him, "Anytime. Here's my card. Give me a call and bring them by the house. I'm always on the lookout for new ideas, new composers, anything to keep me challenged. Right now, I'm practicing until I'm blue in the face, but eager to play the works of new composers, those men and women writing on the cutting edge of contemporary music. In fact, one of my personal goals is to be a conductor, so I'm always on the lookout for new talent whose compositions I could introduce as a conductor. The life of a studio musician is enjoyable, it pays the bills, but contemporary music has no boundaries. I'd like to explore more modern music just like Jackson Pollock extended contemporary painting."

Richard is ecstatic and his eyes brighten as he combs his hair with his hands and adjusts his spectacles. He utters nervously, "By the way, if you have a popular melody or rhapsody that you've written and need an arrangement for your quintet, let me know. I might surprise you with my arrangements. At college my students called me the 'Lalo Shifrin of Chestertown'."

Overlooking all the activities of everyone going in and out of Annette's Antiques is Nellie Fox Boyd, the spinster who runs the B&B next door. Her eavesdropping reputation has earned her the highly respected nickname of 'the Spy in the Sky' by locals who love to hear the latest gossip coming from her lips. The locals never refuse or dismiss her telephone calls, but have learned to take her gossip with a grain of salt.

You can always tell when she's at work by simply watching the movement of the curtains in an upstairs back window of her B&B. If she isn't peering out the window, she's usually on the telephone, spreading tidbits that she heard from tourists and tenants who spend a night with her. Through an open window, you can hear her voice speaking into the telephone, "There's people going in and out of that garage, at all times of the day and night. It's obvious to anyone with a brain in their body that it looks like an affair between Sandy and that former Navy SEAL. And remember, he's a 'chicken-necker'. He's from Baltimore."

Just as Reggie, Richard and Mark finish their business with the guitar, Annette asks Sandy to invite them all to stay for lunch. In a way this is a small celebration. During lunch you can see by the brighter expressions on all their faces and the overall laughter and chatter, that life is looking better, much better this afternoon. Mark says, "There seems to be a change in the air, I feel it. It's just a start here, but I believe that times are changing in Betterton."

Then Reggie adds, "For the better, and next time, I'll bring you some of my father's chicken breast filets. Perdue chickens are considered the best poultry money can buy. In Murlin everyone one says that it's the tender loving care of his workers. They really love their Perdue chickens."

The next morning around 9, Richard telephones Mark to say, "I know it might seem impulsive on my part, but I just wanted to know if you're coming to the Crumpton auction on Wednesday. I hope this time you'll have some consideration for me and my age and limited finances if we should compete against each other again."

Before he can continue, Mark interrupts, "Not to worry here, pal. There's no competition between us, at least not at Crumpton. I hope you're not thinking about moving in on Sandy,"

Richard says, "Whoa, Mark. Actually I was thinking of moving in on Annette whom I find very attractive, fascinating and a bit intriguing."

Mark tells him, "That's a mouthful of adjectives. Why don't you drop over for lunch if you have nothing better to do this afternoon?"

"I've got my motor running and the pistons are pounding away."

"I know the feeling, pal. I'll make sure Annette is here, and both of you can spend some time alone, getting to know each other a little better."

Suddenly there's a knock at the back door and Mark is surprised to find his mother Sara and chauffeur pulling a dolly with two trunks of his clothing. He ushers her into Annette's Antiques and introduces

Annette. They embrace and quickly share a few laughs, then Annette shares details of her daughter's rescue in the Bay.

Sara's quickly brought up to speed here, but is curious to see his new quarters over the garage. She's prepared to be shocked over the difference between these living quarters and his bedroom in Homewood. When she climbs the rickety wooden stairs and steps into his apartment, she begins laughing and says, "This would've made a good set in Barry Levinson's movie 'The Natural'. You know, humble beginnings."

About this same time another delivery truck pulls up, with a new computer that Mark had ordered. Mark tells his mother that he now has to arrange with an installer to install a satellite dish, so he can get higher speeds than the slow speed of telephone dial-up. "I suspect in these rural areas like Betterton, there's not enough demand for fiber-optic or high speed telephone dial-up. That leaves me with the only choice to install a satellite dish like Wildblue dot com., for my new life as an antiques dealer here," he tells her. In a loud voice full of confidence, he professes, "This little town is about to undergo a change. I'll be the first in Betterton to have a satellite dish."

Mark pulls a chair closer to the bed where his mother is checking out the mattress, and asks, "What's new with Dad?"

"That's one of the reasons I came personally this morning...The pressure of running the mill is increasing. I can see it in his eyes and his breathing. He's a workhorse that is running out of energy, not ideas or goals, just energy."

"Just energy? That's enough to choke a horse. He's not 21 anymore, a graduate in metallurgy from Hopkins. At 60 he's probably worked harder than two men his age. If you ask me to join him in the mill, I'll do it."

"No Mark, I can't ask you to do that. That has to be your decision. But I want you to continue with the idea of finding someone with management skills that can help your father run the day-to-day operation at the mill."

"You know, I'm just getting started in the antiques business and I really like it. No one has to lead me, like leading a horse to water. It's exciting, the unexpected joy of discovering a lost treasure, engaging people from all walks of life. It fits into my quest for culture and competition."

His mother looks at her watch. "You're probably hungry for lunch…We better get to the Bay Bridge before the traffic begins to back up and cause big delays. There's nothing worse that wasting you time in line to pay a toll…Take good care of yourself, son. You're always in our hearts," she tells him.

After lunch, with Mark, Richard and Annette take a stroll along the bluffs overlooking Betterton beach where the Sassafras River meets the Chesapeake Bay. They find an old bench under a shady tree where the afternoon sun is not so direct and warm on their faces. They hear a boat whistle and Richard says, "That's a B flat."

"It sounds a little flat to me too."

"With you it seems to be all work and no play."

"I've always believed that hard work will lead to success."

"Yes, but you have to take some time to smell the roses too, like my mother used to tell me all the time."

They talk about music and how music has played an important part of their lives. Annette tells Richard, "I wish you could have met my son Tommy. He never had a father in his lifetime and never complained about anything. Quite extraordinary, really! His birth father was an antiques dealer from Philadelphia who taught me everything I know about antiques, but would not move to Betterton. Since I couldn't live anywhere but here, we were never married, but he always supported me with advice. A few years later I was infatuated with a young music teacher from Baltimore who paid a visit to Betterton. I fell in love with his hands first, then his music."

Annette gazes towards the pier of Betterton and her mind drifts and fades into her memory bank. She says, in a sort of flashback mode: "Picture this if you can. About 25 years ago, the ferry from Baltimore docks at Betterton pier and out steps a smiling striking 26 year old mahogany skinned man dressed in a business suit, hardly the wardrobe for a weekend outing in a country town like Betterton. He moved with the grace of a Roman god, striding up Main Street, with a body 6 feet tall, solidly built, and an aura of confidence like Columbus discovering America. You know the image: broad shoulders, erect head exuding confidence from the top of his dark wavy hair to the bottom of his shoes. Talk about a fish out of water. He seemed out of place here and believe me, he was. But his eyes had a special sparkle in them.

When he eventually came into my shop, he told me that he was born in Hawaii with a sprinkle of Spanish and Philippine blood. He said his name was Joseph Lopez, and in the next few minutes he was playing the Hawaiian steel guitar like nothing I had ever heard before. He found the guitar buried in one corner of my shop, covered with remnants of fabrics.

I immediately fell head over heels and stayed that way during the few months that we dated. But it was clear that he wanted the big city life of Baltimore and I wanted the quiet farm life around Betterton. He never knew that I was pregnant and would give birth to Sandy. I never asked him for anything after we parted. We both went our separate ways. I was an independent woman and enjoying the life of an antiques dealer."

Annette's gaze fades back to the Betterton pier, empty and somewhat solitary except for a large white dove walking aimlessly. She continues, "There was no looking back. So you can see, I've had two wonderful kids, both out of wedlock. I had the confidence that hard work would lead to success. You see, when I was growing up here in Betterton, going to school around these parts, I watched other young girls having love affairs and swore that I would never sleep with a man before marrying him. So I waited for the right man. Well, Richard, 'the right man'. Wish I knew what is 'the right man'. I'm telling you about myself so you can get a clear picture of what you might be getting yourself into."

Richard says, "I get the picture. You certainly don't pull any punches. But you can be proud of yourself and your two kids. You've accomplished something special here. It does take hard work, diligence, dedication, and lots of will power." He caringly takes her hands into his and begins to tell her about his life. "I was a professor of music at Washington College until the bottle eventually forced me to retire early. I really wanted to be a composer, like my ancestor Richard Wagner, but the pressure of trying to live up to those lofty ambitions almost did me in. I continued to teach but the conflict of teaching and composing in my subconscious was unbearable at times, and I hit the bottle.

But now I've been sober for three years, attending meetings with a good support group, and feeling pretty good about myself. One day I will go back to composing when the inspiration leads me to pick up the pen again and write. You might be the inspiration that I've been looking for and needed in my life."

From the twinkle in their eyes and the smiles being exchanged, the chemistry and electricity are flowing between them. Suddenly Nellie Boyd accidentally walks near their bench, interrupts their conversation, and in a somewhat friendly but deceptive manner, asks "Are you both planning to attend the Harvest Moon Fest next weekend? There's always something special going on, isn't there?"

The Harvest Moon fest is the last thing that Richard and Annette have on their minds at this moment, but Annette politely tells her, "You might even be surprised at what's in store for the fest. I'm sponsoring one of the entertainers."

Nellie asks again, "Can you give me any more information? You know, I wouldn't tell a soul."

Annette rises and says facetiously, "I know only too well. I know how you get the word out. Do you still use the telephone or a pigeon?"

Without waiting for an answer, Annette grabs hold of Richard's arm, and they walk slowly away from the shady tree and back up Main Street to Annette's house, where Richard has parked his car. He gives her a gentle kiss on both cheeks, says goodbye, and drives his car up Main Street in the direction of Chestertown.

That same afternoon, while Richard and Annette were together under the shady tree, Knute unexpectedly drops by the shop and offers to watch over the business for the rest of the afternoon, so that Sandy and Mark can have more time together too. He tells them, "Young people like you should be out in the sun, enjoying life outdoors. Oh, how I remember those days when I was courting my first wife."

While in the shop alone, Knute spots an old 12-bass accordion hanging on a hook along a back wall. He takes it down and begins playing very slowly to get familiar with the keys. Playing reminds him of an old favorite from his days as a tugboat captain. He plays softly as Gertie joins in and sings only one word. That word is "Always." While Knute plays the accordion, Sandy invites Mark for a swim on Betterton beach and picks up a yellow colored straw picnic basket.

Once they arrive at the beach, Sandy simply wants to find out what is best for her future and decide if Mark will be a part of it. They talk about her love of sculpture. She asks him, "Have you ever seen the exhibition of the Barye bronzes at the Walters Art Gallery in Baltimore?"

"As a matter of fact, I have. Are you surprised that a Navy SEAL would be interested in bronzes? There's a lot of things about me that you don't know that might surprise you…(pausing)…But Sandy, there's a time and place to talk about bronzes and art and such things. Frankly I would prefer to talk more about you and me going steady or is it too early to think about us as a twosome? I don't plunge overboard without a reason. In fact I don't plunge into anything without a reason."

Sandy confesses, "Well, Mark, it is true that I fell head over heels in the Chesapeake Bay, but for now I'm very content to have you as a friend, a close friend. I think that you're good for my heart."

Mark takes Sandy in his arms, and presses his lips against hers. The caress is tender and long. "I feel the passion coming through my skin, but what's lurking behind it?" he asks himself. Confused and bewildered, his subconscious mind asks, "I can't get the questions out of my mind. Why am I here? Did some of my teammates die in Iraq just so I could be here holding Sandy in my arms? I have this inner conflict stirring around, the guilt of survival, and now falling in love. It doesn't make any sense. What the hell am I talking about anyway?"

Sandy says, "Remember the old adage: time will sort things out. We'll find our place in life. You'll find your place in life. Maybe it'll be with me, maybe not. Time will tell."

As the sun begins its descent over the Bay, they start to walk from the beach back up Main Street towards home when confronted by four black teenagers loitering on the street corner. As Sandy and Mark approach them, they stop dancing to some loud music coming from their radio and begin singing in harmony, 'A Tisket, A Tasket, I Wonder What's in Your Yellow Basket'. One of the kids teases Sandy, then grabs her basket without knowing her purse is inside, and sprints away up Main Street while his other three friends push Mark to the ground and fall on top of him.

Like a race horse that has stumbled at the starting gate, Mark regains his form and is in hot pursuit. It's a straight 200 yard dash but slightly uphill, with both sprinting at full speed, until Mark finally manages to tackle him just inside the chain link fence around the small senior citizen park next to the church. There is no fight here, just good-natured fun and laughter while both regain their breath. Mark looks carefully over this kid with a big smile on his face and sees something that reminds him of delinquent kids near his old neighborhood in Baltimore. He asks, "Hey, pal, what's your name? And don't tell me Jesse Owens."

The kid answers, "You can call me Mo, short for Motor Mouth."

Mark asks, "You've got to be kidding."

The kid answers, "Yeah, I'm kidding. Nobody could ever catch me, especially running uphill, except you, today."

Mark asks again, "And your real name?"

"It's Jesse James, believe it or not."

Mark says, "Really? I would've never guessed it."

"My grandmother raised me. My mother died at my birth and my father left home for good. You know, your chasing me is not like the ones you see in the movies where the robber has the purse in one hand and knocks over garbage cans or boxes in the path of police in pursuit or dodges between trees and cars parked along the street. There are no trees or cars parked along the street here in Betterton that I could zigzag around and try to slow you down. No one could ever catch me before, especially in running a straight 200 yards up a hill. Yes, come to think of it, no one has ever caught me from behind either"

Mark says, "Well, there's always a first time for everything, isn't there? A straight run like today is nothing compared to running for your life in Iraq. No one can outrun a bullet or grenade when it has your name on it. How old are you, Jesse?"

"Seventeen. We're all the same age. We're juniors at Kent High," he answers. So you're a military man. I should have known by your slender build."

Mark asks, "Build? Build has nothing to do with speed. For track and sprinters, you need to be lean and mean. Forget the muscles. It's what's between your ears and inside your heart that counts, things like determination, and the will power never to quit until the race is over."

Jesse continues, "We never meant anything by this snatch and run. We were just teasing and having some fun."

Mark begins laughing and says, "Now that I've met you, I feel better and relieved," then puts his arm around him.

A minute later Sandy arrives at the park along with Jesse's other three friends. Mark introduces her to Jessie who is quick to apologize for the snatch-and-run maneuver and hands the basket to Sandy. She immediately checks to see if her wallet is still inside it.

Mark tells her, "This kid is a born runner. He has talent, big time. I mean, he made me work up a sweat to catch him, at least 200 yards, all uphill." He turns his attention away from Sandy and addresses Jesse's three buddies and asks them why they're wasting their time on street corners, waiting to get into trouble by loitering, when they could be learning something.

He asks them, "Have you ever thought about running track? If you could run half as well as Jesse, you would make a good relay team. Have you ever thought about going out for track in high school? Forming your own relay team here in Betterton? Exercise, especially running will stimulate your brain, give you an induced high, and open up other areas in your brain for creative ideas."

Sandy tells Mark, "Around town, these kids are called juvenile delinquents. Anything you can do to teach or guide them will help to improve the reputation of the town, too."

Mark continues to talk like an older brother. They begin to pay attention and trust what he is saying to them. It seems to them that no one has ever spoken to them like he now speaks to them. They were never offered much encouragement before. Within a few minutes, they decide to give the idea of running as a relay team a try.

Mark agrees to train them in the park adjacent to the senior living and retirement building. Everyone in town calls it the senior park. He tells them, "If we start on Monday afternoon, I want no quitting from anyone until the end of practice each day. You've got to sacrifice something to get ahead. We will take it one day at a time if that's all right with you, O.K.?"

They all agree to meet on Monday afternoon, since Mark has to work at the shop over the weekend.

Finally he concludes, "I like someone who wants a second chance. If you do what I tell you, no one will ever call you juvenile delinquents again."

CHAPTER 6

Sandy and Mark walk from the park back down the slight reclining sidewalk to their home. Along the way Mark tells her, "In the next few days, I'd like to pay a visit to the school here, and find out what they're teaching these kids, and how they're treating them."

"Sounds like they have become your kids," she asserts and pulls his arm closer to her body. "That's a very quick adoption. You hardly know them."

"If I don't take an interest in them, who will? It's obvious that something is missing in their lives. I have the time, correction, I'll *take* the time to help these kids which will also help make Betterton a better place for everyone too. I have a hunch here, just a hunch mind you, but a visit to their school may be necessary. It certainly can't hurt to talk to their teachers, and the sooner I check it out, the better I'll be able to plan my next step."

When Sandy and Mark get back to their respective premises, she goes into her studio while he climbs the stairs to his apartment overhead. He rests his head on a stack of pillows piled against the headboard of his bed. He closes his eyes momentarily and suddenly feels a little flirtatious and lustful. He reaches for his cell phone, and telephones Liz. He says, "You've heard the old expression, 'Wish You Were Here'? Well, Liz, where are you and when will you find time to see me again? I was hoping that we could meet halfway between Washington DC and Betterton, something like Annapolis for lunch tomorrow."

Liz says, "I can't make it for lunch. How about an early dinner at 5?"

"Any special restaurant that you like in our state capitol?

"I know a cozy place called the Blue Heron. Ask for a quiet corner called the nest, overlooking the water."

"Apparently you do know Annapolis, don't you?"

"I'll fill you in tomorrow at 5 if you can make the reservation."

"Leave it to me. If I don't call you back, it's a date. Roger, over and out." Mark closes his cell phone, slides down towards the footboard, and passes out in his bed.

Two hours later a stranger knocks at the back door of Annette's Antiques. He looks at his wrist watch whose dial reflects in the moonlight overhead and indicates exactly 10 pm. He shakes his head from side to side in a somewhat apologetic and hopeless manner. Annette, wearing a light blue oversized bathrobe, slowly opens the door just wide enough to catch a glimpse of the man. She asks, "Do you know what time it is? This better be important."

He asks, "Do you know where my horse is?"

Annette dumbfounded, asks, "Who are you? Have you been drinking?"

He repeats himself, "Do you know where my horse is? And no, I have not been drinking although it might be time for one."

Now curiosity takes over as Annette inquires further, "Exactly what is this all about?"

He replies, "I'm Tom Bowman, owner of the breeding farm down the road a piece. I think one of my horses, a really smart thoroughbred, probably was excited by music coming from the radio of one of my trainers or handlers, and managed to nudge open the latch to the door of his stall and disappeared from my complex.

My guess is that he smelled the fresh air of the Bay or saw some lights or heard some interesting sounds along Main Street. He's a romantic son of a gun. So I'm going door to door, house to house, to find him. You may not realize it but that horse is worth a ton of money. His name is Storm Cat. Ever heard of him?"

Annette says, "Storm Cat? Are you kidding! Yes, I've heard of him. Hasn't everyone? But what's he doing in these parts? I thought he was at a breeding farm in Kentucky."

Tom replies, "Well, he's on loan to us for breeding, but we can talk more about that later. I just would like to inspect your garage if you don't mind. I hear some music coming from inside the garage."

When they enter the side door of the garage, in the center, under a dim single light hanging from an overhead rafter, seemingly frozen in his posture, is the stallion Storm Cat. He is erect and motionless. Sandy stands 10 feet away from the horse and works feverishly with the clay model taking form right before her eyes. Filling the garage are the sounds coming from a LP record that plays a recording of Nicolai Rimsky-Korsakov's "Scheherazade." This particular recording provides the perfect background music for this precious moment in Sandy's life. Almost with the pace of the dazzling, swirling movements of this Russian composer's music, Sandy's fingers press into the wet clay like a pianist playing on a piano keyboard. With one hand she reaches into a pot of clay near her sculptor's table with rotating top, never taking her eyes off the model that she is creating. Her fingers seem to have a life and an energy all their own. It's motion without thinking. It's all a spontaneous feeling, a reaction, a creation purely from impulse and instinct.

Sandy senses that two figures have quietly entered the side door and now are lurking nearby. She can feel them breathing down her neck although they are standing a safe distance away. She continues to concentrate on the clay model, and says, "In art schools, they call it the 'madness' of clay. Sculpting can take over your life. Tonight is an accident that happens maybe once in a lifetime. The clay comes from right here in Betterton but that horse comes from God! Yes, the clay comes from right here in Betterton. Very bad for drainage of water and septic systems, but very good for sculptors like me."

The model stands about 18" high and looks like a horse sculptured in terracotta by the French sculptor Edgar Degas. She moves her eyes, almost in a movement attuned to the music echoing in the background, back and forth, first at the stallion then back at her model, and confesses, "If only that horse could talk!"

Tom sighs, "He did all his talking on the racetrack. You should've seen him at Pimlico in Bawlmer 20 years ago when he came down the stretch, trailing by four lengths, laying back off the pace, then letting go with a burst of energy, hard to believe unless you were there in his saddle like his jockey holding on for dear life. He ended up winning by three lengths, with plenty left in his tank. It was like the other horses were in slow motion and Storm Cat was breaking the sound barrier."

Sandy asks, "A stallion like him must have some special blood in him, right?

Tom answers, "Special blood? His father was Northern Dancer, who descended from Native Dancer. I guess you've heard of Native Dancer, haven't you?

Pulling her wardrobe closer around her neck, Annette says, "Native Dancer? Who hasn't heard of him. I remember when Native Dancer was called the 'Gray Ghost of Sagmor', and in stud at Alfred Vandabill's farm in Glenin, Murlin. A few years ago I even met Kevin Plank, the current owner of Sagmor, but that's another story."

Finally Tom says, "It's getting late and past my bedtime. I should get that stallion back to his barn. The insurance company would be furious if his presence here leaked out. I'll be in touch with you all later in the week."

He puts a halter on the horse and leads him out of the garage, then turns to Sandy and says, "You know, Sandy, it's something about this horse that handicappers and even trainers and breeders don't see, but you see it. Everyone talks about the importance of conformation. You have captured more than what is visible to the naked eye. You've captured some of the characteristics of his heart and spirit, the angle of his head, the shoulder muscles. I like what you have created here. When you are completely satisfied with the finished model and ready to cast it in bronze, I'd like to buy the first one cast by the foundry."

Annette takes a deep breath and bursts out laughing uncontrollably. Sandy adds some finishing touches to her sculpture and wipes her hands clean, and places a wet towel over the model to prevent fast drying of top surface of the clay. She turns to her mother and they give each other a giant bear hug and pat on the back. Together they look up at an old fracture hanging on one wall. It reads, 'It Is Accidents In Life That Bring Out Hidden Talents In People of All Ages'.

The next morning, a beautiful warm and sunny Saturday, during breakfast with Sandy and Annette in their kitchenette in the rear of their store, Mark talks somewhat impulsively and excitedly about the auction in Crumpton and says, "You know, partner, that farm auction is my new battlefield. It is made for me, just right for me, right for someone who has to judge the situation, size everything up quickly.

You have to use basic instincts, with no time to research or look in a book or price guide or to scroll into an iPod or browse everything with Google. There, in that hangar and in that field, I look at it as opportunity knocking at our door. I further predict one day that we will strike it rich, big time. Mark my word. When a dealer or private party drops off his load of junk into the field or on a table inside the hangar, we will eventually get lucky and spot a gem. I can just feel it growing inside of me. It's that hunt for the elusive fox. Do you ever get that feeling too?"

Annette says, "Yes, Mark, I know that feeling well. For me, it's not a fox hunt, but the challenge that requires all your memorization, instincts, and analytical skills: It's what keeps me motivated and loving the antiques business. Also Mark, you'll find this out for yourself eventually, too. It's something to do for the rest of your life. The older you get, hopefully the better you get!"

Before Sandy can get a word in, the telephone rings. Both Annette and Sandy rise from their seats and step across the floor, but Mark takes a giant step and stretches out his long arm, and quickly picks up the telephone and puts it to his ear. Annette says, "You're a little anxious this morning, aren't you?"

"Well, to tell the truth, I have a good feeling about this business and I'm eager to keep the momentum going forward." He brings the telephone to his ear and surprises them by declaring in a loud voice, "This is Annette's Antiques, the Best in Betterton."

A voice on the other end says, "And this is Vera Wayne, the Best in Rock Hall. I've heard through the grapevine that there's a fellow from Bawlmer who's working in Betterton at Annette's Antiques. Would that be you?"

Mark admits that he's from Baltimore and is working with Annette. He then asks, "What's this all about?"

Vera says, "Someone told me you have a model of a ship called Gratitude. Is that true?" Mark explains, "The model's well carved, an exact replica of the *Gratitude*, but I'm not exactly sure of the scale, perhaps one-hundredth. I can vouch that it was obviously carved with tender loving care. It stands about 16 inches tall."

Vera then explains, "Me and my husband Bud own the Swan Point Marina in Rock Hall, where the *Gratitude* used to dock in the 50's. I think it would be a good idea to have that model ship here in our marina office for everyone to see, don't you think? Would you mind bringing it to the marina this afternoon for us to examine? I feel certain that we'll buy it if the price is right, of course."

Mark tells her, "The price is right, $600 plus tax, and a bargain to boot. I could bring it over in the next hour."

Vera says, "Bring it on, I mean bring it over. We're at the end of Route 20, then turn right onto Lawton Road and drive to the end. We're on the right side. You'll see the big sign for Swan Point Marina. We'll be waiting for you."

Vera hangs up the telephone in her marina office just as her husband Bud enters the back door and an older man dressed casually enters the front door. She tells the older man, "I'll be with you in a moment if you don't mind waiting a moment," then turns to Bud and explains quickly, "There's a dealer from Betterton that coming here with a ship model of the *Gratitude* in the next hour for us to see. I heard that he's a Navy SEAL, a new partner working with Annette Antiques in Betterton."

When Bud hears the words "Navy SEAL," his eyes turn sinister, and the thought crosses his mind of another encounter with a military man, something to muddy up the waters of his life again.

He walks behind the counter right next to his wife and grabs her arm tightly. With no hesitation or reservation, he blurts out, "Is this purchase a legitimate one for the office or another one of your seductive interludes with a military man while I'm working hard in the marina, trying to make ends meet?"

Vera says, "You have a cruel streak, Bud, that will be your downfall. Also you're hurting my arm. Let go, Bud. I'm not going to tell you a second time. Let go or I'll bust your nuts."

Bud is surprised but still irritated as he releases his grip and says, "Watch your mouth, Vera."

She answers, "You struck a nerve. It's not easy living with someone like you, but it's the life that I've chosen for myself and my baby. You've provoked me and hurt me with your grip. You better be careful, Bud. If you try to hurt me again or my baby, you'll regret it, believe me. Furthermore, I don't have a clue about this guy from Betterton.

"As far as any encounters with military men, what I do with my personal life is my own business. You're certainly not interested in satisfying my needs in that way anymore. I thought we had that all settled a year ago after Jaime was born. You're jealous of anyone and everyone, especially my partner in the soft crab business, Steve Floyd.

Plus, are you aware that we have a customer in the office, over there, probably over-hearing everything we're saying to each other?"

Bud says, "When you talk about being in business with Floyd, a partner like him is scraping the bottom of the barrel, isn't it?"

Vera says, "What transpired in the bedroom between Pretty Boy and me is over and done with. He's just my working partner in the soft crab business that provides a little extra spending money for me and Jaime that I don't have to ask you for, like paying the baby sitter each month or shopping for toys. Furthermore, you're making a good profit with the marina but you continue to give most of it to your sisters, instead of sharing it with your wife and child."

Bud says, "We've been all through this a thousand times. I have to split the profits with them, 'cause that's the way I got control of the marina in the first place. You know, Vera, it does no good for us to be quarreling in front of Jaime although he's only 1 year old, or in front of a customer who's waiting for you in the front of the office. Settle down. I'll take a good look at that model ship if you want me to, but keep the price down to an acceptable level, so we can write it off as a needed expense for the office."

Bud exits through the back door as Vera walks over to a far corner of the office and says to the older gentleman staring at a wall of photos, "I apologize if you've heard anything personal here. Now, what can I do for you, sir?"

The gent says, "I've had family quarrels too. It's none of my business. I was concentrating on all the wonderful photos that you have hanging on the walls. It's arranged to give someone like me a nice perspective and history of the marina, in days of old up to the present time. Not much has changed in 30 years, has it? I guess it's just like Rock Hall itself. Not much has changed here in 30 years either."

He says, "I'm thinking about berthing my vessel here. It's an easy ride for me from my home in Delaware and an easier ride to take *Pal Joey* out of your marina right into the Chesapeake Bay. No need to navigate up a river. I've seen these old houses lining the Chester River a hundred times and that's not interesting to me anymore. I prefer to start the motor and get as fast as possible into the Chesapeake Bay."

Vera escorts him over to the office counter and shows him a sheet of fees and charges for berthing a boat in Swan Creek Marina.

He finally introduces himself, "I'm Les Huntington of Dover. I'm on the board of DuPont and have a 40 foot power sail called *Pal Joey*. Let's talk business. Being a businessman, I'm interested to see what discount you can give me for a lease of one year, two years, perhaps five years?"

Vera says, "Well, in that case, under the circumstances, with my husband's permission, how about a seven percent reduction?"

Les inquires further, "And for payment in advance?"

Vera says, "In that case, under the circumstances, with my husband's permission, how about 10 percent for a five-year lease? That will save us a lot of time and paperwork."

Les smiles broadly and says, "I like the way you think! I've always enjoyed doing business with a smart lady who knows a good deal when she sees it. Obviously, time is important to you too, although you have your whole life ahead of you and a lot more years to enjoy your life here than I have. Here's my card and my boat's tied up at the far end of your last pier. You can't miss it. Prepare the contract for five years, and after I mosey around town and shop for a present for my wife, I'll be back with a check, in an hour or two."

Vera is feeling exuberant as Les leaves the office. She walks over to a crib containing her one-year old boy and lifts him high in the air, "Well, Jaime boy. Clap your hands, little darling. Your mother just pulled off a sales contract that will last until you're six years old and ready to enter the first grade. In fact, I think I'll begin teaching you the letters of the alphabet and numbers so you can help me here in the office. How would you like that, Jaime boy?"

She then returns him to his crib and telephones Steve "Pretty Boy" Floyd to get the results of last week's production of soft crabs. The line is out of order or off the hook. So Vera takes Jamie in her arms and flips the sign on the door so that it reads, "Office Closed. See Boss on Pier." She walks with her baby in her arms to her red Cadillac, parked near the front door of the marina office.

After strapping her baby securely to his seat behind the driver's seat, she drives only about a quarter mile from her marina office to the soft crab shed complex that was her former home before she married Bud. Although she's not living there anymore, she still owns it, lock, stock, and barrel.

Vera parks her Caddy between the main house on the left and the crab shed on the right side. She marches into the shed, about 18 by 20 feet, the shape of a Quonset hut, but with a concrete floor that is cool and damp from water dripping everywhere. Compressor motors are humming in the background along with water pumps that beat in a steady rhythm. Long white plastic PVC pipes hang down from the ceiling and run around the inside periphery of the shed like track lighting. Six large metal tanks, each 3 by 6 feet by 10 inches high, supported by heavy metal legs, are half-filled with water.

These crabs are a special specie of crab, called 'peelers', all different sizes, some swimming around, some stationary, some alive, some dead. The water is temperature controlled at about 50 degrees, with control valves leading to overhead tanks containing a salt solution. The water is constantly circulated and re-circulated through filters to remove impurities and contaminants. There are no automatic alarms in case conditions of the water change. This is a hands-on operation, almost primitive in nature.

When everything is working properly, each crab inside the tank thinks it's still in the Bay. Floats inside each tank keep the level of water at a height of about nine inches. While the peeler crab is living inside the tank, one of the small miracles in life occurs. It undergoes a transformation called sluffing or moulting.

By means of a special enzyme created within its body, the peeler crab dissolves its smaller cavities, then lifts its entire body, with all of its organs intact, completely out of its larger cavities including its hard shell and grows an entirely new shell that is soft. The entire transformation usually occurs within two days or less while the peeler is in the tank. But the soft shell remains in the soft condition for only about two hours. If not removed from the tank within that time period, the soft shell develops into a hard shell again

Vera inspects each tank, which now contains at least five dozen crabs. The total number of peelers in the process of sluffing is over 360. Her blood begins to boil as she realizes that no one is around to supervise the operation.

"This soft crab business requires constant monitoring," she says to one of the soft crabs while lifting it out of the water. "There's a lot of money at stake here because I pay the watermen a dollar each for you. If you develop into a savory soft crab, I can sell you for $3 wholesale."

She feels the texture of the shell and returns it to the tank. She says, "You're close but not close enough. The Murlin blue crab, Calinectes Sapidus, beautiful swimmer! How I miss caring for you." She moves to another tank and mutters, "Now where in the world is Floyd? If he's not here to remove you when you're soft, I lose money, clear and simple. And I have to pay the utility bills and insurance and God knows what else. From what I see here in these tanks, there's about a thousand dollars at stake."

Vera reaches down into the last tank and notices the color of the shell of a peeler has darkened. She removes it, feels the weight in her hand, and smiles at the excited movement of its spiny legs, claws, and eyes. She says to herself, "Well, little darling, you're not going to grow back into a hard shell crab today, that's for sure!" She finds a small cardboard box bottom and carefully places the soft crab on its end, with its eyes upward, against one side of the cardboard box.

In the next minute she picks out eleven soft crabs and stacks them at an angle on their backs like books facing upward in a display.. The dozen soft crabs are large and fully packed, all about the same size, 'whale' size, each weighing nine ounces or more. In a good restaurant each one would easily sell for $20 when sautéed in butter. She says, "My mouth is just watering with the thought of you on a whole wheat bun with lettuce and tomato and a side order of coleslaw."

She places the box in a cooler and slams the door shut, and says, "Now where in the world is my partner, who should be monitoring these peelers?"

She is steaming mad when she exits the shed and walks across a small yard between the shed and main house. She opens the back door and barges into the kitchenette, cluttered with dirty dishes everywhere. She quick-steps down a small corridor leading to a back bedroom, thrusts opens the door, and finds Floyd slightly tipsy or drowsy, and in bed with Bonnie Bratcher, her 17-year-old babysitter.

Floyd shouts, "You have no right to come barging into my private quarters when I'm resting."

Vera orders Bonnie, "Get your clothes on and come with me now. You and I have a lot to talk about during the drive back to the marina."

Then she turns to Floyd who rushes to put his clothes on, shakes her head from side to side, and cries out in a much louder voice, "Resting?

Is that what you call resting? What you do on your own time is your own business, but we have crabs that demands constant supervision when those peelers are sluffing, and you have to answer the telephone in case there's a client ready to place an order."

She pauses to catch her breath and continues her tirade, "Same old Pretty Boy! Up to your same old tricks! But you must be scratching the bottom of the barrel with this high school drop-out, aren't you? Look, I can't risk my reputation as co-owner because you have your sexual needs in the middle of the day. What you do on your own time is your own business but not this thing, in bed, with an under-aged girl who is also half your age. I can just see the headlines in the paper, 34-year-old waterman caught in love nest with 17-year-old high school dropout, and my baby-sitter to boot. In a small town that spells disaster and scandal for me, and I simply won't have it. I don't like scandal. I will not permit scandal!"

Floyd says, "I wasn't neglecting the peelers. I checked them an hour ago and everything was O.K. in the tanks. We have 50 ready for pick up at 5 o'clock by a restaurant that placed an order this morning."

Vera says, "An order of 50 is peanuts and you know it. You have over 360 crabs sluffing right now in those tanks and you're out here indulging. For the first time in your life, try to be honest with me and tell me why you left the phone off the hook and for how long was it off the hook. We not only lose business today, but a customer will turn to someone else to do business if he can't get through and place an order. You simply cannot leave the phone off the hook while you tend to your afternoon delights."

Floyd replies, "I was just taking a break."

"A break?"

"A break in the afternoon was alright for you a few years ago, wasn't it? I never heard any complaints from you when you wanted some pleasure in the afternoon."

"Well, Pretty Boy, that was then. This is now. And this is pretty much the end of our business together. I'm ending our partnership in the soft crab business here and now. No more excuses from you. It's not 'shape up or ship out' anymore. It's 'ship out' for you at the end of October. I'm giving you your marching orders."

Floyd apologetically says, "It is what it is."

Vera counters, "You mean, it was what it was...your fired!"

Floyd says, "You can call it the end in our crab business if you want, but you cannot deny me my rights to see my son Jamie "

Vera says, "That's all over and done with a year ago. I chose Bud, married Bud, and as far as I'm concerned, Bud is the father of Jaime, period. So when you come to your senses, remember this tune, 'Hit the road, Jack, and don't you come back, no more no more no more no more'."

Vera concludes, "One last thing here. When you calculate the totals and close down the business, I want you out of my house. No more free lodging as part of our soft crab business. I want you to clear out all your possessions from this house, and get out of town, away from me and my baby, the farther the better. I don't want to see your face again. You and I are history. At the end of the month, if there are any peelers that have not sluffed, you can have them, get whatever you can for them and keep the money for yourself. It's your termination bonus."

Vera walks back into the sluffing shed, scans the tanks and peelers and running water, and curses, "Damn it! Screw the crabs and the crab business. It's a seasonal business anyway. I have bigger and better things ahead."

She slams the door to the shed and walks back to her car where Bonnie is already sitting next to Jaime in the back seat. Vera starts the engine and pulls sharply out of the dirt road and onto the asphalt road leading back to the marina.

On the brief six minute drive back to the marina office, Vera asks Bonnie, "Aren't I paying you enough money for baby-sitting Jamie? At least it gives you a cushion until you can find something better. You know, as a drop-out, no one will hire you for a good paying job unless you get your GED. How many times have I told you that I would help you with your studies? At some time in your life, you have to stop falling into bed with every Tom, Dick and Floyd in town."

Bonnie is silent as usual and only reaches over to touch Jamie's fingers. Jamie grabs hold of one of her fingers and holds on tightly and won't let go of it.

CHAPTER 7

Within 10 minutes of leaving her old home and the confrontation with Floyd, Vera is once again inside the marina office, telling Bud about finding Pretty Boy in bed with her baby sitter Bonnie. Bud says, "Did you expect anything different from that bastard? You know what he was like years ago. A leopard doesn't change his spots, does he? And you still think he is the father of Jaime? I wouldn't have him anywhere near my child, Vera! He's just no good, period. Furthermore, if word gets out about him and Bonnie, it's just more fuel for gossip. You know how these local big mouths in Rock Hall like to spread the word."

Vera tells Bud, "It's not only scandalous, but possibly criminal. You'll be pleased to know that I fired him on the spot and we're no longer partners in the soft crab business. And he will move out of my old home, too."

Bud says, "Good riddance."

Back in Betterton, Sandy has the afternoon free and offers to drive Mark to Rock Hall to meet Vera and Bud, and show them the model ship Gratitude. She mentions that afterwards, she could show him the town and perhaps the wild life refuge outside the town of Rock Hall. Annette agrees to watch over the store while they try to sell Vera the model ship.

Annette says, "Mark, you could be embarking on your first wild goose chase! I heard that Knute will be coming by to see Gertie, so I'll certainly have some fun this afternoon."

Mark wraps the model ship *Gratitude* carefully with soft tissue paper and places it in a large Hutzler-of-Baltimore box for transport to Rock Hall, then tells Sandy, "I would like to be back in Betterton by 3 so I can keep an appointment in Annapolis at 5."

Sandy raises her eyebrows, smiles, and asks with a slight touch of jealousy, "Is it animal, vegetable or mineral?"

"What are you talking about?"

"Your date in Annapolis."

"It's a military matter. She's a Major at the Pentagon."

Sandy says, "I'd like to meet her. Why don't you invite her to Betterton? I'll get her a discount at Nellie's B&B."

Mark says somewhat facetiously, "I'll take it under consideration. A discount won't be necessary. The military pays the Major a very good salary, with an almost unlimited expense account, too."

Finally they walk to the pickup truck parked in the driveway. He turns to Sandy and says, "I have a surprise for you. Let's take my new BMW convertible!"

With complete surprise and relief, she says, "I saw that car delivered late last night and wondered why it was parked on the curb between us and Nellie's B&B. I thought it belonged to one of her overnight guests!"

He brags a little, "I really don't own it. A long term lease is economically better for me, which leaves me lots of money to spend at Crumpton. I'll drive from here to Rock Hall, and then you can drive us to Eastern Neck Wildlife Refuge with the top down, and I'll just relax and watch the geese."

Mark drives the 30 mile distance from Betterton to Rock Hall. Along the way Sandy tells him a little bit of the history about the town. She says, "Supposedly around 1787 George Washington and his crew sailed from the capitol in Washington DC up the Potomac River and into the Chesapeake Bay, and eventually dropped anchor in Rock Hall harbor.

He scratches his head and asks, "How is it that you remember the date 1787 so well?"

"I've always had a knack for numbers and dates, I guess. Probably a spillover effect from my physics class, where I had to memorize lots of numbers and formulas."

"You know it's rare to find a beautiful girl with a beautiful mind too. Usually the two don't go together for some reason."

"Well, look at you, Mr. Know-it-all. Who are you to judge people by their looks?"

He raises his hands and hollers, "Hold it, Sandy. I wasn't inferring anything. Actually I was just trying to pay you a compliment and make good conversation. It's a beautiful day for a drive in the country, so why not enjoy it, right? Frankly if I had my choice, I would've preferred to take a horse and buggy, but 30 miles each way is a long hike for the poor horse. Remember one horse power is not much power, is it?" Sandy giggles and all is calm inside the car.

Soon Mark pulls up into the gravel parking lot of Swan Point Marina. As he retrieves the box containing the model from the back seat, Sandy says, "Look over there. Isn't that magic? Beautiful boats tied up to the piers, with a sandy beach and cove of high grass and birds everywhere, all chirping in the light breeze. Just smell the fresh air of the Chesapeake Bay, and over there, you can see the Bay Bridge on the horizon."

Mark says, "Yes, Sandy, this is a paradise."

Sandy says, "They call it Swan Point Marina but I've never see any swans here, unless they're nesting in that high grassy area over there." Sandy opens the front door to the marina office as Mark carries the model ship behind her and proceeds to walk over to the corner office area where he places the model ship carefully on the countertop.

Vera leaves her desk and introduces herself, "I'm Vera Wayne. Nice to meet you, and that's my pride and joy, Jaime Boy, over there in his crib. I apologize that Bud was called away unexpectedly just a few minutes ago. He'll be disappointed, but I'm delighted to see the model ship Gratitude. It's truly a fine replica, right down to the exact scale. I'd say about one-one-hundredth scale. Whataya think?"

Mark says, "You have me at a considerable disadvantage since I've never seen the *Gratitude* in person, or even in photographs."

Vera points to a wall and says, "Well, you should have a look at the wall over there. You'll find a pretty good history of Swan Point Marina in those photos."

Sandy meanders through the office looking at photos of celebrities and their boats, along with larger photos of the Wayne family, owners of the marina for over 30 years.

Mark reaches over the countertop and places his hand in Jaime's crib. The baby's hand grabs Mark's forefinger and won't let go. Mark says, "What a grip! How old is your baby?" Vera turns her attention from the model ship and focuses on Mark, and asks, "What did you say?"

He says, "Your baby has an incredible grip around my finger. He doesn't seem to want to let go."

She counters, "Just like his mother. When you find something special, why would you want to let go of it?" Vera now spends more time studying Mark than the model ship on the countertop.

He suddenly turns his attention away from the baby and towards a row of black and white photos lining a wall. Vera nudges him slightly and draws his attention back to the model ship. She moves her finger over her lips and into her mouth.

Vera says to herself, "Now how in the hell am I going to get Sandy out of the picture here?" She then declares, "Back to reality. I like the ship and will buy it if the price is right, and my husband agrees."

Mark tells her, "The price is $600 plus tax, the same price I told you over the telephone. The price hasn't changed. I can't leave it with you since it's not insured off-premises."

Vera tells him to reserve it until Bud gives his approval. Mark repacks the model ship and follows Sandy in the direction of her pickup truck. While they're walking away, Vera is already plotting her next rendezvous with Mark. She says to herself, "I'll simply have to find a way, accidentally on purpose, to bump into him another time, another place, without Sandy and without Bud around. I've had more challenging situations before. This Mark is my mark, the new man on my compass. He's hot and so am I!"

Sandy looks at her wrist watch and tells Mark, "We have time for a cup of coffee at Java Rock on Main Street, my treat. It's not Starbucks. Maybe better."

A few minutes later Sandy and Mark are enjoying a cup of freshly brewed coffee under an umbrella stand on the outside deck of Java Rock, a relatively new addition to Rock Hall. While relaxing in light-weight, plastic chairs, Sandy says, 'This corner was an old time gas station, then ambulance garage for the old fire house next door, until 2004. You should've heard about the problems Jim and Joanne Rich encountered with the Planning and Zoning Office in Chestertown, about their converting it from a rusty old and dilapidated gasoline filling station and ambulance garage into a wonderful and modern

Starbucks-type coffee house that not only brews the best coffee in Kent County, but the best panini sandwiches as well.".

Mark studies the arched bay window that blends in with the windows of the Methodist Church across the street and the teal-colored siding of Java Rock, and says, 'Teal for Two'. Isn't that a song by Cole Porter? Or was it Irving Berlin?"

In a comic mood, Sandy tells him, "Mark, the song is 'Tea for Two' and it was written by neither Cole Porter nor Irving Berlin."

"Don't keep me in suspense, Sandy. Tell me quickly before I die, who wrote it, please?"

"The music was written by Vincent Youmans, with lyrics by Irving Caesar. Furthermore, the song is sung from the viewpoint of a love-struck man, who plans his future with a new woman in mind. That man might be you, Mark, but I'm not sure of the woman you have in mind."

"Very perceptive of you, Sandy. But I'm disappointed to think that you lack some confidence in me, or yourself, when you should know that the woman in my life is you and not Liz. .But I'm as curious as all hell about how in the world you know so much about that song."

"Mark, I'm an artist who's interested in all things musical and artistic. Sometimes I surprise myself by remembering such things."

"You'd make a good contestant on Jeopardy."

"Getting back to reality, here we are sipping coffee for two, not tea for two. Ah! There's nothing like a fresh brewed cup of Gimmee Coffee. Now, isn't that funny. What a name for a coffee, but it's the name that the Rich's gave to their special blend. They also serve it at their B&B called Huntingfield Inn, down the road about 2 miles, one of the best B&B's on the east coast with fresh baked muffins for breakfast, great service and early American furnishings. They also cater Weddings and all sorts of parties on their farm."

Mark shakes his head in wonderment, still digesting her revelations that now surprise and please him. He momentarily is at a loss for words. He turns to watch a foursome of tourists holding ice cream cones and licking the ice cream dripping down the sides of the cone and onto their fingers. He tells her, "Maybe we should have had an ice cream cone from that old store on the corner. The way those tourists are licking the sides of their cones tells me that the taste must be heavenly."

Sandy notices that Mark is now engaged in people-watching, and says, "People-watching here is nothing like watching people on the fancy boulevards of Paris. About the most exciting thing that has happened in Rock Hall was a terrapin crossing the road without getting squashed by a car or bicycle. You'll find out soon enough that Rock Hall is just a slow moving sleepy little town on the Eastern Shore, like Betterton."

A few cars drive along Main Street at this late noon hour. Sandy continues, "Not long ago those homes were converted into B&B's for tourists wanting to spend the weekend here. Eventually these people liked the slow pace of things, bought a boat that they would haul back and forth from their cottage that was rented for summer vacations. It would be nice to see them retire and spend their life full time here, but right now, only about 600 out of 1,500 people live here full time. It's hard for chicken-neckers to settle here permanently."

Mark says, "Hold it, Sandy. Would you mind telling me exactly what a chicken-necker is?"

Sandy explains, "Well, in essence, it's an outsider, anyone not born locally. I guess the expression came from local watermen in these parts who all use clams or eels cut up as bait for their trot lines or pots. But outsiders use chicken necks for their bait. So the watermen then started calling them 'chicken-neckers'. But the name carries other implications too. Watermen resent anyone changing the way things are done around here."

Mark says, "I never did like name-calling. When you get right down to it, it's a form of racism, petty jealousy, and envy. Perhaps the watermen are jealous and envious of the wealthy boaters. There's more than enough for everyone in the Bay if they would just cooperate with each other and help to keep the bay clean."

Sandy tells him with some trepidation, "I think the watermen just worry about losing their traditions and livelihood. Look over there, across the street. It took a long time before an outsider from Philadelphia could get permission to convert his property from a residence in the middle of Main Street into a Kayak and Bicycle Rental Shop for tourists downstairs and an apartment overhead."

Mark says, "I see a sign on the corner: Durdings, founded in 1890."

Sandy says, "Yes, they're still famous in these parts for making the best chocolate sundaes with scoops of homemade ice cream topped with fruit and whipped cream. And on the opposite side of the street, across from Java Rock, is Smiling' Jake's. The owner named his place after his dog, can you believe it? And they're a Haberdashery, with a huge selection of Hawaiian clothes."

Mark says, "Wow! Hawaiian clothes in a fishing village like Rock Hall. I wonder how I would look in one of those Aloha shirts."

Sandy chimes in, "They're sold to tourists, not the local crowd from Rock Hall. At the end of the block is Bayside Market, owned by Jeff and Debbie Carroll, who sell the best quality meats and locally grown produce at bargain prices. Finally, right in the middle of this block, to our right, is the local saloon with a small dance floor where locals can unwind and have a good time. It can get pretty wild inside."

Just as they are about to finish their last sip of coffee, a stunning beauty exits the Java Rock coffee shop while humming a tune. As she steps down onto the outside deck beside Sandy's umbrella stand, Sandy says to her, "Excuse me but are you in the Wayne family?"

The beauty answers, "Yes, I'm Ruth Wayne."

Sandy says, "I just saw a photo of you and your family at Swan Point Marina a few minutes ago, of you in a bathing suit. I'd like you to meet Mark."

He says, "Now, that's something I would like to see, I mean, you in a bathing suit, not a photo of you in a bathing suit. I would say six foot, 150 pounds blended all in the right spots, and fancy free at 26, right?"

Ruth answers, "You look like you're beginning to drool a little, but you've sized me up quickly, accurately, and boldly, Mark."

Sandy invites Ruth to join them for a few minutes and help her explain what it's like to live in Rock Hall.

Ruth takes a seat and continues, "In a nutshell, it's Dullsville with a capital 'D'. Nothing changes here. Tourists come to eat oysters and crabs and do a little sailing on the Chesapeake Bay. There's got to be more in life than eating oysters and crabs and go sailing on the Bay. I remember attending a town meeting last year when, during a discussion of a resolution, the question of syntax came up. One of the councilmen from Rock Hall suddenly stood up and shouted, "I ain't paying no tax on sin, even if the devil himself comes to collect it! I guess he thought syntax was a tax on sin."

Mark asks, "Are you trying to tell me that Rock Hall, like Betterton, is really a way of life, a state of mind, a psychological complex? If so, why are you still here?"

Ruth answers, "I'm not still here. After high school, I couldn't wait to get away and see the world, so I joined American Airlines. I just felt there had to be more in life than running a marina or running around town with nothing to show for it at the end of the day. When you get down to it, to be completely honest and frank, I have my eyes set on a millionaire, but the chances of finding him in this town are pretty slim to none, so I decided on a career in the air, so to speak."

Suddenly another young girl exits Java Rock as Ruth rises to say, "Sandy and Mark, this is my younger sister, Jean. She's 24 and still fancy free. You probably saw her in the bathing suit photos at the marina office too. She still helps Bud and Vera whenever they need a little extra help in the office answering the telephone, whatever or whenever."

Jean grabs the belt of her tennis shorts that are shortened and ragged, exposing almost all of her thighs and gives it a tug, trying now to cover her bare belly button. She bellows for all to hear, "Help out? That's a crock! No one can work beside Vera who has her own way of doing things. It's her way or no way! She's a bitch to work with."

A car pulls over to the curb in front of Java Rock with two young men in the front seats. The passenger sitting in the right front seat calls to Jean and waves her over to the car. She moves a few steps and sways her hips like a Hawaiian hula dancer. She leans over beside the open window of the car to give both of them a closer look at her cleavage. With dark hair and a face resembling Ben Affleck, he asks boldly, "What's going on tonight, Jean? Wanta go for a drive or walk on the beach in the moonlight?"

Jean answers, "Sorry. I've got a date tonight, but I could squeeze you in tomorrow night, one at a time."

The driver, who resembles Kurt Russell, leans forward and says, "Ever tried it with three at a time? I think they call it ménage a trois!"

Mark, Sandy, and Ruth along with other passersby cannot help but notice Jean's shorts, stretched to their limits and now exposing her rear end.

A horn blows from a car directly behind them because they are blocking the street. Jean leans back away from the window as she waves the car behind them to go around them when the coast is clear. Then she prances 20 feet to the car waiting to resume their conversation with her. As she walks towards the car, Jean sways her hips even more widely than before, reminiscent of a Hula dancer in slow motion. She's well aware of her action and flaunts it openly. .

Meanwhile, back at the café, Sandy asks Ruth if she'll be home for the Harvest Moon Festival coming up in a week or two. Ruth confesses, "As a matter of fact, I will be off that weekend and plan on attending the fest, especially the dance."

Sandy tells her, "Ruth, we have a special friend by the name of Reggie Perdue that I'd like you to meet. He's good looking, a professional musician, and he'll be the featured attraction at the Harvest Moon ball."

Ruth says, "That sounds wonderful. I'll look forward to meeting him"

Sandy smiles and confesses, "Well, I'm not sure if he can dance, but I guarantee you his music will floor you."

Ruth says, "Well, that's a new one on me. I've never been floored before, although many men have tried to get me floored. Well, let's just leave it at that. You can use your own imagination here." They all break out laughing as Ruth heads off down the street towards Jean. Mark and Sandy walk in the opposite direction back to their truck.

Now Sandy is driving Mark's convertible slowly down Sharp Street. When they can go no further, she confesses, "Here's the place where George Washington supposedly came ashore in 1787, probably ate some oysters to get his daily requirements of iron and potassium, maybe a few steamed crabs too, before going inland 12 miles to Chestertown. As president of these United States, he probably needed all the vitamins that he could get his hands on for his battles with Congress."

She pauses and begins laughing, then continues, "Over there to our left, you can see yachts with charter captains waiting to take people fishing, and over there to our right are 'buy boats' where watermen bring in their catch of the day to sell to distributors waiting with refrigerator trucks to transport it to wholesale seafood markets in Baltimore, Dover, and Philadelphia, and Jersey City. We'll have to come back here for dinner some night at Waterman's Restaurant. It's really quite beautiful to dine outside on the deck and watch the spectacular sunsets here on the Bay."

Mark asks, "Look across the harbor at all those yachts and sailboats swaying gently in the wind."

Sandy answers, "That's the Sailing Emporium, owned and run by the Willis family. It's a showplace, featured in magazines as the number one place for tourists. They keep it in pristine condition, and have a gift shop full of souvenirs."

In another minute Sandy makes a U-turn and drives back up Sharp Street to Main Street, makes a right turn and says, "Main Street becomes Eastern Neck Island Road and further down, about 6 miles, is the Wildlife Refuge. I'll be your chauffeur and tour guide for the next ten minutes. I think you'll find this area heavenly. No dozing off, please."

During the drive to the refuge, Sandy explains, "Except for the Wildlife Refuge, most of these corn and soybean farms have been owned for generations by the same family. Income from these farms is scant and hardly pays much of a profit over the increasing taxes and high costs of seed, fertilizer, and insecticides. But farmers are reluctant to sell their land. Only the deer, geese, and ducks enjoy the freedom to roam at will."

Over the next few minutes both are suddenly silent as Sandy concentrates on driving and Mark admires the landscape around them. Soon they cross over a wooden bridge where some of the old wooden boards of the bridge pull away and lift upward from their placement. The rattle of the boards is noticeable but last only a few seconds when their vehicle has passed completely over the wooden bridge.

On the other side of the bridge is an island of about 10,000 acres of dense woods and open fields of marsh and wetlands, a government tract of land used as a nesting ground for Wild Canada geese and Artic Tundra swan.

"I bet you didn't know that the Tundra swan flies all the way here from Alaska," Sandy suddenly blurts out.

"You have me at a considerable disadvantage," replies Mark. "I wouldn't make that bet with you. I've never even heard of the Tundra swan."

"Well, Mark, next month, these fields will be littered with them. But how they managed to fly thousands of miles has always astounded me. One of the staff in the Refuge Office told me that they have an uncanny ability to sense wind currents and will suddenly take off like a 747, reach a certain altitude, and let the high winds do the rest. I get goose pimples just thinking about it."

A minute later Sandy turns right onto a gravel road and drives about 200 feet more until the road reaches a dead end, a slight bluff above the sandy shore. They leave their car which is the only one parked in this area and walk arm in arm through the high grass and wetlands right up to the sandy shore.

"Bicyclists pedal their little rear ends here from the town limits, about six miles each way.," says Sandy. "But for me, this area is truly a photographer's paradise, an infinite source of picture-taking on open trails, don't you think?"

"I've never seen or felt anything like it before, so peaceful, truly a paradise," confesses Mark. "I see and feel the Good Lord working everywhere here. Why can't people get along with the same harmony as God's creatures here?"

"Harmony. That's a good word but so hard to implement."

"Take a look at all those butterflies."

"They're called Monarch, and in a few weeks they'll fly 2,000 miles to nest in El Rosario, Mexico."

"I know that spot because I went scuba diving for lobsters off the coast there."

"We're not done yet, Mark. Over there you'll find a two foot tall white heron with yellow bills and a wing span of three feet called Cattle Egrets. They started arriving here in the early 1940's all the way from South America."

"Listen to those geese cackling."

"It's called 'gaggling', and once you've heard it, you never forget it. They gaggle all the time, on the ground, in the water, in the air."

"They must be very contented here with room to roam at their leisure and plenty of food to eat."

"It's nice to see those geese in flight or walking on land if you're a photographer or artist," continues Sandy. "I like the symmetry when they're all facing one direction and marching in unison, like an army of soldiers. But to make a profit or break even from the expenses of running a farm is another thing. There are a few rich families, like DuPont and Carnegie, who are conservationists and never have to worry about making money from farming. For these families, all they seem to care about, especially in the winter months, are the hunting parties and weekend outings. They descend here in their expensive camouflage outfits and shotguns for a weekend of shooting.. Their battle cry is: 'After two geese each, break out the champagne and caviar'. I guess it's a special place and time for them to unwind."

CHAPTER 8

After Sandy and Mark return to Betterton, Mark showers quickly in the bathroom of his apartment, changes into a dark orange Ralph Lauren shirt, complete with western-styled angled pockets, and Levi slacks. "Casual, but kind of classy for my date with Liz," he says to himself. He sits on his bed and puts on a pair of leather boots with his initials MH on the heel. He had them custom-made in Texas by Tony Lama himself during a SEAL exercise there a year ago.

He stands up, reaches up for a Stetson hat hanging on the wall near his bed, and looks inside at the colored label of a cowboy kneeling beside his horse and the triple X marking on the inside band. When he puts it on his head, he looks in the mirror, and says, "Mirror, mirror on the wall. Who's the fairest of them all? Lie a little and tell me it's me and only me, please, but I won't believe you.

"If I had one wish, I'd like to look like Clint Eastwood." He releases a frown. "I think the Stetson is not for me tonight," he says apologetically. But he catches a fleeting thought. The hat reminds him of his younger days riding alongside his father on fox hunts in Western Maryland. He says to himself, "I wonder if there's a ranch nearby where I can go horseback riding one of these days."

He hangs the Stetson on a clothes tree, slams the door of his apartment, and hops down the stairs and into his BMW for the 60 mile drive to Annapolis.

One hour and ten minutes later Mark finds Liz at the bar of the Blue Heron Restaurant. She holds in one hand a Navy grog cocktail with a pineapple slice leaning over the edge of the glass, and in the other hand a stop watch. She presses the stop watch and it plays the song, "Just In Time, I Found You Just In Time." I always thought that the best music boxes were made by the Swiss, but this one is Chinese, and precision made. I can't believe it, Mark. You're exactly on time. You're aware that it isn't good form to keep a lady waiting," she tells him satirically and bursts out laughing.

"It's my SEAL training. Precision counts, otherwise lives are at stake. Liz, you look like a million dollars, after taxes. I can see where all those Pentagon dollars are spent and well worth it."

"Wrong, Buster. I wore this number to try to impress you. I can't write it off either. Tonight's not a date for business, but maybe we'll figure out how to make it so."

"The night is young and you're so beautiful. Aren't those the words to an old Cole Porter ballad? I know I'm reaching into history on that one."

"I love those oldies but goodies, but were those words written by Cole Porter? Let's get to our table where we can have some privacy. I'd like to learn as much as I can about you in the next hour."

Before leaving, Mark tells the bartender to send over a gin Martini and an icy Navy grog with extra Jamaica rum to the Nest.

After both are seated in a secluded corner with only a partial view of the waterfront, Mark asks her, "Do we have to rush things? We have the rest of our lives, unless one of us doesn't live up to expectations."

"Let's not go too far into the future. Let's just enjoy the moment."

In this special corner, Liz continues the conversation with, "On a first date, the man usually begins by telling a joke, slightly risqué and off color."

Mark responds, "Well, Liz, I'm not that type of man, but I do have an interesting story if you'd care to hear it."

Slightly anxious and curious, she tells him, "Fire away, Mark, but I still want that off-color ending."

"Well, a man with a strip of bacon dangling over each ear rushes into the psychiatrist's office and tells the receptionist, 'I've got to see the doctor right away'. The receptionist asks him, 'Do you have an appointment?' The man says, 'No, but this is an emergency'. The receptionist turns to her intercom, presses a button, and says, 'Doctor Freud, there's a man here who says he has an emergency and has to see you right away.' From the intercom comes the voice of the doctor, who gives the order, 'By all means, send him right in.' The receptionist tells the man, 'You're very lucky because the doctor is in between patients.

Go right in.' The man rushes into the psychiatrist's office, and the doctor looks at him with a strip of bacon still dangling over each ear, and says, 'Please take a seat. Now what can I do for you?' The man says. 'Doctor, I want to talk about my absent-minded father!' Mark is the only one laughing at his own joke.

Liz groans, "Oh Mark, that's a terrible story. I'd keep my day job if I were you."

Both break out in laughter and take a sip of their drinks.

He takes a deep breath and tells her, "I had intended to tell you the one about the athletic director who is so naive that he thinks foreplay is a quartet on the golf course!"

Liz laughs and responds with a sheepish grin, "Oh Mark. That's even worse than the first."

Marks blushes a little and apologetically asks, "I better leave the joke telling to others. Without getting too serious in our first date, would you mind telling me about your goals and expectations?"

"You certainly don't waste any time, do you Mark?" She pauses to look around to ensure no one is eavesdropping, and continues, "Despite the initial impression that you might have about me, I'm basically an honest and straight-forward person, but I expect a great deal out of people, including myself. In my line of work, if people fail or I fail to deliver, it can cost someone his life."

"Without probing too deeply, can you give me an inkling of your line of work at the moment?"

"Let's just say that it's usually chaotic since I move around a lot. Right now, it's ISMAD, which stands for Intelligence Surveillance Management And Dissemination. "

"Wow! ISMAD certainly is mad! Are you sure you're able to reveal this information to me? I certainly don't want you to get into trouble."

"It's science applied to counter insurgency and terrorism around the world. At the moment, we're focusing on the Middle East. At the Pentagon they look at me as a technocrat. It's very challenging work, believe me."

Mark leans back in his chair almost to the point of falling backward and out of his seat. He lets out a sigh, then looms up, "That's a big responsibility for someone of your age."

Liz says, "Age is not important. I was lucky to be in the right place when my boss needed me, and I had the talent necessary to do the job."

Mark inquires further, "And what's your background, education wise?"

Liz says, "A degree in metallurgy from Hopkins, then, with my ROTC there, I saw an opportunity to join the Signal Corps assigned to the Pentagon. I've always wanted to work in or near Washington DC. Eventually I maneuvered into the Corps of Engineers and led a small team of engineers and scientists doing research on the Panzer tank. One of our first problems involved the heavy casing and how to make it safer, but lighter, so it could carry more weight in weaponry. I have to admit here that it was my idea to introduce the right amount of titanium to pig iron."

"You're probably understating your contribution here, aren't you?"

"Understating, yes, but it was recognized by my superiors, and I leaped in rank from Captain to Major overnight. But enough about me, what's a Navy SEAL doing in Betterton of all places? You must feel like a fish out of water. I bet you've heard that line before."

"Betterton is my new battlefield. You'll probably be surprised to hear me say it, but I'm in the process of becoming an art and antiques dealer. I find it quite interesting and challenging, in a different sort of way. At least I'm not dodging rockets and missiles in Iraq anymore. Do you know Betterton?"

"Do I know Betterton?" Let me tell you, brother. I can call you brother since we were in the military together at one time. I first went to Betterton many years ago with my family, at least once a month on the ferry from Baltimore, just to ride the carousel with those horses, carved so beautifully by Dentzel and with such dazzling colors too.

"I also know a bit about antiques. Our house is filled with them. I was also a frequent visitor to the Walters Art Gallery while studying piano at the Peabody Conservatory across the street."

"I know you said you went to Hopkins. Did you grow up in Baltimore?"

"I went to Polytechnic High, and after graduation, my senator arranged a scholarship to Johns Hopkins."

"I was at Hopkins too, a psych major. I'm certain I would never forget a face or figure like yours on campus. Maybe you were an upperclassman when I was a freshman?

Liz smiles and asks, "You're not trying to find out my age by any chance, are you?"

"No. As you said before, age is not important. It's our interests and backgrounds that will bond us."

When their appetizers arrive, Mark suddenly grows solemn, and tells her, "I've run out of questions and words. Perhaps it's time for us to enjoy this food. You're right, Liz. The nest in the Blue Heron Restaurant is a cozy spot to dine."

After appetizers and a glass of wine, both pass on selecting an entrée. Perhaps the excitement of getting to know each other has filled all their needs at this moment. After the waiter hands Mark the bill, he slides it halfway across the table and asks Liz, "Would you mind picking up the tab? I'm saving up for our next date." He laughs and quickly picks up the bill and says, "Just kidding. But I am saving up for our next date when you can spend some time in Betterton."

A suspicious smile crosses Liz's face. She knows what's implied here. It's not the first time she's heard such an offer.

As the last traces of sunlight disappear and lights are automatically switched on to illuminate the parking lot next to the restaurant, Mark concludes, "Speaking of spending some time in Betterton, I would be remiss if I didn't tell you, probably like a hundred guys before me, that you're one of the most beautiful women I've ever seen. Five foot six, 135 pounds, 35, 22, 32, all the essential figures, figures that remind me of those marble statues in museums."

"Obviously you're very good with figures. Actually you're right on the mark. But stats are for statisticians and economists, not for us." She hesitates a moment, then confesses, "I've been checking you out as well. I bet the girls go gaga over you."

"Whatever the statistics, you're too good to be true. Talk about beauty and brains. You have it all, Liz. What a package."

After Liz opens the door to her car, she turns to him and they both embrace and exchange kisses on both cheeks. Although there may have been the expectancy of a long passionate kiss at this concluding moment of their first date, the feelings and expressions on their faces tell all you need to know about their date tonight.

Early the next morning, a Sunday full of sunshine and blue skies, Annette along with Sandy and Mark attend church services at the Catholic Church in Betterton. During the mass the priest mentions the passing of Private Tommy Wells in Iraq a few weeks ago, his sacrifice for all Americans, his willingness to put his life on the line to protect those back home, then closes with expressions of his condolences and along with those of his parishioners to his family and friends in Kent County.

Following the service, all three are invited to the church hall for coffee and doughnuts and to meet other parishioners who want to console Annette and Sandy and meet Mark, their new tenant in Betterton.

What is most unusual here is the sudden silence by Annette, Sandy and Mark. They are waiting for the parishioners and neighbors to express their condolences first. But their wait is in vain. The parishioners, including neighbors, cannot find the words to even greet or introduce themselves to Mark. Perhaps later they'll have time to drop by Annette's Antiques.

Ten minutes after coffee and doughnuts at the church hall, all three take up their posts at Annette's store, together with Knute who drops by to see Gertie and help out if needed. Annette tells Mark, "Sundays are important because it's the last day of the week for selling things to tourists. What we don't sell on Sundays may end up in Crumpton on Wednesdays. We have to turn over our inventory until we either sell it or auction it off. The fall season is coming to an end, and we should clear out things to make space for new inventory."

Mark says, "Why not try a season ending closeout. We need space for higher quality, higher priced items for clients with deep pockets. It's too late to place an ad in the local newspapers, but we could print up some circulars and flyers to hand out to people as they get off the ferry, and put them on posts or poles around the town. A 'Once-in-a-Lifetime' clearance sale like Epstein's in Baltimore."

Sandy chimes in, "And Mark, how about asking your track team to join in and distribute the flyers, especially at the dock?"

Mark says, "Why didn't I think of that? That's a good idea, Sandy, and I think my kids will love to get involved in something productive in Betterton."

In a matter of four hours, from about 1 to 5 pm, they sell over $10,000 of merchandise and everyone is bursting with joy and pride. Annette credits Mark for his major efforts in achieving one of the highest gross sales that she can ever remember.

But Mark brings everything back to reality when he says, "There's something very obvious here and you don't have to be a genius to recognize it. From the looks of our sales receipts, we didn't sell anything to the local people of Betterton. In fact, I don't recall seeing any of our neighbors in the store during the sale. Aren't they interested in antiques, or at least curious enough to stop by and say hello?"

Annette responds, "I've never counted on people living in Betterton for my sales. The tourists and a few special clients make the business enjoyable enough. For me right now, knowing and working with you, and meeting Reggie and Richard is almost beyond comprehension. We're so lucky to know someone so talented, aren't we?" She pauses to study again the final calculations, smiles, and says, "Any other ideas to improve our business, Mark?"

He says, "As a matter of fact, I've been thinking about adding a word to the sign in the front of your store."

Annette asks, "Do you want to add your name to the marquee so it reads 'Mark and Annette's Antiques'?"

He says, "No. Forget Mark. The sign now reads, 'Annette's Antiques' on one line and below it 'Buy Sell'. I'd like to add the word 'Trade'. It's a small step up where we might catch someone who wants to trade something instead of a straight buy or sell proposition."

Annette says, "Mark, I like the idea. Your suggestions are always welcome."

Everyone is filled with smiles and a feel-good mentality until fatigue sets in and everyone fades away to their respective bedrooms.

The next Monday morning, Sandy, Mark and Annette are having breakfast and discuss plans for the day. Annette agrees to watch the store while Sandy works in her studio and Mark drives the truck alone to the local high school.

After convincing the principal that he has an interest in some teenage kids in the school, he gets permission to monitor a few classes in the morning session. He sees first hand what the instructors are teaching and how the kids are reacting. He learns quickly that the kids are not paying attention nor is the teacher concerned that they are not paying attention. He realizes that he can do nothing at the high school, but instead will work one on one with each of them during the afternoon training sessions at the senior park.

Later that afternoon, Mark and his four runners are training at the senior park, starting with calisthenics and short wind sprints. He tells them, "Today I want you all in the long straight-aways to extend your legs, lengthen your stride just little until you feel like you are literally flying down the stretch to the finish line. But when you approach each turn, put your legs in reverse and slightly shorten your strides so you can make the turns comfortably. Got it?" In unison, they call out, "I hear you, coach."

Mark says, "I don't want you to say 'I hear you, coach'. I want you to say, 'I understand you, coach'. There's a big difference in hearing and understanding."

Sitting nearby on a bench under a shady tree and watching the runners are three seniors. The slender lady in the middle of the two men gets up and walks over to Mark and says, "My name is Mo, short for Maureen. You see those two other buzzards over there on the bench under the tree? That's Manny and Jack. We're all from the senior citizen house behind the cemetery. I like living there but I never thought I would be living each day one step from the graveyard.

"We're all carefully watching those kids, monitoring their every move. Now Manny claims that he clocked the tallest kid wearing the white trunks sprinting 40 yards in five seconds. They're still arguing whether or not he is either Jesse Owens or Jesse James. I think that you've given some inspiration to those buzzards too, perhaps a better way to spend their time in the park than just feeding and watching birds, or waiting to die."

Mark says, "That's a morbid thought. Call your friends over, and let me introduce you all to my team."

Mark calls his team together and introduces them, one by one, to Manny, Mo, and Jack. The faces of his kids light up with broad smiles and their bodies seem energized knowing that these seniors show an interest and care about them. Mark says to his team, "Over the weekend, I have been thinking about a name for our team. I like the name 'Flyers' but that's taken already by the pro hockey team in Philadelphia. How about the 'Breeze' of Betterton?"

The kids look at each other with a puzzled look, while the seniors smile and nod approvingly. Mark says, "Since I'm the coach, I hereby christen you the 'Breeze' of Betterton." The kids change their puzzled looks to smiles. Mark says, "The name is just the beginning of things to come. It's just a start, but you have to take pride in being a member of the Breeze."

While still huddling around Mark and his kids, Manny suddenly says, "How about letting us buy you some track shoes? You need the right equipment in order to compete properly, don't you?"

Then Jack says, "We'd like to become involved too. Be a sort of booster club."

Mark asks his kids to continue running sprints while he takes the seniors aside, and tells them, "We want them lean and mean. But regarding your offer of track shoes, we'll take this offer under consideration. We don't want to get in trouble with someone accusing us of being professionals and accepting things that might jeopardize our amateur standing.

"However, I have an idea here. Whenever you talk to these kids, one on one, try to get inside their heads and hearts. Let them know that you are here to help them, not just today, but for as long as they want you to help them. It's only a start here but it just might work out for the good. What do you think?" The seniors are very pleased and give Mark a thumbs-up.

Right about now Mark's kids are feeling pretty good about themselves, but he reminds them that they have a long way to go, and still have a responsibility to complete their homework later.

Mark says, "We want some muscle in your brain too, not just in your legs. From now on, you have to be a little more serious with everything you do, starting with your studies. But we'll take it one step at a time."

The kids look at each other and realize Mark might know what he is talking about and decide to give him more respect, starting with addressing him as 'sir'.

As they leave the park, Mark remembers hearing something about a county-wide amateur race coming up in Rock Hall at the Harvest Moon Festival. He calls the kids back and asks them, "Would you be interested in competing against other teams in Maryland?"

His kids like the challenge and look forward to the Harvest Moon Festival track meet coming up in a week. Each one seems to grow more confident in himself, but Mark reminds them that it's a team of runners, not individuals, that's important.

Although Mark spends every weekday afternoon at the park training his kids, he is always with Annette on Wednesday mornings at Dixon's Auction in Crumpton.

On the next Wednesday, at about 7am, they unload outside in the fields a truck load of boxes containing items removed from the store, including framed Gibson illustrations, porcelain figurines, carnival glass pitchers, dinner dishware, magazines and small cabinets.

Annette says, "You mentioned that we should create a theme in our store and not have it cluttered so much, simplify and make it a little more upscale. Isn't that what you had in mind?"

Mark agrees, "We have to make some space in the store for something special that will bring in a better class of buyers."

It doesn't take more than 20 minutes to drop off this load in the outside field. Around 7:30 am they are both inside the main hangar for the 8 o'clock auction. Mark walks over quickly to Table 1, where he surveys an assortment of porcelain figurines and baby dolls piled on top of a small table, a lowboy. He glances around to find Annette, who is in the middle of the hangar talking with some people unfamiliar to him. He shakes his head from side to side at the sight of 40 tables all piled high with art and antiques.

He says to himself, "I better concentrate on this piece and forget the other tables. I have a hunch that this lowboy is something special. It seems to talk to me." He checks his watch and realizes he only has to wait less than 20 minutes for the auction to start, plus it's early in the morning, and many bidders have not yet arrived for the 8 o'clock start. He puts his fingers into his mouth and lets out a loud whistle, the kind used for hailing a taxi. Annette comes running over to him from the middle of the hangar and together they examine the lowboy very carefully.

Mark says, "I've seen a piece like this either in a museum or in an exhibition catalog."

Annette looks more carefully at the piece, then quietly mutters, "It's in mint condition, never been touched, all original hinges too. Let's give it a try, Mark. Since you found it, you do the bidding."

He says, "That lowboy is talking to me."

She asks, "And what is it saying to you?"

He answers, "It says, 'take me home. I want to go home with you'."

Within another minute or two, Mark and Annette move closer until they are about six feet away from the auctioneer, Albert Hobbs, who's now wearing a bright orange and black Orioles cap. They are positioned in his direct line of sight, and almost close enough to touch the lowboy as it stands in front of them on top of Table 1.

Hobbs begins in a loud voice, "Remember I don't miss you. You miss me, so if you're interested in bidding, let me know by waving, shouting, or whatever means available. But don't throw anything, please. And once I say 'Sold', you own it. Everything is sold 'as is, where is'. And have your client number ready if you're the winning bidder. No cash, please. You have to register at the office before you can bid here. We'll have over 3,000 things to sell inside this morning, and have to move quickly. Everyone ready?"

He pauses and smiles at his anxious crowd around him, as Dave Bloom points to the lowboy and shouts out, "Table 1, four legged table."

Hobbs begins, "Now how much for this four legged table? A hundred dollars to start off?"

Mark raises and waves his right hand, and leaves it extended in the air, in full view of the auctioneer. The bidding moves upward rapidly in 20 dollar increments, with Mark bidding against a five foot elderly lady looking eager and hungry. She has that look of determination in her eyes and stands on the opposite side of the table. She looks at Hobbs without any emotion whatsoever, and stares only at him, except for a slight forward nod of her head, as if agreeing with the number he calls out.

She turns her head slightly to look across at Mark and realizes that she's bidding only against one bidder, Mark, who stands on the other side of the table, equidistant from the auctioneer. The volleys between the two bidders are enjoyed by the viewers gathered around Table 1, until her bid reaches $480, which it's immediately topped by Mark's bid of $500. Now the bid increments switch to $50, and the volley of bids continues between Mark and his elderly rival, until she nods at $950, but is quickly topped by Mark's bid of $1,000.

She shrugs her shoulders and turns away from the auctioneer to take a final look at Mark, and gives him a look of distaste, as if she's bitten into a bitter lemon.

Mark continues to keep his hand raised in the air and concentrates his eyes only on Hobbs, who lifts his Orioles cap, wipes his forehead, and says, "eleven hundred...any more, anyone?"

A new bidder calls out from a crowd about 15 feet away, "Yea." It's a voice that only the auctioneer recognizes as a dealer who wants to conceal his identity.

Hobbs continues, "I have a bid of eleven hundred. Any more, anybody?"

Mark lowers his hand momentarily, cocks his head in a peculiar way, almost like a rooster ready to take on another cock in the chicken coop. This time he keeps his hand in front of his chest and waves it somewhat secretly again at the auctioneer, and renews his bidding against this unknown bidder.

But the bids are now in $100 increments, until the auctioneer says, "It's yours at $2,000" and points to Mark. Then he asks again, "$2,100 anyone?"

Suddenly, a new bidder, well acquainted with the auctioneer, and standing in a crowd of spectators 20 feet away, calls out in a woman's voice, "21."

The auctioneer says, "I have you, Madame, at $2,100. Anymore, anyone?"

Mark waves his hand at the auctioneer again, in a somewhat disgusting gesture, and continues the bidding battle, against this third competitor, still in one hundred dollar increments, until the bidding reaches $3,000.

The auctioneer points to Mark and says, "It's your bid at $3,000. He sighs a little, squirms in his seat, takes a deep breath, and says, "What a way to begin the auction this morning!" He pauses to catch a few laughs and surveys the crowd for a new bidder, then remarks, "$3,100 anyone?" This time he pauses only a second or two, then pounds his table top with his fist, and says, "Sold!"

Everyone crowded around Table 1 claps their hands and whistles excitedly. Before the auctioneer can utter any more words, Mark is overcome, and with a gust of emotion, shouts out in a voice that echoes throughout the hangar, "Annette's Antiques number two three three."

The auctioneer Hobbs breaks out in laughter and says, "We can hear you. We're not deaf. Congratulations, young fella" He turns to look at the middle of the crowd and says, "Folks, here's the new guy on the block. If you're smart, you'll watch him."

Mark says to him, "Now you've just blown my cover." He pauses and cups his hands to his mouth to direct his words only at the auctioneer, and continues, "I don't need the publicity. I could be just a flash in the pan. Everyone will expect me to discover something special every week, but it's just not going to happen."

Tony Wanderer, hiding behind the auctioneer, steps away so that Mark can catch a glimpse of him and gives him a thumbs-up with his right hand along with a big smile and slight nod of his head. Mark makes a fist and thrusts it high above his head. Everyone who looks at Mark can tell that he's tickled to death.

Annette turns and gives Mark a big hug and says, "Welcome to the big leagues, if you want to call Dixon's the big leagues. Let's get that piece out of here now before someone scratches it. I have some furniture pads in the cabin of the truck. Can you manage to carry it alone to the truck?"

He says, "No problem. Just make a path for me, like running interference on a football field."

Annette cautions him, "Mark, try to keep the piece level so that the drawers don't fall out."

After leaving the hangar and arriving at their truck, they spread two furniture pads in the center of the bed of the truck, then carefully turn the lowboy upside down and place it carefully on these pads. They use two more pads to cover the lowboy completely. Mark secures everything with a special fabric tape, about three inches wide, that is wrapped around the entire package.

He threads the tape through a fitting in each corner of the bed of the truck to secure it to prevent any movement, especially bouncing during the drive back to Betterton. Mark shows his military training by looping the tape in special knots that he can easily pull to take up the slack on all the lines. He tells Annette, "This baby isn't going anywhere."

Annette tells him, "What would you say if we call it a day? Let the vultures have their way inside and outside today. I have a suspicion that you discovered something special and I can't wait to get it home."

Mark answers, "Whatever you say, partner. I am getting good vibes from this piece."

On the drive back to Betterton from Crumpton, Annette tells Mark, "I have a client in mind for that lowboy. Her name is Lois Carnegie, an heiress of the steel empire in Pittsburgh, who lives nearby, has good taste and a love of antiques. I can't wait to call her. In fact, if you can take over the driving, I'll call her on my cell phone right now."

Mark tells her, "Let's take our time, get it home and cleaned up, study it, make sure what we are selling is the real thing. No rush to judgment here. This could be our first big score."

She says, "Our purchase today was like trading up and I think we got lucky, because not many buyers were here for the 8 o'clock start of the auction."

"I wonder if anyone saw us intensely examining the lowboy table, you know, drawing attention to an item."

"I wouldn't give too much importance to that, unless you're a well known expert. Then the collectors and dealers will surely watch you tip your hand, so to speak."

"It seems like the lowboy needs no repair, perhaps only a light polish."

She quickly advises him, "But in this business, collectors want originality. Never tamper or restore the finish. Leave it as original as possible."

After arriving back in Betterton, they carry the lowboy very carefully through the back door of Annette's Antiques and place it in a back corner area, where it is given appropriate space and a position of importance. Mark adjusts an overhead spotlight so that it shines directly on the top and front surface of the lowboy.

Annette prepares to telephone Lois Carnegie, but Mark stops her and says, "We haven't discussed a price yet. If you call your client, let her know that it's just a courtesy call to alert her about our new discovery. We should consult with an expert before putting a price on this piece. To do otherwise is pure guesswork. I think caution is needed here.

While you telephone Lois, I'll run up to the senior park for a session with my track team. Tell Lois that she has first dibs on buying the lowboy, but let her know, in your own words, that we have another interested party."

Annette asks, "And who might that be?"

He counters, "Well, my father, of course. He always told me to be on the lookout for good investments and he certainly has the resources. It's good to put the seed into a buyer's mind that he or she has some competition. This piece, from my viewpoint, is museum quality and collectors will jump at the opportunity to own it."

Mark leaves by the back door and jogs up the hill to the senior park, where his track team is ready and waiting for him. During this session, while his runners are still limbering up for a mile relay medley, he has a chance to talk again with Manny, Mo, and Jack, watching everything again under their favorite shady tree. He learns that Jack is a black retired builder and carpenter, and an ace when it comes to building and remodeling.

He tells Jack, "Sandy is interested in converting a garage into an art studio. Would you like to make some extra money and give me a price on the remodeling? What do you think?"

Jack says, "Sounds like music to my ears. I've got nothing but time on my hands nowadays. Just let me know when I can get a look at the project."

Then Mark turns to Manny who says, "I helped Mom and Pop Muller in their seafood restaurant on Bond Street in Fells Point. Those were the days before it was called Fells Point, but I have to confess, it served the best seafood in the city. When they closed the business about thirty years ago, I retired and moved to Betterton.

Mark asks, "What made you think of moving to Betterton?"

Manny says, "One of our customers at Mullers Restaurant was a big baker. I mean this man, Harry Gerstung, was big in size like the Pillsbury dough man, not dough boy, and only five foot tall, but his bakery made the best bread, rolls, and sweets in Baltimore. His muffins were to die for. He trained in Germany to become a baker and brought all those fabulous and famous recipes with him. He usually came to Mullers for steamed crabs with his close friend, a fellow German, William 'Willy' Haussner, who owned the best restaurant in the city, with its fabulous art collection hanging on the walls and enclosed in showcases everywhere.

Gerstung built some weekend rental cottages on the bluffs over Betterton Beach, and I went there for weekends on the ferry, and later took up a hobby in photography. Eventually I moved to the senior home about 15 years ago."

"And how do you like living there?"

"With my two friends here, it is surprisingly good, but there's still so much that I'd like to do with my life. Everyone says I have a natural talent and good instincts with the digital camera. One of these days I'll probably have to take a course in photography to reach the next level. I'm looking forward to our senior field trip to the Eastern Neck Wildlife Refuge outside of Rock Hall."

Mark turns to the smiling face of Maureen Greenspand, and asks, "And what about Mo?" She modestly confesses, "I'm a widow who raised two kids alone and I'm very proud of them, too. After they graduated from high school, the itch to see the west..."

"The itch was a catalyst, huh?"

"They were always dreamers at heart and wanted to be on their own. So after they went west, I was left on my own too and returned to the University of Baltimore to complete my law degree, then worked with trial attorney Peter Saltair in the preparation of his law suit against the manufacturer Johns Manville and the harm from asbestos He ended up winning millions for himself, but very little trickled down to lawyers like me who did most of the investigation and preparation."

Mark thinks to himself, "Wow, these seniors are treasures, something very special here. What a reservoir of talent and fountain of knowledge for me and the kids. I'll have to find a way to use their talents and experience to help to restore some pride in the lives of everyone involved here. As the Good Lord says, 'The seeds of hard work will reap their rewards'."

CHAPTER 9

The next morning, precisely at 10, Mark carries a cup of freshly brewed coffee into the main showroom and removes the cover over Gertie's cage just as two women in their early 30's enter the front door. The taller one, standing six feet in off white casual low heels, wears a loose-fitting sporty canary yellow, two piece light-weight suit, with a pleated skirt. On her neat dark hair, trimmed very short like an Italian model, rests a bell shaped cream-colored hat with a three inch brim. Real daisies are scattered around the brim.

The entire outfit, suit and bonnet, are all trimmed with an off-white flower overlay. Her entire figure is a replica of the 1920's flapper era. Covering two-thirds of her face is an oversized pair of white rimmed glasses with a double G insignia, a touch of the bygone Great Gatsby era. When she takes just a few steps, the impression of culture, wealth and vitality is immediate.

Mark thinks to himself, "Can this be Jordan, the six foot tower of dazzling beauty from Fitzgerald's 'The Great Gatsby', or am I just dreaming? She's a living doll. And look at those legs!"

Mark turns to both and announces in a slow and deliberate voice of a circus barker, "Welcome, layyyy-dddiieess, to Annette's Antiques of Betterton. It's nice to have you here today."

The taller lady says facetiously in a slightly baritone and well cultured theatrical voice, "You must be Mark. I've heard about you from Annette. I'm Lois Carnegie. This is my dear friend Clowie Bankhead."

She lowers her eyeglasses and surveys Mark from head to toe, then releases a pleasing nod of her head. It's obvious that this tall and handsome figure of a man now standing before her is something special.

Mark says, "Tell me, Lois... Carnegie? Are you related to the Carnegie's of Pittsburgh, the steel magnates that are now USS Steel?"

Lois answers, "Yes, I'm on the board of the firm founded by my great grandfather."

A pleasing smile covers his face as he confesses, "Well, we have something in common. Your firm in Pittsburgh and my grandfather's firm at Sparrows Point were once fierce competitors, but lately I've heard some rumblings and rumors about a possible merger."

"If what you say is true, and I have no reason to doubt you, we have much in common. So, tell me Mark, does this commonality entitle me to a discount on the highboy that Annette has recently discovered?"

"Annette discovered?" Mark laughs and turns slightly to look at Clowie, who is about five foot four inches in loafers and wearing a conservative and subtle light-maroon colored blouse and trousers. She stands erect, like an officer inspecting her troops, by a clothing rack, and carefully examines an antique beaded dress with sequin overlay, probably from the roaring 20's.

Lois walks over to a vintage designer clothing rack and playfully picks up a long silk scarf, off white and transparent, stretches it out, and brings it up to her face like a veil. She turns to Clowie and confesses, "Did I ever tell you about my days on stage at Northwestern, when I did the 'Dance of the Seven Veils'?" She spins around 360 degrees, and the veil forms ripples and waves and turns into something quite exotic. "I was playing the part of the youngest and most beautiful wife in the harem of Sultan Pasha of Istanbul and..."

"Yes, please continue. You have me in suspense, daw-lin."

"Well, to make a long story short, I gave only one performance."

"Why one performance?"

"There's something unnerving about unveiling in public, right down to your bare skin, that was terribly embarrassing. I mean, there I was, momentarily alone in the harem set on stage, with nothing on. Not a stitch of clothes, only seven of these veils."

Clowie prods her, "But Lois, I've known you for years, and we've had exotic parties at your pool and everyone there was stripped to their bare skin."

"I guess it was a question of vanity. The difference is that it becomes fun when everyone participates."

Clowie stops and freezes momentarily with a curious look on her face, then smiles and says, "Well, daw-lin, I'm sure it was all for the best, I mean, to walk away from that play."

Lois says, "Well, I just didn't walk away from that play. I was set to play the part of Daisy in the university's next production of 'The Great Gatsby'. It was not as easy as you think. Right there and then, I switched majors from drama to business, which surprised and pleased my family immensely. I guess it all worked out for the better, all because of this veil."

Suddenly Gertie, the squawking bird of Betterton, blurts out, "Take it off!" There's a few seconds of silence, then Gertie burst out again, "Take it off. Thirty percent off, Doll!"

Both Lois and Clowie turn sharply in the direction of the birdcage.

Clowie, in a voice and accent like Tallulah Bankhead, asks whoever is nearby, "Who said that?" She spots the parrot in the birdcage and begins laughing at Gertie, and says, "For impromptu openers, are you a live bird or one of those mechanical automated birds made in Switzerland? What's your name, daw-lin?"

The parrot answers, "Gertie…Doll!"

Clowie says, 'Well, Gertie Doll. Better be careful around Betterton when you tell someone to take it off. The local sheriff might arrest you for inciting a riot with the local watermen."

Finally Lois watches Clowie as she holds up a beaded dress up to the light to see if there are any tears or moth holes in the fabric. With a slight touch of exasperation, she sighs, "As much as I love looking at dresses from the Great Gatsby era, I hate to tear myself away from you. I thought we came here to see that lowboy that Annette called me about yesterday."

They return all the clothes to the rack, and affectionately hold hands as they meander together through the store looking for the lowboy.

Clowie tells Lois, "Sometimes, Lois, you surprise even me when you drop everything and rush to see an antique piece for your collection. I know you want to be the first one to see it, but we still have so much work in preparation for our swim fest this weekend."

Lois tells her, "That's the difference between being a collector, like me, and an admirer of fine art, like you. If I missed out on the opportunity to buy an important piece of art simply because of our swim fest, I could not live with myself, at least not for an hour or so."

Clowie follows Lois like a poodle on a short leash. By observing their physical movements and whispers, one could easily surmise that they obviously have a great deal of affection for each other, and perhaps a lesbian relationship.

Finally, in a somewhat isolated corner of the shop, Lois finds the lowboy, and immediately begins to study carefully the surface construction. She removes the center drawer and examines the dovetail carpentry on the edges, then smiles and recognizes immediately the lowboy maker as a late 18 to early 19th century Philadelphia carver. She whispers to Clowie, "For an exact date, I'll need a little time to research it and consult with the curator of American furniture at the Winterthur Museum in Delaware."

When Mark creeps up and looks over her shoulder as she is bending down to look at the hinges of the lowboy, Lois suddenly straightens up and stretches out her arms as if to shake a kink out of her muscles, and says, "Well, Mark, I usually rely on my instincts and first impressions. I like the piece. I'd like to own it too. What would you say if I handed you a check right now for $15,000? I think that's a good price."

Mark says, "It might be a good price for you, but it's more important to establish the date and origin of the maker, don't you think? So if you don't mind, I see no rush to make a sale this moment. Surely you would want to have an expert's opinion too, wouldn't you? Plus I have a responsibility to get approval from my partner Annette who has an interest in this sale as well. Having said all this, however, you have my personal guarantee that I'll give you first option to buy it and get back to you in a day or two."

Lois says, "Well, Mark, I respect your position. A quick offer from my lips is one thing but fairness between a buyer and seller is more important, don't you think? Therefore, would you kindly give me your best price in a day or two at most, and surely before Friday, because I have the perfect spot for it and want to show it off at our swim fest this weekend."

Mark sizes up Lois as a very astute business woman, highly-educated and cultured. He carefully leads her and Clowie to their classic

1958 burgundy-colored Bentley parked at the curb outside Annette's Antiques. He opens the front passenger door for Clowie, then walks around the sporty chrome grill of the Bentley and opens the driver's door for Lois. As she takes the drivers seat, he glances through the rear window at the chrome and burl wood pullout tables attached to the rear of the front seats, a touch of luxury enjoyed by English gentry when they attended the races at Ascot. He tells them, "In Baltimore, when a Bentley like yours is parked outside an antiques store, tons of customers will gather around to see what celebrity is visiting inside. Such a situation can do wonders for business."

The following day, Annette telephones Wendell Garrison, the curator of American furniture at the Winterthur Museum in Delaware, who is persuaded to drive about 50 miles to Betterton and give his opinion on the lowboy.

Annette tells him over the telephone, "Time is of the essence here. The trip will be worthwhile, I assure you. After all, you might be surprised by discovering something rare in American furniture plus we'll certainly pay for your consultation and reimburse you for your expenses."

Within two hours, Wendell Garrison, who's a splitting image of Arthur Schlesinger, is hovering and peering over, under, and around the lowboy like an expert on the 'Antiques Roadshow'. Annette and Mark watch his every movement from a safe distance away

Mark whispers, "No one likes to have someone watching over their shoulder."

After 20 minutes, Garrison looks around and calls Mark and Annette over to the lowboy, and declares, "The trip was worth it. You have a rare American lowboy, Philadelphia, circa 1810-20, or perhaps earlier. If you can research the provenance, and find the identity of the family, probably Rittenhouse Square, we might be interested in exhibiting it in a future exhibition at Winterthur. It's very close to matching the craftsmanship in our 18th century high boy, perhaps a companion piece."

Mark asks him, somewhat facetiously, since he already knows the answer, "And what would you say about the value or price?"

Garrison answers abruptly, "Are you trying to test me, young man? You know that I'm prohibited from offering any suggestion about the value. If I were pressed into giving you a monetary value, it would cost me my job. Nice try anyway. I suspect you already knew how I would answer you, didn't you? I'll send you my written report and bill in a few days. Thank you for the pleasure of this appraisal assignment."

After the expert leaves the shop, Mark asks Annette, "Do you now have a price in mind?"

She responds, "I haven't a clue. In my 30 years as an antiques dealer, I've never owned anything like this baby."

Then he says, "If you want my opinion, mark that baby $77,000 and tell Lois it's a bargain compared to New York prices."

Annette telephones Lois and tells her, "The curator of Winterthur just completed his examination of the lowboy and told us that it is authentic American, Philadelphia, 1810-20, and possibly a companion piece to the highboy in Winterthur."

Lois asks, "And what did he say about the value or price?"

Annette says, "You must know him, don't you? If so, you know that he cannot offer any type of valuation, otherwise it would cost him his job."

Lois asks, "Have you a price in mind now?"

Annette says, "We're prepared to offer it for sale for $77,000, plus tax. The piece really is Mark's baby, his discovery, and he's setting the price here. He's standing nearby and wants me to tell you…"

Mark says, "Tell her, when you buy a fine piece of furniture…"

Annette says, "When you buy a fine piece of furniture…"

Mark continues, "…that brings you enormous pleasure when you look at it…"

Annette repeats, "…that brings you enormous pleasure when you look at it…"

Mark continues, "Every time you look at it, you don't remember the price you paid for it!"

She says, "Every time you look at it…

Lois interrupts, "O.K. Annette. I can hear Mark's echoing clearly in the background. I get the point. That's very well stated, and I will buy it for $77,000 plus tax. But Mark has to deliver it to me in time for my pool party this weekend, O.K.?"

Annette tells her, "Mark will deliver it to you tomorrow afternoon, if that's satisfactory?"

Lois says, "Tell Mark to handle it carefully, and I'll see him tomorrow afternoon, say between 12 and 2."

Mark and Annette give each other a hug that seems to last forever. "It was your coaching at the auction that led me to take the risk and buy it," says Mark.

"Success is never achieved without the element of risk," says Annette with pride.

"Instincts and intuition go hand-in-hand in the antiques business," answers Mark as he leaves the store and heads to his apartment.

The next morning around 11:30, Mark is outside, enjoying the peace and quiet as he takes the final steps of adjusting the lowboy with furniture blankets and special cloth tape to keep it secure in the bed of the truck. He backs out of the driveway along the side of Annette's Antiques into Main Street, and drives slowly out of town towards Rock Hall. Along the way he is bombarded with questions bouncing and racing around in his head. The thought of meeting again one of the descendants of Andrew Carnegie flash around his mind.

He thinks to himself, "This is the big leagues now. What's she really like in the privacy of her mansion? What can I expect to find inside her home? What does she expect from me?"

Finally he admits, "I'll just be myself. After all, I've met important people before. The main thing is that she's buying the lowboy. Stop worrying about something over which I have no control. The hard part is over. Now, it's simply delivering her purchase and picking up the check."

After about 30 minutes of driving along the main road, halfway between Betterton and Rock Hall, he turns left and enters a gravel driveway, past a wrought iron sign that reads "Heavenly Manor." He drives slowly up a slight incline which leads upward to a mansion of gray stone, leaded glass windows, and slate roof. The mansion is entirely secluded by a grove of trees. He soon arrives at a circular driveway in front of a one story building, all constructed in a bygone era where craftsmanship meant something.

As Mark slows his vehicle to a halt, he looks over at the façade, something reminiscent of the mansions of Long Island. Before Mark can turn off his engine, he is met by two workers waiting to unload the lowboy and carry it inside.

Mark follows them into the foyer, where he overhears a lot of activity coming through the stained glass windows of the living room. Suddenly Lois appears out of nowhere, dripping wet from a plunge in the pool and wrapped in a large Turkish bathrobe. With a wide smile on her face, she walks briskly up to him and says "Welcome to Heavenly Manor. I must look like a mess, don't I?"

Mark says, "In the words of Yves Saint Laurent, you look 'RAV-A-SHING'. You look dazzling!"

She bowls over in laugher, and her towel opens slightly to show that there's nothing under it. Her cleavage is noticeable. She says, "Compliments are always appreciated, Mark."

Mark asks, "Where are you hiding Jay Gatsby? He must be around here somewhere."

"Obviously, you didn't realize that Clowie is my Gatsby, did you? I'm grateful to you, Mark, for bringing me this magnificent piece this morning. I have an ideal place for it. Did you bring me an invoice?"

Mark nods and says, "I put it in the center drawer of the lowboy. Here it is, Madame."

Lois takes the receipt with one hand and tucks it into her pocket, then takes a few steps to a circular table in the center of the hall. She adjusts a bouquet of flowers in a blue and white Chinese vase, and retrieves an envelope on a small but elegant and richly chased ornate sterling silver tray. She tells him, "Excuse my wet hands. Here's your check. Bet you've never received a check on a sterling silver platter before, have you?"

"When you're in business, like my partnership with Annette, we'll take the check anyway we can. But on a sterling silver platter? Yes, that's a first for me. I won't forget it. I hope this'll be the first of many sales between us."

"I hope you're as pleased as I am, but I'm a little curious about how you arrived at the price of the lowboy, with those two sevens in the price."

"Seven is always a lucky number, for the buyer and the seller. I just added a second one for good measure."

"How clever of you, Mark. Would you like a spot of tea or glass of champagne?"

"If you don't mind, I'll take a rain check."

Lois takes Mark's arm and walks him to the front door and tells him, "We're in the middle of our little fall fest, and I've neglected my guests more than I had anticipated. Sounds like 'Stairway to Heaven' coming from the pool, which means it's time for champagne and caviar.

She pauses and reaches for a bottle of champagne resting on a table nearby and hands it to him, and whispers, "This is for you and Annette to celebrate your sale to me. Now I hope you'll forgive me. You must bring Annette and Sandy here one day soon. Thanks again, Mark."

On the drive back to Betterton, Mark is thrilled about the quick sale and fascinated in seeing Lois again. "The Crumpton auction can be challenging, but the conclusion of a sale is pure fun, especially in meeting people like Lois Carnegie along the way," he confesses. "Lois is culture and class with a capital C. I wonder if she'd be interested in knowing me a little better, or am I just imagining things here? Perhaps it's the devil in me. I don't even want to think about the profit here. For me it the satisfaction that I used my instincts and memory to spot a gem, buy it at a reasonable price, and with Annette's contact, make my first big sale."

In the middle of his ride back to Betterton, he begins to feel ambitious and lusty. He pulls his vehicle off the road and, instead of calling Annette to give her an update, he brazenly calls Liz on his cell phone. He reminds her of his earlier invitation for a weekend in Betterton, with accommodations at Boyd's B&B. To Mark's surprise, Liz tells him she just had some plans cancelled and could arrive at noon the next day.

Precisely at 12 noon, when the church bells ring out over town, Liz parks her car in front of Boyd's B&B, but walks next door and enters the front door of Annette's Antiques. Near the front entrance she is drawn immediately to the vintage designer dresses hanging from a polished aluminum rack.

Sandy watches nearby and is struck immediately by her beauty and poise as she holds a dress close to her body and gazes into a mirror on the wall. Twenty seconds later Sandy approaches and says, "I'm Sandy Wells, at your service this afternoon. It's nice to have you here in our little shop. Is there anything special that you're looking for?"

Liz introduces herself, "I'm Liz Carter, and just browsing this afternoon, if you don't mind. Actually I'm here to see Mark Hopkins."

Just as she finishes mentioning his name, Mark enters the shop from the back door. Sandy says, "Speaking of the devil…" She hesitates and announces in a loud sustaining operatic voice like Ed McMann introducing Johnny Carson on one of his television shows, "Hheeerrrreee's Mark."

Sandy pauses to look at Mark but studies Liz, and says, "Wow, Liz. You look great. How do you do it?"

Liz answers, "Strict diet, strenuous exercise, and good genes. My mother was something special. She could have been an actress, exceptional vitality and intuition, with a face and figure like Rita Hayworth. But she wanted a family, married at 21, and had twins. My twin sister died in an auto accident when we were 12. I survived. I was the lucky one."

Sandy turns to Mark and asks, "Would you mind if I borrowed Liz for twenty minutes? I'd like to show her my studio and discuss a project I've had in mind for a long time. If we're not back by then, I've hermetically-sealed her in a capsule all for myself, and you'll never see her again."

Mark bows in an acquiescent gesture, with one arm sweeping outward in the direction of the garage, and says, "Take as long as you want. I'll freshen up and change my clothes. I thought we'd all go for a swim at Betterton Beach this afternoon."

Sandy takes Liz by her arm and leads her from the rear door of the shop into her studio to see her latest sculpture of Storm Cat.

Once inside, Sandy boldly asks Liz, "I hope that I won't shock you, but would you consider modeling for me? I've always wanted to create in clay a life size figure of a young Goddess, something approaching the Venus de Milo, but with all the body parts. I've been searching for the classical young woman with the perfect figure."

Liz replies, "I'm flattered that you would like me to pose for you but I'm not prepared to pose in the buff. Perhaps you could loan me a leotard, like ballet dancers wear."

"Exhilarated," Sandy answers. "Good idea, Liz. I have been saving this costume, made out of spandex, just perfect for the project."

A few minutes later the door to the studio is locked and curtains drawn across all windows. Liz is put at ease by Sandy who explains the process between model and sculptor. Together they come to an agreement on the pose, especially the stance, and position of her arms and hands. Cameras and lights are maneuvered to capture everything on film that will enable Sandy to study the photographs and translate the images into a three dimensional model. Surprisingly her hands and fingers are very expressive. Sandy comments, "You're a natural beauty and a fabulous model. I just hope I can capture your expression like I captured the expression of Storm Cat."

Liz asks, "What's Storm Cat?"

Sandy laughs and replies, "Storm Cat is a Thoroughbred racehorse that has retired and is now one of the highest paid studs in the world, somewhere around a half million dollars with a guarantee of a foal."

"Since I'm competing with a horse, how much are you paying me today, Sandy? Remember, I only have two legs."

"You'll just have to put it on my tab, Liz. Just another five minutes, please, and I'm happy with shooting everything that I need for my model in clay. In about a week or two, perhaps you can return and pose for the final session and finished product."

Inside of ten minutes Sandy uses her digital camera to shoot about 25 still photographs, plus a one-minute video with a camera used for 3D virtual reality. When Sandy finishes, she says, "Cut and print."

As Liz starts to dress again, she spots a set of wind chimes hanging in the corner of Sandy's studio. She confesses, "I've always loved the sound of chimes. Perhaps it's the delicate, whimsical magic of the Orient."

Sandy says, "I made it."

Liz asks, "I assume it's for hanging outdoors? You could add a remote electronic vibrator in the top that would trigger the chimes, like door bell chimes. Have you thought about that?"

Sandy says, "Are you kidding? That's way over my head. I was just playing around one day."

Liz says, "Well, Sandy, why not take it one step further and automate them."

Now Sandy is grateful that Liz not only posed for her but suggested an improvement in her chimes. She tells her, "Mark likes to use the term 'forge a bond' between friends. It's a term he picked up from his father who owns a steel mill in Bawlmer. Well, Liz, I think you and I could become good friends."

Before Liz can respond, Mark, dressed in swimming trunks with a Hawaiian shirt, knocks at the studio door. When Liz opens the door for him, he pretends to be disappointed that he didn't get a chance to observe artist and model at work. He turns to Sandy and says, "Hey! How come you've seen her body, almost naked, before me?"

When Sandy tells them that she needs to download her photos of Liz on the computer, Mark tells Liz, "No reason why you and I shouldn't take a swim at Betterton beach. Perhaps Sandy would let you change into your swim suit in her studio. I'll be waiting for you on the porch if you don't have any objections."

During their beach session, after they've splashed in the Bay and exhausted all their energies, they drag themselves to their towels placed in a secluded part of Betterton Beach, away from tourists. It's suddenly very peaceful.

Liz suddenly blurts out, "Are you going to kiss me, like in 'From Here To Eternity'?"

Mark says, "Huh?"

She asks, "If you're not going to kiss me, I'm going to kiss you."

They embrace long enough until Mark senses a twinge of guilt. Up until this moment, Sandy was the woman in his life. It's not in his character to play around or play one woman against another. He pulls away from Liz's embrace gently and says, "I think the dip into the Bay has energized me. I've always loved the act of swimming. But I can't help in confessing that, at this very moment, you make me feel good. I've never met anyone quite like you."

Liz says, "I like you, Mark. Perhaps it's just the beginning, the newness of two people getting to know each other. If nothing develops in a serious way, I think that I'd like to have you as a friend. You're going places, Mark. Who said, 'The world is your oyster'?"

He answers with a laugh, "Probably a clam." He sighs, gazes up at the sky, combs his hair with his fingers, and continues, "I never could quite figure out what that expression means." He leans back as Liz lays her head into his chest and he begins to run his fingers through her hair. Their eyes are studying the expressions on each other's face until they both turn to watch the sun descending on the horizon.

Despite Mark's interest in Sandy, he cannot easily dismiss an opportunity to know Liz better. He thinks of it as purely impulsive behavior, seizing the day or night or moment at hand. For him, it's a combination of atmosphere, environment, emotions and feelings. For him it's just a form of exploration. The problem is: Will this new plunge with Liz turn into something serious to rival Sandy? That's the million dollar question.

Eventually both walk arm in arm back up Main Street from Betterton Beach. Liz strolls into Boyd's B&B while Mark heads back to his garage apartment next door. He lingers on the stairway long enough to catch an evening kiss thrown by Liz from an open downstairs window.

CHAPTER 10

Mark notices Nellie Fox Boyd spying with binoculars from an upstairs window above Liz, and says, "The 'Spy in the Sky' is still at it. Doesn't she ever go to sleep?"

Meanwhile, inside Boyd's B&B, Liz greets Nellie, who leads her to an upstairs bedroom, and says, "I trust you'll be comfortable here. The front room is surprisingly quiet and the views out your windows are romantic for sure. You have a full moon tonight too."

"You know about measurements of the moon?"

"I like to watch heavenly bodies."

"And what about earthly bodies?"

"That too," she answers with a smile. "I'll get you some fresh towels. The bathroom is just down the hall."

Liz follows Nellie through the hallway leading to the front of the house, but something makes her turn around. She glances towards the opposite direction and is drawn towards a back room with the door slightly ajar. Although the sign on the door says "Private," she pushes it open and discovers what amounts to a small control room with audio and video equipment, well organized and concentrated mostly on the garage next door.

She glances at a shelf with boxes clearly Marked and, when Nellie enters the room, asks, "What's this box labeled "213 Main – WC"?"

Nellie laughingly says, "My audio equipment captured some sort of wind chimes from the garage…I suspect Sandy was developing wind chimes about a month ago."

"And here's a box labeled "Garage – SM AM&PM."

"That's the spring mattress in the garage apartment, morning and night!"

Liz says, "Ops."

"It's all very innocent I assure you."

"Are you sure about that? You know it might be construed as an invasion of privacy. You could be letting yourself in for a very dangerous and costly lawsuit. It's called invasion of privacy without permission."

"Who am I hurting here."

"In effect, you are hurting yourself by spying, eavesdropping, wire tapping. These actions all come with conditions that must be first approved by the court."

Nellie says, "Oops!"

Liz says, "You have all sorts of digital equipment here, but it's more than just a hobby, isn't it? It seems that I overheard someone talking about the 'Spy in the Sky' in Betterton? Would that be you?"

Nellie is embarrassed and says, "You know the door to this room is Marked 'Private', and I think we should leave it at that for now."

Liz advises, "Before saying goodnight, let me give you some good advice, something to think about. You know, Nellie, the telescope makes things larger than life, magnifies them. But the use of the telescope to spy on neighbors makes you small, very small in life. Is that what your conscience wants? Maybe you should try your hand at photography. You have a marvelous natural habitat at Eastern Neck Wildlife Refuge where you could spy on birds, butterflies and geese nesting. I bet in no time you might become an award-winning photographer."

On Sunday morning, Annette, Sandy and Mark have already attended church services and are now enjoying breakfast at home with homemade pancakes topped with a sprinkle of crab meat. Sandy, surprised and anxious blurts out, "I just realized that Liz's car is missing this morning from her spot in front of Nellie's B&B"

Mark, appearing unconcerned, says, "Liz had to return to Washington DC. Something came up, unexpectedly. This is common in the military."

Sandy is curious and asks, "I found her to be a perfect woman with a perfect body and a perfect mind. What do you think, Mark?"

Mark answers, "You're right on the mark. I've been tossing and turning in my bed, and finally realized that she's looking for the perfect man. She deserves the perfect man, and I'm certainly not that man. It would be difficult to live with such a person on a daily basis. Perfection has its drawback, too. But maybe Reggie is the man for her."

Mark pauses when no comments come forth from them, and offers, "Nevertheless, I'd certainly love to have her as a friend, wouldn't you?" When again he fails to get a response from either Sandy or Annette, he asks, "Did I say something that I shouldn't have said?"

Sandy says, "No, Mark, I am still dazzled by her beauty. You have no idea, or maybe you do, about how beautiful she is, physically speaking. She is a sculptor's dream model. I can't wait to get back to my studio and work on the clay model of her while my heart is still fluttering. Also I wouldn't stand in your way if you have intentions of pursuing her, except to tell you, in the old days, in those old western movies, I'd tell her that this town is not big enough for the two of us, find a way to lasso her and run her out of town."

She begins to laugh, turns to Annette and apologizes with, "Sorry that I won't be much help with you in the shop this afternoon."

Mark agrees, "I was just going to say the same thing. I have to check out two ladies in Rock Hall who telephoned me yesterday and think they have something precious in their attics. It will probably be a wild goose chase, but I have to check them out. There will be a service charge of $77 for my appraisal. They both agreed to pay me even if I tell them their ancestor handed down a piece of junk that they should take to the Crumpton auction!"

Annette, comforting as usual, assures him, "Not to worry. I don't expect much in the way of tourists here today. The winds are kicking up on the Bay, and the commercial watermen will be at home with their families. There's probably a sailboat race going on somewhere. You'll see lots of the small boats motoring around the Bay today, filled with hungry crabbers out to snag their dinner tonight. I might telephone Richard and see if he'd like to spend an afternoon here or perhaps take a drive to Centreville, rent a rowboat, and mosey along with the tide of the Corsica River. Depending on how the afternoon goes, we might even have dinner together later."

It takes Mark about 40 minutes to drive his truck down Eastern Neck Road until he sees the RIDGEFIELD FARM sign on his right. He turns onto a dirt road and drives another quarter mile and parks in front of a two story colonial house that looks like something out of 'Gone With The Wind'. An elderly lady, somewhat frail and very gaunt, greets him and says, "I'm Judy Ridgefield. Welcome to Ridgefield Farm. I appreciate your taking the time to visit an old hen on such a beautiful Sunday afternoon. Won't you take my arm and let me lead you into the living room to see if any of my hand-me-downs are worth anything,"

Mark says in a high pitched voice and slight cockney accent, "Judy…Judy…Judy." He gets no reaction.

She asks, "What did you say? My hearing is not as good as it used to be. I really should have a hearing aid."

He says in a louder voice, "It's nothing. I was just feeling a little playful this afternoon. There's so much room on your farm to play, isn't there?"

Mrs. Ridgefield opens a screen door and politely ushers him into the front living room which is overflowing with over 200 duck and goose decoys, sitting on shelves, dangling from wires attached to the ceiling like track lighting, and on every table top.

Mark, astonished by the size of the collection, says, "This almost takes my breath away. It reminds me of my uncle's collection of decoys, I grew up playing with them and remembered everything he taught me about carvers, their names and where to find their best works. Most of the best decoys are in the museum in Havre de Grace, outside Baltimore."

Mrs. Ridgefield explains, "Everything here was collected by my late husband, whose family farmed this land for over 100 years. During his lifetime, even before we were married, he developed a passion for decoys. He just loved to touch and study them, especially after he met the carver and acquired one of his carvings. Here's a pair that was carved by Charlie Joiner of Betterton, who later moved to Chestertown, and over there you'll see another pair carved by the Ward Brothers of Crisfield. At the far end of the room is his last purchase, just before he died in 1989. It was carved by Craig Ginn of Earleville, another Murlin carver. I probably have a file somewhere in the house with all the invoices. My husband was a stickler for keeping good records."

Mark is still stunned but always the businessman, says, "Well, Judy, from our phone conversation, my fee today for an informal appraisal is $77. I'll take a moment to look in my pocket guide of prices for decoys while you look for that file of invoices. It's important for purposes of authenticity and provenance." He pauses to walk over to a window where sunlight makes it easier to read his guide. He continues, "I'll start with some of the most expensive decoys you've shown me today. First off, the Ward Brothers of Crisfield would start at $8,000 to $10,000, for a humpback duck, and $6,000 to $8,000 for a canvasback duck. The Charley Joiner decoys start at $450 and go up to $5,000 for a pintail duck. Finally the Ginn decoy is worth $500 in today's market. If you intend to insure or sell them and need a written appraisal, that fee could amount to over $2,000. I can recommend a member of the American Society of Appraisers who's an expert in appraising decoys, or someone like Mike Stranahan who's a local dealer from the St. Michaels area."

Judy says, "Thank you, Mark. I'll have to think hard about this appraisal fee. I just don't have that money budgeted right now."

Mark, feeling sorry for the elderly lady, suggests, "You might also think about another possibility. Whenever I undertake an informal appraisal, I have to be careful to remain unbiased and cannot become involved in the items appraised. In other words, I can't appraise them and then buy them for myself. Do you understand?"

Judy nods, "I think I understand what you're saying. As far as I'm concerned, this visit is just a consultation, isn't it?"

Mark assures her, "You could call it that. If you need funds for the formal appraisal fee, you might consider a consignment of one or two decoys to Annette's Antiques in Betterton. Annette Wells is my partner, very knowledgeable in antiques, and has a nice clientele. She might have a collector in mind, and if sold, would give you the funds for appraising your entire collection. It's something to think about, so take your time. If you have any questions, call me or Annette. You already have our number. Now if you don't mind, I'll ask you to write a check for my fee today, $77."

Judy writes out the check and hands it to Mark, then walks him to the front porch. She draws her hand to her forehead to shade the bright sun from her eyes and watches him drive his truck away from her farm.

Once inside his vehicle, Mark picks up his clip board and stares at his next and final appointment. He thinks to himself, "Well, that certainly wasn't a wild good chase! I wonder what we'll uncover in our next appointment. Let's see...6167 East Dorlon Drive. That's in the Edesville area." He starts his engine, looks at the hood, and thinks to himself, "Gittyup, Bucky. One more appointment and we're done for the day." He whistles the tune 'Whistle While You Work' while driving back along Eastern Neck Road into the town of Rock Hall.

Within 10 minutes, he's parking his truck in front of a small, modestly built house, in a conclave of six identical houses, each approximately 25 by 25 feet, all with the same off-white vinyl siding, obviously built by the same builder.

Mark notices the numbers 6167 on the mailbox as he walks up the concrete pathway leading to the front door. As he reaches for the doorbell, he notices a handwritten sign above it that reads 'Bell Out Of Order - Use Back Door'. He walks around the side of the house and knocks at the back door.

Within seconds Mark sees in the doorway a lady with long blond hair, dressed only in a negligee. Her shapely figure seems to fill the entire doorway. He says, "Five foot ten, one hundred fifty five pounds, 42-30-38."

Rubbing her eyes as if she's been unexpectedly awakened from a deep sleep, she asks, "What did you say?"

"It's just a bad habit I have of sizing up someone. One of these days I'm going to get a slap across my face or a bust in the mouth."

"A bust in the mouth? You're very frank, aren't you?"

"No, I'm not very frank. I'm Mark, your friendly appraiser."

She asks, "Are you my two o'clock appointment?"

Mark is a little alarmed by her greeting in the form of a question and draws his head slightly back like a turtle returning his head to his shell. He blinks his eyes and says, "Yes, I'm Mark Hopkins. You called me to look at some of your things."

He can't help himself from gazing upward at her negligee that has no bra beneath it to hold her protruding bare breasts in place.

Marks thinks to himself, "She has a doll's face, perhaps a little top heavy, but what a woman, at least from the waist up." He guesses that she's about 40 and wearing a little too much makeup to make her look fifteen years younger, say around twenty five. But she's certainly one of the largest women, almost Amazon size that he has seen in a long time.

She smiles and says, "I'm Eloise, rhymes with breeze. Won't you come inside? The neighbors might get the wrong impression."

"What impression?"

"They might suspect that I'm propositioning you out in the open on my back steps."

"I know how neighbors can spread gossip, especially neighbors in a small town."

Once they are both inside a small kitchenette, Eloise says, "You look a little tuckered out. Would you like some refreshment?"

Mark asks, "What did you have in mind?"

She pauses a few seconds to collect her thoughts, looks down at her breasts, and says, "Well, I was thinking of several things but, for starters, perhaps you'd like something to drink."

Mark agrees, "As a matter of fact, I am a little thirsty. What do you have?"

"I have Coke, Pepsi, ginger ale…and I make the best butter milk around these parts."

"I'll try your buttermilk if you don't mind."

Eloise, a cordial hostess, says, "Rest your feet over here at this breakfast nook," then opens the refrigerator, removes a bottle of milk and places a glass on the table. She begins to pour him a glass of fresh buttermilk, and, while pouring, turns to look at Mark's eyes, which are now focused within a foot of her breasts, both about to fall out of her negligee. A second later, milk spills over the glass and leaves a small puddle on the table. She utters, "Oops. Is there anything else I can get for you?"

He now pauses a long time, thinking to himself, "What am I getting myself into here? This looks like an invitation. This sounds like an invitation. Then it must be an invitation, but an invitation for what?"

With a smile on his face, he says "Could I have a cookie, please?"

Her shoulders droop suddenly and she says, "Please? I always aim to please. But I must be slipping, losing my touch. Of course you can have a cookie if that's what you want. But I had something entirely different in mind. Are you sure that there's nothing else of interest to you here?"

He answers, "In the words of the great Billy Wilder, 'I have neither the interest nor the inclination'." Mark leans back in his chair and grows cautious, then asks, "Aren't you afraid of what your neighbors might think? Doesn't it bother you that your neighbors might talk behind your back?

She says, "I'm a chicken-necker, so I'm not ever going to be accepted in this town. I've lived here almost 20 years, and admit I'm a little tattered around the edges after two divorces and three kids. Frankly, I could care less what these neighbors in Rock Hall think about me."

"Eloise, you're a beautiful woman and obviously very gifted, physically speaking. You probably have talents that you've never realized you have, all buried inside your body, waiting for the chance to express themselves.

"With a little work and inner retrospection, you could be on the path to finding a good man and developing a strong and lasting relationship. As for me, I've been flirting with you, trying to have a little fun this afternoon, but I know it wouldn't be fun if I continued down the path toward your bedroom. It wouldn't be fair to you or to me. Do you follow me here?"

She says, "You've right, Mark. You've given me something to think about."

He utters, "So perhaps you better show me whatever you wanted me to appraise this afternoon."

Eloise says, "One of my boyfriends gave me that bronze statue over in the corner in exchange for the chance to play with my peaches, on a rainy night. Oh, those rainy nights. How they bring out the beast in me."

She continues, "He said that he inherited it, but it was a little too big for his farmhouse, and his wife didn't like the bare breasts of the nude model. I suspect that his wife was jealous and couldn't live with it."

Mark looks at the 20 inch tall statue and tells her, "It's late 19th century, probably French, good chasing, and nicely modeled, but I can't find a signature or foundry mark on the bronze anywhere. It's always easier for an appraiser to value something like this bronze when it's signed."

She asks, "And what's it worth?"

"Probably around $1,000."

"Would you give me $1,000 for it?"

"You owe me $77 as the fee for my consultation, and you have to remember that I'm a dealer and have to buy it and resell it, hopefully for a profit."

"Then how much would you pay me for it?"

"Ordinarily I would be prevented from buying something that I appraised, but since this is considered a consultation, I'm permitted to act as a buyer."

"Cut the legal crap, Mark," she exclaims. "Just tell me how much you would pay for it?"

"I'll give you $300 and a waiver of my consultation fee of $77."

"I'll take it," she says with relief. "That's fine with me. I'm $300 richer and it'll come in handy right now for some unexpected bills."

She smiles as he opens his wallet, and carefully counts out the cash. Mark pulls out a pad labeled 'Invoice Forms" and begins to write a statement in handwriting so illegible that it reminds her of a doctor writing a prescription that only a pharmacist could read. He tells her, "I'd like you to sign this statement that you're the legal owner of the bronze and paid in full."

She takes the cash without counting it, signs the receipt, and adds, "Are you sure that you don't see anything else you might like today?"

He hesitates and looks around the room, and back again at her tempting body with the protruding breasts ready to escape her negligee. He shakes his head from side to side, raises his eyebrows, and smiles like Walter Matthau with an added smirk, and says, "The devil was definitely tempting me here today but fortunately he didn't get the best of me. However, I saw three bushels of peaches outside your back door. Would you like to sell your peaches?"

Eloise appears disappointed and looks down at her protruding breasts and back at Mark, and says, "Peaches? Peaches are not exactly what I had in mind. I worked all day yesterday picking those damn peaches before they fully ripen on my trees and now all you want are my peaches. Hell, take all three bushels with my compliments for your visit this afternoon."

Mark puts a $20 bill on the kitchenette table, turns around and takes another look at her negligee, nods his head from side to side in a little whimsical and puzzling gesture. He tucks the 20 pound bronze statue under one arm, and exits through the back door. When he reaches his truck, he puts the bronze on the passenger seat, and then returns to tote the three bushels of peaches to the bed of his truck.

On the drive from Rock Hall back to Betterton, he is smiling all the way as he peers occasionally down at the nude bronze. He says to himself, "I think that I'll keep this bronze for myself. It reminds me mostly of Sandy and a little of Liz."

On Monday morning at 10 am, after a late breakfast, Mark is having a second cup of coffee alone in the shop when Vera calls and asks him to bring the model ship *Gratitude* to her marina office again, for her husband, Bud, to see and approve.

Vera says, "He's too busy to come to Betterton this afternoon and can't leave the area, so I put an anchor around his foot this time and he'll definitely be here when you come, say around two? And I guarantee that he will buy it. It's a done deal."

When Mark arrives at the marina office, he places the model ship on the office counter while Vera calls Bud on her cell phone. Mark meanders around the office and asks Vera, "Where is the photo of Ruth in a bathing suit?"

Vera replies, "You like to look at girls in their bathing suits? I thought you and Sandy were going steady. Better watch out, Mark. I could blackmail you with her." She bursts out laughing.

Mark says, "There's nothing more striking than a beautiful girl in a swim suit, is there?"

Vera counters, "How about a beautiful girl without a swim suit?"

Mark blushes, then continues to study and admire the photos hanging on the office walls, all of them depicting the history of the marina and the Wayne family, circa 1955. In a large framed black and white photo on one wall is Les Wayne Sr., the family patriarch, appearing tall and slender with gray hair, and holding a motor in his hands beside his petite wife, Mary Jo.

Other photos show them operating the marina, with over 30 years of yacht owners, a Who's Who in Boating. Finally he finds the photos showing daughters Ruth and Jean in bathing suits, and Bud at a workbench repairing an outboard motor. The telephone rings at the opposite end of the office and Vera scurries to her desk to answer it.

While she's on the telephone, Bud enters a side door, begins wiping his greasy hands on a dirty rag, and confronts Mark, still gazing at the photo of Bud repairing a motor.

Mark asks, "How old where you in that photo?"

"15, I guess."

Mark looks closely at Bud's face and sees the wear and tear taking its toll.

"Another case of pressure and tension aging a person beyond their years," Bud answers.

"After the death of my folks, about 10 years ago, neither of my sisters were interested or qualified to run the marina. With a few bucks in my savings account and a friend who knew carpentry to repair the piers, I took control of the entire estate with the stipulation that Ruth and Jean would share equally in all profits generated from the marina business. Jean helps out when she can or when we need some extra help, here and there."

"But essentially you're the boss of the marina?"

"I'm the boss and fully in charge until I married Vera about a year ago. That added more pressure too, as you'll soon see. She's a loose woman. No one has ever been able to rein her in, although I keep trying. It's like bouncing your head against a wall, after awhile, you get used to it and don't feel any pain.

Vera's basically very complex, maybe impossible to please entirely. I'm reluctant to offer you any more background, except to say that my biggest problem may be our baby. Frankly, only a DNA test would determine Jaime's birth father since Vera was dating me and Floyd before she married me and gave birth to him. Do you follow me so far, Mark?"

He quickly answers, "Yes, every word."

Bud continues, "I just want you to know what might lie ahead for you if Vera makes a play for you. Does that shock you?

"A play or flirting is one thing. But I won't take her seriously. Anything serious is out of the question for me."

"She thinks she's getting away with murder, flaunting herself, especially at military men, and right under my nose. But believe me, every man has his breaking point, after which rage takes over. Don't you agree?"

Mark asks, "Breaking point?"

"I think she feels restrained, restricted, unfulfilled, perhaps an estrogen imbalance or overactive libido. She makes no pretensions about trying to catch a man in her net."

"Your marriage is like a Lifetime movie."

Vera returns to where Mark and Bud are talking, just in time to hear Bud's last words, and says "What's that about catching a man in her net?" That'll be the day. Catch a man? Is there a man in Rock Hall?"

Mark says, "I think you both should take a look at the *Gratitude*."

Bud says, "Yes, let's take a look at the *Gratitude*. Vera's been raving about it."

Vera says, "I haven't been raving about it. I just feel that it would be a good object to own. It would spruce up the office and let people see some history from the 1950's."

Finally Mark unveils the model, and Bud takes a closer look with a magnifying glass lying on the desk. Bud admires the details in the rigging, but needs some persuasion when it comes to the price.

Vera simply tells him "I want it and that's it."

Bud asks him about some newly carved areas on the stern of the model and Mark explains that he restored that area with a special knife. Bud asks him more about the knife and Mark opens his shirt and removes the dagger from its waist-belt sheath. Bud glances over at his wife, who releases an unusually big sigh with eyes bulging at the sight of Mark's bare muscular chest. Then Bud looks over at Mark, who is unaware of his innocent stretching, until he glances again at Vera and realizes that she is glued to his every motion.

Suddenly Bud asks if he could examine the dagger. Mark hands it to him, then watches Bud's eyes turn into a sinister look as he studies the shiny blade and rotates it mysteriously to catch unusual reflections of light. The blade is as reflective as a mirror.

Mark says, "Watch out for the blade. It's sharper than you think."

Bud is fascinated with the dagger. He weighs it in his right hand and grips the jeweled handle tightly. A more intriguing, beguiling look covers his face, much more sinister than before. "I wouldn't be surprised if this is worth a ton of money," he remarks. I've never seen anything like it, except in the 'Arabian Nights'."

"You surprise me, Bud," replies Mark. "But the book was 'One Thousand and One Nights'."

"What a combination of beauty and craftsmanship, "mutters Bud.

"And I thought you only fooled around with motors, and boats, and such things," says Mark.

"I dream a lot. I read fairly tales and books of fantasy when I have the time. I get a kick out of the exotic nature of things. There's a lot of things about me that might surprise you, Mark. I bet you didn't know that I have a small collection of hunting knives, but nothing like this one," murmurs Bud. He takes an apple out of his pocket and begins peeling the skin with the dagger, and continues, "I've never seen a knife that could peel wafer thin, or cut with more precision than this blade. What do you call it?"

Mark says, "It's my carving tool but it can also be my equalizer. I hope I never have to use it as an equalizer." Bud looks at Mark, Vera and the dagger again with that sinister expression still on his face. It's the unexpected look of a devil, a fiendish, scary face you might see in a nightmare.

As Bud attempts to hand the dagger back to Mark, he flips it in his hand and grasps the handle. When Mark extends his hand, the blade strikes his palm, causing a small cut.

Vera quickly grabs a clean cloth and tells Mark, "Let me have a close look at your wound. I don't think it's deep, just something like a paper cut." She applies a band-aid.

Mark looks suspiciously at Bud. Bud doesn't apologize. After Vera applies a band-aid, she looks upward at her husband, and says, "He's always messing up something in the office anyway. If it's not misfiling bills and records, it's dropping and breaking something."

Bud says, "There you go again. Can't you leave our business private or do you have to broadcast it for everybody to hear?" Turning to Mark, he says, "I'd like to use it sometime."

Mark asks, "You want to carve something special?"

Bud says, "You never can tell."

Finally Vera says, "I'm going to write a check for $600, Bud, because I think it should be on display here. Is that agreeable to you?"

Bud sighs and consents, "All right. I guess we can deduct it as a legitimate expense, for promotional purposes for our business, can't we?"

From this moment forward, Vera will make it a practice of finding out when Mark comes to Rock Hall, making it seem like they are always "bumping into each other." But the encounters are all carefully and skillfully planned, cunningly so, by Vera.

After Mark leaves the marina office with his check in hand, Vera gets a telephone call from Floyd, who wants to apologize and have a serious talk about the future of their soft crab business.

Vera tells him bluntly, "Pretty Boy, get yourself a new life and hit the trail out of town. By the end of next week I want you to close down the business and move out of my house. You can have all the peelers in the tanks, too. No use in letting them die for your blunders, is there? Bring me the final statement and I'll give you your last check. The sooner you do this, the better for everybody."

CHAPTER 11

It's late October, time for the Harvest Moon Festival, the biggest weekend of the year in Rock Hall. People from all over Murlin, mostly from Kent County, are well aware of this festival and put it on their calendars every year as a 'must see'. It's a one-day, free, and free-for-all festival, full of fun and games, contests and prizes for young and old, including a mile relay track meet. In the evening, musical acts appear on a small stage erected near the harbor.

Events begin at 10 in the morning with a kids-and-parents walk-and-run race, and a two-in-a-sack race for kids and adults. In the afternoon, there are pie-and-watermelon-eating contests, followed by a track meet for youths under the age of 18.

Precisely at 6 pm, after the temperatures have cooled a little, the crowd gathers around a track that circles the park for the one mile relay race. This track event is open to all comers, as long as each member of the team is under 18 years of age. The race is one mile, with each runner circling the track for a quarter of a mile, holding the baton in one hand and handing it off to his teammate until the final quarter mile lap and sprint to the finish line by the fourth member of the team.

Manny Meyer, from the senior center in Betterton, looks like a photo-journalist-reporter for Hearst News, with two cameras dangling on straps around his neck. He is full of smiles as he takes shot after shot of participants and families celebrating the festival. But now he must be on his toes. He gets into position to photograph the relay team from Betterton.

Mark's team, the Breeze of Betterton, is entered as the only entry from Kent County, to compete against teams throughout the state. Mark's team is nervous and jittery but ready for the race, having limbered up all day with stretching exercises and small talk between themselves. Finally Mark brings them into a huddle and tells them, "This event is just like the practices in Betterton. Don't do anything differently tonight. Just run like the wind is at your back, and you'll all be winners. Now, go out and do it for yourselves, for your families, and for your friends. It'll be something that you'll remember for the rest of your lives."

The crowd surrounds the entire track so closely that the spectators can almost reach out and touch the runners as they fly by. Mo Greenspan stands near the starting line, looks down at the shoes she bought for the Breeze. They're Under Armour "Fast and Fusion Power Lift" track shoes, in predominantly white and orange with a black trim. She smiles with the satisfaction of knowing that she gave these youngsters a little lift in their run in life, not just for today.

An announcer steps onto the track and announces the race will consist of 8 teams of runners from all of the state. At the starting line is the State Commissioner of Athletics, Bucky Larimore. He walks to the far end of the starting line, shakes hands, and wishes each participant good luck. His shaking the hands with all 32 runners resembles a politician running for election. The Breeze are the last and only entry from Kent County. Mark decides that Jesse will run the last quarter of a mile for the Breeze.

Within a few seconds, the starting gun is fired and the first runners in the relay take off down the track. At the halfway point in the first quarter mile, almost all runners are even in their lane, with no clear runner ahead of the pack. After the first runner hands off the baton to the second runner of his team, only the second runner of the Breeze trails the pack by 10 feet. After the second runner hands off the baton to the third runner of the relay team, only the third runner of the Breeze trails the pack by 20 feet. The runners from the competing teams are all incredibly even, almost unprecedented in racing.

Now the stage is set for one of the greatest comebacks in amateur track. After the third runner hands off the baton to Jesse, the fourth runner of the Breeze, he is behind the entire pack by at least 30 feet. Accelerating like the thoroughbred Mine That Bird in the Kentucky Derby, he moves like lightening, and not only catches the pack but leans his chest at the finish line, a photo-finish, to win the event for the Breeze of Betterton.

When the final time is verified by two judges and read to the crowd, Mark's team has set a state record for the relay event. Everyone, including the opposing track coaches and runners, erupt in applause when they hear the record announced over the loud speakers.

After the team and Mark accept their medals and trophy from Commissioner Larimore, Mark gathers them together for a private huddle. He offers them a new challenge, "What do you think about hitting the water and training as a relay swim team? I've been thinking about it and have a good name for our team, the BETTERTON HYDRO-NUTS!"

They all burst out laughing while still contemplating the feeling of ecstasy that comes from winning unexpectedly. No one ever gave them a chance to succeed before. Finally Jesse says, "Sir, if you don't mind it, how 'bout letting us enjoy this moment together, and, as you always say, 'we'll take it under consideration'."

Precisely at 8 pm when the moon is full over the Bay, everyone gathers around the stage for a concert and dance session. The Master of Ceremonies, Annette Wells, introduces the Kent County Marching Band to lead off the program with a rousing medley of John Phillip Sousa's patriotic marches, accompanied on stage by young and athletic drum majors, twirling their batons high in the air.

Annette thanks the crowd for making the event such a success every year and says, "This year is something special because we've just broken the record for attendance. I won't read the exact figure written down on this piece of paper, but each one of you can take a guess and write the number down with your telephone number for a drawing later tonight. The lucky winner will get free ice cream for one year, courtesy of Helen Durding of Durding's Ice Cream Parlor of Rock Hall.

And as I said before, tonight is special and for special nights, we have a special act. The next act is an experiment tonight. If you like what you are about to see and hear, we'll take this act to Bawlmer and the Hippodrome Theatre. I guarantee that you'll pay a lot more to see it in Bawlmer than here in Rock Hall tonight. So without further adieu, here is 'Gertie, the Bewitching Bird of Betterton' with her friend on the accordion, Knute Runagrun."

Gertie sings while Knute plays a song on an old accordion for all the old timers at the pavilion called "Always." Knute begins singing the opening phrase, "I'll be lovin' you…"

Then Gertie sings "Always."

Knute continues "With a love that's true…"

And again Gertie sings "Always."

The repetitive sequence of Knute singing the phrases and Gertie squawking "Always" brings cheers and laughter from the crowd.

During this song, the trumpet player of Reggie's quintet joins in with a hat mute over his horn. When the song finishes, the crowd erupts again in another long thunderous ovation and laughter. The duo of Knute and Gertie is a smash hit tonight.

Annette takes the microphone and says, "I think those two are headed to the Hippodrome Theatre in Bawlmer, don't you agree?" She pauses and announces, "We've saved the best for last. From the far away region of Betterton, we proudly introduce one of our own gifted musicians, Reggie Perdue and his quintet, sponsored by Perdue Farms, makers of 'Yummy for your Tummy' chicken tenders! Ladies and Gentlemen and all you young people, straight from New York City by way of Betterton, Reggie Perdue and His Quintet."

As members of the quintet, consisting of drums, trombone, clarinet, piano-organ keyboard, and guitar, arrange the microphones on stage, Reggie takes the center mike and says, "For everyone who wants to dance with his special gal or guy, we've set up a dance floor, especially for you."

Reggie and his quintet begin the session with his instrumental rock and roll arrangement of Otis Redding's "Respect," with the Breeze substituting for Aretha Franklin. Now, that's something you have to see to believe it! Jesse and his three friends dance on stage like it was home away from home, or on a street corner of Betterton. A small group of spectators gather around and admire this naturally gifted foursome with sporadic applause.

Standing nearby is Little Mac, who's covering the story for the Baltimore Sun papers. Between making notes on a pad, he's rocking and rolling to the music too. He says to himself, "There's nothing better than covering a story and enjoying every moment."

When the song is finished, Reggie says, "By the look on some of your faces, you all didn't realize the talent waiting to be developed in Betterton, did you?"

Then Reggie takes the mic again and says, "And now I have a surprise for everyone, that even our master of ceremonies doesn't know about. When you ask a friend to join you for a session like tonight, but he's in the middle of a recording session 400 miles away, you never know if he'll be able to interrupt his schedule. But he did for us and here he is, in person, for our Harvest Moon Festival, right from New York City, Mr. Johnny Mathis."

The crowd erupts in applause followed by incredible silence. Johnny takes the mic and speaks softly, "For a change of pace, I'd like to slow things down a bit and offer you all a sort of revival of two standards that never grow old. They're as popular today as they were fifty years ago, so if you want to dance along with me, there's the floor."

Without an accompaniment, Mathis begins alone with the words, 'In the still of the night', and then the quintet joins in very quietly in the background. After almost 50 years in the music business, he still evokes a special style. Like a good wine, it seems to get better with age.

Within a second or two of the end of the first song, he segues immediately into the ballad, 'Tender is the Night'.

The audience is stunned. Reggie scratches his head, takes the mic, and tells Johnny, "Silence is golden. I think they've never heard you singing before. It was magic. Take it from me, pal, you were magnificent tonight."

Afterwards, Reggie brings Johnny over to Mark standing by the bandstand with his Breeze. Reggie tells Mark, "Johnny wanted to meet you and your track team. You probably didn't know it, but Johnny ran track in high school in San Francisco, and he wanted to thank you for what you've done with your kids in Betterton. At one of our recording sessions in New York, I told him all about your work, and your rescue of Sandy, too."

Mark is speechless, but Jesse speaks up and asks, "How did you go from track into the music business, Mr. Mathis?"

Johnny says, "Well, my boy, that's a long story. We'll leave that question for another time and place. Right now, I want to get out of town before the musicians union knows that I've appeared here."

Johnny then turns to Mark and says, "I expect you to keep me informed about the Breeze, too."

They all walk Johnny back to his limo and watch him disappear into the night. Reggie looks around for Sandy, who wants to introduce him to Ruth Wayne. As he is walking back to the stage, he finds her and tells her that he has one last session on stage. He breaks the secrecy code by informing Sandy, "Ruth's the Harvest Moon Queen, as if you didn't know already, and I'll get the first dance with her on stage."

Taking center stage next once again is Annette who proclaims, "Ladies and Gentlemen, I give you the Mayor of Rock Hall, Stanley Piotrowski, a man who needs no introduction in Kent County."

Nick-named 'Stash', he is known far and wide throughout Kent County as the Jolly Green Giant, because he stands six feet eight inches and weighs 300 pounds. When the spotlight shines on him, his shadow is cast over Reggie and his quintet playing softly in the background. The Mayor says, "Hello, everyone. Tonight I'll try to be brief, which will come as a big surprise to everyone who knows me. I have the honor of announcing and crowning this year's Harvest Moon Queen, Ruth Wayne."

He turns around as Reggie hands him a box containing the gold-colored plastic crown, which he holds in two hands. Suddenly he looks as if he will drop it because it's so heavy. He says, "It's pure gold or at least it *looks* like pure gold. Heavy too, but not too heavy for our Queen to wear tonight."

He turns to Ruth Wayne, looks down at her six foot frame, places it on her head, and turns to the audience, "As Mayor of Rock Hall, I crown our Harvest Moon Queen, Ruth Wayne, six feet of beauty and charm, locally grown, born and raised right here in Rock Hall, with golden hair like the husks of corn on the cob. She's a stewardess, now working for American Airlines. So look for her on your next flight. By the way, we should get something for that publicity plug for American Airlines."

The crowd erupts in thunderous applause, and the lighting specialist who maneuvers the center spotlight says, "Same ol' Mayor. Always a little long winded, but always in a good way."

On stage, Reggie sets his guitar aside and steps forward to have the first dance on stage with the new Queen. While Reggie introduces himself to Ruth, the Mayor takes a harmonica from his pocket and plays the lead along with the quintet, minus Reggie on guitar, of an original ballad by Richard Wagner, especially written for the occasion. Richard takes the microphone, turns his eyes towards Annette, and says, "This ballad was written for a special someone. I hope you'll like it." He taps his baton and leads the quintet into the song, 'It's Like Heaven'.

When the song ends, Reggie takes the mike, and announces, "That's a new ballad written by Joseph Szymanski in the 1960's but given a new arrangement by Richard Wagner, one of our bright rising stars in the music business from Chestertown. If it sounds somewhat familiar, like 'Miss America', that's purely coincidental, but we're hoping it will catch on and get recorded soon, so you can listen to it over and over again. And here again, is our Master of Ceremonies, Annette Wells."

Annette has the final word for the evening, thanks everyone for coming, and wishes them a safe journey home.

Sandy greets Ruth and Reggie as they descend the stage together, and tells them, "I guess you won't need any introduction, will you? So you're on your own. It looks like a beautiful night to gaze at the stars, the stars in the sky, and the stars in your eyes."

Reggie takes Ruth's arm for a short walk along the harbor, and tells her, "Here's my Shangri-La for tonight, nicely tied up, waiting just for you. Let's watch the harbor and stars from the upper deck. On a clear night like tonight, you can almost reach out and touch them."

She says, "I bet you take all your girls here for their first date, don't you?"

He counters, "What would you say if I told you that you're the first?"

She asks, "The first what?"

He says, "The first and only one I've asked to lounge besides me on the upper deck. This is where stars collide, where and when the conditions are right, magic happens, life begins." He leans over and caresses her gently.

She says, "In the moonlight things look different, don't they. You're a very attractive and persuasive man, Reggie. I hope we'll be good friends...Settings like this, aboard your yacht, under the stars, all get me in the mood, but I need something more to keep me in the mood. Things like honesty, sensitivity, devotion."

Reggie says, "I think this is the beginning of a beautiful friendship."

Ruth answers, "For reasons that I can't explain, my heart is unexpectedly skipping an extra beat or two. Any suggestions as to what I should do about it?"

Reggie says, "How 'bout a change of scenery."

She says, "In that case, if you'll escort me to your master stateroom, I'll show you where life begins."

He takes her hand and ushers her below deck and into the master stateroom. He claps his hands twice and automatically soft lighting and romantic music from his state-of-the-art surround sound system provide a background for romance about to blossom. A moment later the stateroom door closes behind them.

As the evening wears down and the moon is still in its full cycle, Mark and Sandy find a quiet spot overlooking the Chesapeake Bay. It is a special time for two people to be alone, away from all sounds except for the heartbeat inside your body. Mark is somewhat hesitant here but hopeful, and a little anxious. He takes a deep breath and manages to get up some courage to make a proposal of marriage. He feels comfortable with his life now and is looking ahead to a future that includes Sandy. Would she consider an engagement leading to marriage? Would she be willing to set some goals together?

He tells her, "I've never been in love before, but I feel something special about you that leads me to say.... I'm IN love with you. Will you marry me?"

She sighs and tells him, "I love you too Mark. It's something that I've been thinking about too, but the suddenness to hear you propose marriage tonight..." She pauses to catch her breath, and continues, "You've taken my breath away. What do you expect me to say here?"

He replies, "I would expect you to say what's in your heart, and let the Good Lord take care of the rest."

"I still have a responsibility to take care of my mother."

"Richard is now becoming the new man in your house who can carry the load of your mother's personal and business needs, don't you think?"

Sandy is cautious and reluctant to make a decision tonight, which leaves him reeling and disappointed. She finally confesses, "Is your goal in life to make more money than your father, have more power than your father? You still seem to harbor some frustration in wanting to be your own boss and some resentment about your father's offer to join him at the mill. It's like you're carrying a lot of unnecessary baggage around, weighing you down, preventing you from expressing yourself and following your dreams.

"Your resolve to make it on your own, prove to everyone around you that you can make it on your own, and on your own terms, these things stand in our way right now. Until you can moderate your goals and can take the time to understand those friends around you, including me, it's best to wait a while longer before we plunge into an engagement. Mark, you don't have to prove anything to me. You are and always will be my true love."

He listens carefully and tries to understand everything that she has just spoken to him. With a slight groan, he tells her, "Sandy, you're very perceptive. Perhaps being an artist gives you special instincts, and a better perspective into the minds and hearts of people, especially me."

"This is not a rejection, but merely a pause, like getting a second breath of air. Neither of us has been in this situation before, so we're treading on new ground, aren't we?"

"You may not know it, but I'm still not sure about living in Betterton." He pauses to collect his thoughts and says, "I need some of the big city life, and intellectual and cultural stimulation occasionally. I'm getting to know and love the art and antiques business, just like I'm getting to know and love you. It's far better to be a big fish in a small pond like Betterton than opening an antiques business and fighting the competition in Baltimore."

As they walk back to their car, Vera accidentally bumps into them along the way and tells them, "News of your business skills has permeated into Rock Hall. Have you given any thought to opening a small shop here? There's twice as many people living here than in Betterton, and there are more wealthy tourists, especially from Annapolis, Philadelphia and Wilmington. I think we should talk about it, and soon. How about next Saturday night at the saloon? The drinks will be on us. Say about 9 p.m. I'll call you during the week to confirm it. See you next week."

After Vera leaves their company, Sandy turns to him and says, "There's something fishy about that woman."

Mark says, "You aren't a little jealous, are you?"

Sandy says, "Of her? Never."

He says, "Good. Let it rest. There's nothing more to be said. There's nothing to it."

The following day the entire front page of the Kent News is plastered with colored photos taken by Manny Meyer beside stories compiled by Little Mac, cub reporter for the Sun, of the track meet won by the Breeze. When Mark turns the front page to read page 2, there are photos of people, young and old, at the Harvest Moon Festival, starting in the upper left and moving clockwise, that show the rollicking fun at the pie eating contest, the horseshoe ringer contest, Reggie and his Quintet, and in the center of the page, a close-up of Mayor Piotrowski crowing Ruth Wayne as Queen.

Mark says, "I can't believe it. Manny captured all the important moments and expressions of the Breeze. He's pushed all news about farmers and watermen to the back section of the newspaper. The Breeze victory will inspire other kids, black and white, in and around Betterton, to form teams and compete in other sports. I wouldn't be surprised if all the seniors are howling a little today when they see Manny's photographs. He's put Betterton on the map, and his photos will become a permanent record. I'd like to see them in an exhibition someday. Manny really has a special knack for photography. He must be tickled pink."

Realtors are suddenly getting inquiries about the availability of houses and schools for families interested in relocating to Betterton. The winds of pride in the town are blowing across the state. Finally, gossip about a Navy SEAL living above an artist's studio becomes a thing of the past. Nellie Fox Boyd is unexpectedly 'out' of words and action for the time being. If this were baseball, she'd be placed on the 'disabled list'.

The next Thursday, after breakfast at the shop, Annette tells Sandy and Mark that she's been invited for dinner at Richard's condo overlooking the Chester River in Chestertown. Just as she finishes her remarks, the phone rings, and Sandy tells Mark that Vera is on the phone for him. She wants to remind them of their Saturday date at 9 pm at the Saloon.

After she hands the phone to Mark, Sandy tells him with a touch of jealousy, "You can go on alone. I've got an appointment with Tom Bowman to show him my finished clay model of Storm Cat. I am thinking of asking him to help me with the costs of making an edition of 10 bronzes of that beautiful Thoroughbred, which will cut the cost of each bronze almost in half. Go on alone with Vera and her husband, but watch out, Mark. As I said before, there's something suspicious about her, but I trust you'll be on guard. Perhaps I'm a bit jealous here, but Vera's reputation proceeds her."

Mark explains to Vera, "Sandy is busy with an important project, so I'll be coming alone if that's all right with you and your husband?"

Vera is ecstatic and can hardly control her joy as she leans back in her swivel chair behind her desk. She looks up just as Bonnie Bratcher, her baby sitter, comes through the back door of the office. She picks up her baby and hands him to her and says, "You'll have to take care of Jaime until I get back from the hair dresser. Understand?"

Bonnie tells her, "Jaime will be all right with me. Not to worry about us." She wraps him in a small blue cover, exits the office through the back door, and climbs the stairs to the apartment above the marina office.

Then Vera puts a sign on the front door, "Office Closed - Manager on Duty Outside." She locks the marina office door, and walks to her red Cadillac with the white hardtop parked nearby. She drives about 5 minutes into a cul-de-sac of clapboard homes and pulls into the driveway of one in yellow vinyl siding.

She walks up the side porch, knocks on the door, and is greeted by Greta Wowl Howell, a middle aged woman and part time stylist, who has a small back room in her home converted to a hair salon.

Greta bellows out, "Vera, where have you been, girl?

Vera replies, "Around, here and there. If you've heard anything scandalous about me since the last time I was here, it's probably true. I know that sooner or later all the gossip flows into your shop like the incoming tide" As Vera hangs up her jacket, she continues, " I'd like to brag a little about my latest exploits, but it's been hit and miss for me lately, and mostly miss. But now I want the Works! Shampoo, a little trim, platinum tint to make me look a few years younger, anything... Can you make me into Gwen Stefani?"

Greta says, "That's a tall order, girl, but I'll give it a try. You must have something special brewing inside, right?

Vera bellows out, "You are psychic! How do you know such things? Or is it just your suspicious nature?"

Gretta says, "Instincts, girl. I picked it up from reading everything I could get my hands on about Shirley MacLaine. Someday I would like to be the Psychic to the Stars, too. Not stars in the heavens but real movie stars, like Brad Pitt and Matt Damon. So tell me, Vera, is the big day tonight or tomorrow?"

Vera says, "Tomorrow night will be my night to howl."

Greta probes deeper, like only a stylist can probe, "You once told me you could do anything to anyone, anywhere, anytime, whenever you wanted to, right? I can see you beginning to blush, girl."

Vera pauses, lets out a sigh, and says "You remember the last time when you told me that I was on a collision course with that ensign from the Naval Academy over in Annapolis? Well, you were right on the money, honey! Damn, that was like opening a bottle of lightning! I must have a way with watermen. I have my sights on a Navy SEAL. His name is Mark and he lives in Betterton. When you have a chance, how 'bout checking out your astro-lo-gee-galgical…" She stumbles in her pronunciation and begins to laugh, "That's a tough word to pronounce, 'astrological'. Check my chart and see if all my stars and planets are in the correct alignment, or am I heading into another collision?"

Greta says, "While you are drying out from the shampoo, I'll see what's coming up for you, *besides* my bill for making you into Gwen Stefani. You know, I used to tell everyone, 'Never make love or fall in love during a total eclipse'. But I'm not so sure about that anymore. What the hell, if you have the chance, I say, "Go for it, girl!" Greta scatters all her astrology charts on a table and screams out, "It's true. It's right here in these charts. You are about to collide with the Planet Mars. Make that Planet Mark."

As Vera hands the cash to Greta, "I don't know what it is about coming here and telling you all about my exploits with military men. Perhaps it's entering another world, a relaxing, peaceful world of innocence. No tension…like when I first lost my virginity. Do you remember when you first lost your virginity, Greta?"

"Are you kidding? I think it was in high school, in the tenth grade, in the back seat of a car."

"You too? Didn't it feel natural and enjoyable?"

"You never forget the first time, do you?"

"No, you don't." Vera pauses and sighs after recalling and relating good memories of her high school days.

After three hours at the hair stylist, Vera finally gets back home around 7 pm. She climbs the stairs to her apartment above the marina office, and immediately notices that the door is not fully closed. She pushes it gently open enough for her to fit through and walks quietly across the small living room towards the bedroom. Along the way she gazes at Jaime asleep in his play crib beside a couch.

When she reaches the bedroom door, it is slightly ajar, probably intentionally to hear whether or not the baby is stirring. When she pushes the door completely open, she finds Bud in bed, with Bonnie on top of him. Their clothes are scattered on the floor. She surprisingly is not shocked, doesn't utter a word, just slams the door shut and returns to the living room to fix a stiff drink. She puts the whiskey bottle down with a loud bang.

Seconds later Bonnie rushes out of the bedroom, fully dressed with her shoes in one hand, and streaks across the living room and down the outside staircase.

Bud comes out of the bedroom in his bare feet, yanks the zipper of his trousers upward and calmly says, "I think she lured me into it, so innocent and enticing. Funny, I did the exact thing that I've accused you of doing. I really have no excuse."

Vera says, "And no apology either. I'm glad that you've found something or somebody to satisfy your needs. But does it have to be in our bed and with our baby sitter? That's unforgivable. Caught red handed, whatever that means. You should've been a little discreet, Bud. But your real self is finally emerging. This might be grounds for a divorce, an expensive divorce for you. I can hold it over your head and take everything, just to hurt you like you tried to hurt me. You might even have to sell the marina to pay for half of our assets and alimony. I could break you, Bud. I hope the sex was worth it!"

Bud asks her, "Whata ya want me to do? From your reaction, especially the look in your eyes, are you threatening me?"

She replies, "For starters, you can find another place to sleep tonight. It's been a long day and I sure didn't expect it to end like this tonight. I'll talk to you in the morning."

Vera mixes herself a strong whiskey and looks closely in the mirror at her beautifully styled hair, and says, "Here's to better days ahead, and not with Bud. This might work out better than I could have ever planned."

Meanwhile, Annette is enjoying the end of a beautiful dinner cooked entirely by Richard at his condo overlooking the Chester River. She tells him, "Everything is perfect tonight, the presentation of dinner, the candles in sterling silver holders, the centerpiece of fresh flowers, the view of the river, even you in a cook's apron. You don't look like a professor of music, but your dinner was a symphony. Thank you, dear friend."

"I thought you might look upon me as more than a dear friend. I was hoping and praying that we might take the next step in our lives and walk down the aisle together."

"Are you thinking what I'm thinking?"

"I've been thinking about what it would be like to be married to you from the first time I saw you. My life has taken a sudden upswing. Reggie has shown an interest in some of my compositions and wants to see and hear more of my writings."

'I've always let my intuition lead me in these situations, and it tells me I should say 'yes' before you change your mind."

"Remember Reggie at the Harvest Moon Festival when he mentioned that I arranged the song 'It's Like Heaven', I'll play it for you on my baby grand and hope my fingers hit all the right keys." Richard takes Annette over to a corner of his condo and plays his arrangement flawlessly, with a concerto crescendo at the end. Annette sheds a tear along with Richard, who rises from the piano, takes her by the arm to the balcony, and kisses her passionately as the moon and stars overhead brighten the night.

It's the last Saturday in October. Vera opens the marina office at 9 in the morning. She answers the telephone, takes some orders from boat owners who want to moor their yachts at Swan Point Marina, and, for the next eight hours, manages the office without showing any bitterness or hostility.

At precisely 6 pm, as Vera finishes up some paperwork in the office, Bonnie comes in. Vera tells her, "You and I will have a long talk at another time when things settle down. In the meantime, I want you to take care of Jamie tonight until I get back home. It'll be late, but how late I can't tell you because I have a date at the saloon with Mark, and possibly Bud, too. If you need me, you can always call my cell phone.

Bud won't be sleeping here for the time being." She winks at Bonnie, and continues, "You might have to spend the entire night here with Jaime, so you can sleep in my bed if you want to, and I said 'sleep', not play around. At some point in your life, Bonnie, you have to get your act together."

Bonnie has heard these instructions before, when Vera plans some nighttime adventures, and she takes Jaime out the back door of the office just as Bud pops in the front door. Vera tells him that Bonnie is baby-sitting tonight, and she means 'baby-sitting'. She advises him to spend another night away from her until they can have a serious talk about their relationship, from a marital and business standpoint.

She finally reminds him about their scheduled date with Mark at 9 pm at the Saloon, and tells him "Despite everything that has erupted in the last 24 hours, life goes on, and sometimes we have to pretend that we have a good marriage when it may be crumbling on the inside. So if you want to come tonight to meet Mark, and see for yourself that I'm not out to *make* every military man like you think I'm out to do, meet us at the saloon at 9."

Although she utters these words, she says them facetiously, just to give Bud the impression of her turning over a new leaf. She asks herself, "I don't think it's out of character for me to think or feel this way, is it?"

Bud says, "I've got the marina to run, and that's my number one priority right now. Furthermore, I have to wait for a customer to bring me a big check for a slip rental that's three months overdue. I'll stay tonight until I get my money. You can go on alone, and I'll catch up with you as soon as I finish my work here. It's no big deal to have some drinks with Mark, as far as I'm concerned."

At the bewitching hour, precisely at 9, Mark walks into the saloon in Rock Hall. Vera, sitting with her husband Bud in a back room booth, sees him coming through the front door and rushes through the crowded saloon to grab his arm and escort him into the back area.

Bud tells Mark, "I just arrived a few moments ago, too. I was supposed to pick up a check from one of my tenants, but he never showed up. He's another guy trying to stiff me, so Vera and I came in two cars. What a waste."

Drinks are ordered, music blares out, and customers are gyrating on the dance floor, letting loose all their frustrations in a Texas line dance.

Vera whispers into Mark's ear, "Maybe it was not such a good idea to meet here to talk about business. Much too noisy and no privacy. What do you say if we just let our hair down and unbutton our shirts, first yours, then mine."

Bud sees the way Vera is flaunting herself again in front of him. He emits a menacing smile, shrugs his shoulders, and says to himself, "I've seen this thing happen one too many times before, but tonight could be the night. She's pushing me over the edge. I won't stand for it any more. Maybe it's time to think about eliminating her once and for all from my life. At least I'd collect the life insurance money, but how and when to do it?"

After a pause in the music, Vera hands Mark a quarter and says, "Why don't you pick out a good tune on the jukebox."

He says, "One of my favorites is Patsy Cline singing 'Crazy'."

Vera hesitates to digest the meaning, if any, behind his words, and looks at him with a strange curiosity, as if he might be looking for the same thing she's looking for, hot sex!

As the music begins, she pulls him by his shirt onto the dance floor.

Bud gets up from the booth with the intention of going to the Men's Room, but hides behind a latticed partition with triangular cutouts to watch Vera, who begins to rub her body sensuously against Mark's body.

After the recording is over, Mark, now perspiring, walks Vera back to their booth, and then excuses himself to go to the Men's Room. When he gets inside the Men's Room, it's empty. He splashes some water on his face and, with wet hands, combs them in his hair to dry them off.

While Mark is still in the Men's Room, Vera carefully looks around to see if anyone is watching her, then tears open a paper packet containing a Mickey, a sedative strong enough to choke a horse and pours it quickly into his beer stein. She doesn't realize that Bud has noticed her actions, which now seem to trigger a deathly impulse in his mind. He says to himself, "Be patient. This might be the opportunity to avoid a divorce settlement that could financially ruin everything I've worked for."

When Mark returns from the Men's room, he is thirsty and downs the spiked beer in one long, continuous swallow. Within a few minutes the fast-acting sedative leaves Mark unable to lift his arms and legs. He begs for help to get some fresh air outside the Saloon. Vera finds Gretta nearby and together they manage to get him outside and into Vera's Cadillac parked nearby.

She tells Gretta, "I'll drive him back to Betterton in my car."

Gretta smiles and says "Good girl. I told you before that your planets and stars are all in their proper alignment, ready for one giant collision and explosion. This is your night to howl."

It's nearly midnight. Vera takes her time driving on the two-lane road leading from Rock Hall to Betterton. As she is driving, she looks quickly over at him, slumped against the car door.

She says to him, "Mark, it won't be long now. I'm going to take you on the roller coaster ride of your life. You know, they say I have a way with men, especially military men. I don't know what it is but they seem stronger, more energetic.

"Yes, come to think of it, I do have a way with military men. I guess I get them to snap to attention, stand *up* to attention. Do you know what I'm talking about here? You think, I'm just mumbling, but soon, mumbling will turn into rumbling."

While continuing to drive, she turns back and forth to watch Mark and the road, and eventually glances over and down at his thigh. She places her right hand against it and starts to massage his thigh. She says, "Just a little while longer. We're almost there. Soon, you're going to come to Mama." There's not a whimper from him. He is out cold.

Another minute later, Vera suddenly pulls off the main road to the right and parks on a gravel path along side a grove of trees near Lovers Lane, a quiet secluded place that is well-known for privacy. A long row of trees provides peace and quiet on both sides of a car when it is parked there. She turns off the motor and headlights. The only light here comes from a full moon overhead that bounces off the front bonnet of her Cadillac

She looks over at Mark and in a loud voice, proclaims, "It's Showtime, baby, time to find out what you have hidden below your waist, and below that belt with the dagger." It takes a lot of effort, but Vera manages to get his shirt completely off. He is still slumped in the corner of the passenger seat. He remains unconscious when Vera swings her body around and sits on top of him. In desperation, she begins to slap his face several times in an effort to wake him, but absolutely cannot get a response. He is comatose. Frustrated and growing more impatient, she grabs him by his shoulders and shakes him to no avail.

Finally, Vera turns and falls back into the driver's seat, slightly ashamed for administering such a potent sedative, and totally exhausted from the mental strain of planning for this night, under the moonlight. Unfortunately, she did not anticipate the power of the sedative, and would never do anything to hurt or harm him. Her intention was purely to get him in a relaxed state where he might be led, not forced, into a state of readiness for seduction. Perhaps booze alone would have done the trick.

In retrospect, Vera confesses, "Obviously I didn't calculate the double whammy of combining the sedative and alcohol." She looks over at him again and whispers, "You're no good to me in this condition, are you?" She sighs heavily and begins to pass out. Her arms drop from their grip on the steering wheel to her lap, and her head falls backward into the driver's headrest as she slips into a deep sleep.

A minute later, footsteps quietly press into the gravel stones with a crunching sound. A hand reaches through the open window on the passenger side and reaches down to Mark's waist belt and removes the dagger from its sheath. A dark silhouetted figure moves around the back of the Caddy towards the driver's side. The bright moonlight reflects off the side-view mirror and is angled at Vera's head. Her throat is especially illuminated by the moonlight, a ghastly foreboding sign of lurking evil.

A squeaky sound of a rusty door hinge is heard as the rear door behind the driver's seat is opened. A hand holding the dagger moves from behind Vera's head and slits her throat, from her left ear to her right ear, but the killer pauses momentarily before withdrawing the dagger. He wants to be certain that blood slowly drips over the slit. The sharp blade makes an incision that cuts the carotids, the two great arteries on each side of the neck that carries blood to the head.

The result is fatal. There is no movement or motion whatsoever by Vera. No groan. Not a whimper. Not even one last breath of life. Her head is locked against the headrest of her seat.

The dagger is pulled out of her throat and wrapped in a handkerchief. The rear door is again closed quietly without a squeak. The assailant walks down the gravel road to a car hidden in a cluster of trees. The night suddenly turns pitch-black. Clouds completely block the moonlight. The sound of an automobile motor breaks the silence of the night. The vehicle is driven slowly by the assailant away from the trees and onto the main road back towards Rock Hall.

CHAPTER 12

It's now 30 minutes past midnight. A policeman in a cruiser drives along the road from Betterton to Rock Hall and spots the Caddy parked in the gravel road. He drives his cruiser into the road, parks directly behind Vera's car, and turns on his overhead spotlights. As the officer cautiously approaches the car, his badge reflects off the bright light and reads, "Lt. Stephen Moorehaus."

He unbuckles the strap around his pistol and uses his flashlight to look inside the car. He immediately sees two occupants, both immobile. Because he is closer to the driver's side of the vehicle, he first examines the woman passed out in the driver's seat, her throat cut ear to ear. He walks around the front of the car and puts his flashlight in the face of the bare-chested man crumpled in the passenger seat. He puts his finger to Mark's throat to check his pulse, then runs back to his cruiser.

He reaches through the driver's window, grabs the microphone, and shouts frantically, "Code 1, Emergency, Cruiser 7, Moorehaus calling dispatch." While he waits for a response, he checks his watch and continues, "This is Moorehaus in Cruiser 7, on Route 44 and Lovers Lane in Rock Hall. Get an ambulance here as fast as you can. I think we have a deadly situation, one individual dead and another immobile. Get me some backup. This is Code 1. I can't tell you what's around me. Do you read me?"

A few seconds pass before the dispatcher acknowledges everything, but Moorehaus doesn't hesitate before repeating everything, this time in a louder voice, and discloses the license plate tag number of the Cadillac. The sense of urgency is clear as he can hardly hold his hands from shaking.

The dispatcher tells him that medical personnel and back up are on the way and orders him to secure the crime scene.

Within 10 minutes two emergency rescue vehicles and personnel are on the scene to remove the individuals from the Cadillac and transport them to the Chester River Hospital in Chestertown, about 20 miles away.

Moorehaus remains at the crime scene and gets additional instructions from the dispatcher to maintain a quarantine of the crime scene until advised otherwise. Minutes later homicide detective Jack Donnelly arrives in his unmarked vehicle and confers with Moorehaus about details of his findings. After Donnelly completes his questioning and drives to the hospital, two additional police arrive to relieve Moorehaus who is informed by the dispatcher to take on an additional task.

He is told that, based on a trace of the license plates, the Cadillac is owned by Vera Wayne, and orders him to notify the next of kin, Vera's husband Bud, residing a short distance away. He records the address, and drives to the Swan Point Marina. As he begins to climb the stairway outside the marina office leading to the upstairs apartment, he notices a pair of bright yellow high-top waterman's boots, wet and covered with grass and mud, on the lower landing area.

He continues to climb the stairs and soon is let inside the apartment by Bud Wayne. Moorehaus finds Bud in his pajamas and Bonnie standing nearby in her robe, and informs them that Vera has been murdered. Bonnie is hysterical and begins sobbing uncontrollably, while Bud is frozen in disbelief.

He remarks, "How could this thing happen? I was just with her a few hours ago at the saloon." He doesn't ask for more details and turns his attention towards Bonnie.

Meanwhile at the hospital, the dolly on which Mark is still unconscious is rushed into the emergency room for examination. Vera's body is taken into the same room, but an accordion curtain is drawn to separate them. After she is pronounced dead on arrival, the Coroner's Office is notified by the attending physician on duty. While attendants transfer her body to the morgue for an autopsy, hospital emergency personnel prepare to give Mark intravenous solutions to counteract the overdose of sedative in his blood.

A police officer suddenly appears and takes his position outside the emergency room, with instructions to guard the room and refuse admittance to everyone except hospital personnel.

An hour later, the gurney with Mark hooked up to intravenous feeding tubes is moved to a recovery room nearby. The police officer follows the gurney and takes a seat just outside the recovery room door.

At 8 in the morning, a doctor enters the recovery room and takes the clipboard from the footboard of Mark's bed. She studies the charts and paperwork and moves to Mark's head. A stethoscope dangles from the upper pocket of her white uniform. On the pocket is an identity badge bearing the name "Vicky Steele MD." She takes Mark's left hand and, at his wrist, begins to measure his pulse while glancing at her wrist watch. A smile crosses her face. His pulse registers a normal level. She places his hand beside his body, and places her right hand on his forehead to get a feeling of his temperature while her eyes gaze at an array of video monitors near his bed. She says to herself, "Thank you, dear Lord," and sighs with relief as his eyes begin to twitter and open. He is in a daze and looks up at her angelic smile. She leans over to a position where her face is almost six inches from his, and says, "Everything went well."

Mark puts both hands up to massage his cheeks. He is still drowsy but asks almost in a whisper, "Where am I?"

Dr. Steele answers, "You're going to be all right. Not to worry. You're in the hospital."

"What am I doing in a hospital?"

"You've had a bad night. There was a huge amount of a sedative in your blood, and you passed out. The ambulance brought you to the emergency room just after midnight. I can't tell you anything more. I'd like to raise your head up if you don't mind. The intravenous tube in your arm contains a solution to neutralize and flush out that sedative, and must continue for at least another hour or two.

We may have to keep you here until noon, depending on how you feel in a couple hours. In the meantime, drink as much water as you possibly can. If you need me, just press the call button attached to your gown. Don't get out of bed until we check you again. Do you understand what I'm telling you?"

"My head is spinning. I feel dizzy. Perhaps if you raise my head a little higher, it will help to clear the cobwebs. How and why and what in the hell am I doing in the hospital?"

"All I want you to do right now is try to relax, and let the neutralizer circulate to all parts of your body again. If you continue to feel dizzy, you can take some oxygen from this mask. Are you allergic to anything?"

"No. Not to my knowledge. But what's going on here? Why am I in the hospital?"

"Everything in due time, Mark. Please try to get some rest, and maybe you should take some oxygen now. It will do you good, believe me."

As she reaches the door, she turns and tells him, "Try to get some rest and let your body recover from that nasty overdose. By the way, all your vital signs are perfect, just where they should be, except for your heart rate that has a slight flutter. It's very understandable, under the circumstances. A cardiologist is monitoring your vital signs from the main control station outside your door. In a few minutes you'll have a visitor, a detective from the Sheriff's Department, interested in questioning you."

Two minutes later there's a knock at Mark's door, and in walks a 40-year old tall, lean and handsome-looking man, dressed in a wrinkled suit, swinging a notepad in one hand. Pinned to his top lapel pocket is a police badge with his name below the insignia. He smiles and says, "I'm Detective Jack Donnelly of the Kent County Sheriffs Department. I'd like to talk to you… First off, how are you feeling this morning?"

"I'd feel a lot better if you told me what this is all about."

"Well, Mark, I have to read you your rights under the Miranda Act. You have the right to remain silent and the right to have an attorney present at all times, and anything and everything that you say could be written down and used as evidence against you."

"In that case, I'd like to call my father before proceeding any further. But before I call him, tell me please what's this all about, what the hell is going on here? You're driving me crazy. I still don't know how or why I'm here in the hospital."

"Last night, a little after midnight, Vera Wayne was murdered in her car parked outside the town limits of Rock Hall. You were found unconscious in the front passenger seat."

"Vera murdered? I don't believe you. My mind is a little fuzzy, but off the top of my head, the last thing I remember was dancing with her at the Saloon, and drinking a large stein of beer. I must have blacked out. I can't remember anything after that beer."

"It doesn't look good for you, Mark. Vera's throat was cut with a sharp blade, and when we examined you last night, you were wearing a waist belt with an empty sheath. Normally that sheath holds some sort of knife. Then we discovered that you're a Navy SEAL. From what I've read, SEALS are trained to kill, aren't they?"

"Are you nuts!" he cries out in anger. We're trained to kill bad people, not good people, and Vera was good people. Am I a suspect?"

"Yes, at this stage. We're not leaving any stone unturned. I don't like this any more than you do, but I've got my orders and a job to do."

"But I liked Vera. We were doing some business together. How in the hell could I or would I kill her and then pass out on the seat next to her? That doesn't make any sense."

"Well, we're thinking, it was a murder suicide. You killed her, then took an overdose to kill yourself."

The monitors around Mark's body, especially those monitoring his blood pressure and heart rate, suddenly begin beeping as Mark's grimaces.

He has no fear as he shouts, "And the murder weapon was my dagger? Is that what you're inferring here? Where's my dagger? This doesn't make any sense whatsoever to me. This is a nightmare. Get out of the room while I telephone my father in Baltimore. He'll know what to do."

"Right oh! You better make that telephone call to your father now. There'll be no further questions until you give me permission to continue. I'll be waiting in the reception area."

"I don't want to talk to anyone about this case until my father hears all about it from me."

Donnelly leaves the room so Mark can telephone his father and tell him, as best he can, of the events leading up to his sedative overdose last night and recovery in the hospital this morning.

Mark telephones his father, who is surprisingly calm and collected. Mark anxiously shouts into the telephone, "I'm in the hospital in Chestertown and accused of murdering a lady who owns a marina in

Rock Hall. The last thing I remember was dancing with her at the local Saloon last night, having a good time, and drinking some beer. They told me I was found unconscious in her car, passed out on the seat next to her. She had her throat cut."

Before he can continue, Mark's father says, "Stop, Mark. Slow down, son. We're way ahead of you. Annette telephoned us last night when she permitted the police to search your apartment. She told them that there was nothing to hide. I believe that they were looking for the murder weapon, possibly the dagger that you wear around your waist.

"I want you to know that everything will be fine. Mike Bloomburg is already in a helicopter on his way to you. He should be arriving at the hospital within the hour. If the police question you, you have the right to have Mike with you at all times. Try to stay calm. We'll get through this nightmare, believe me.

"I love you, son. I know that you could never have committed such a horrendous crime." He begins to sob but continues, "All I want you to do right now is to take care of your medical situation and listen to your doctors. We'll take care of the legal situation and be back in touch with you. Keep me posted, please. Bloomburg will know how to take care of the legal issues."

Entering Mark's room and overhearing some remarks to his father is George Panas, handsome and good-natured 40 year old cardiologist. He tells Mark, "I'm Dr. Panas, your cardiologist. How are you feeling?"

"I'd like to ask you for some medicine to make this nightmare and all of this talk of murder go away."

"We all face crises in life, but I can tell you, everything will be fine, everything will work out to your benefit. I have been doing a little spying the past few hours, and the suspicions of you as a suspect are way off course, in my opinion. I'm your cardiologist. It's my job to make sure that your increased heart rate and blood pressure are a result of your talk with the detective and not related to the transfusion and flushing procedures. From the looks of the monitors, you appear as if you're ready to take on the whole world. Wouldn't it be better if you let us get you healthy and back on your feet, and ready to fight your way through a nice crab cake sandwich at Osprey Point in Rock Hall?"

Mark smiles and nods his head in agreement.

Dr. Panas continues, "For added precaution, I want you to take this pill."

"What is it exactly?"

"An anticoagulant used to treat abnormal heartbeat, such as atrial fibrillation. Have you heard of it?"

"Doctor, I'm aware of almost everything that I put inside my body because it's the only one I have."

"Good for you, Mark. Since you've been cooperative, here's another pill that I want you to take to treat high blood pressure. You've heard the expression, 'It can't hurt to take it.' Well, it's true in this case. We're going to keep you here at least anther four hours. We want to make sure you're back to normal, if that's possible under these circumstances. By the way, is there any history of heart disease in your family? Is there anyone in your family with heart trouble?"

"My father has been in and out of hospitals in Baltimore, but it's related mostly to the tension and stress of running Bethlehem Steel. Both of my grandfathers and grandmothers died before I was born. As far as I know, my mother's in good health."

"That's good news, Mark. By the way, when you get back on your feet, I'd like you to meet my wife. She's decorating our little home on Eastern Neck Island Road and looking for a nice sporting painting, something with geese in flight. Keep us in mind if you find a subject with geese in flight or a similar motif." He pauses to check the records again on the clipboard attached to the footboard of his bed, then walks towards the door and tells him, "Try to relax. Remember that your best days are still ahead of you, my boy. Your lawyer is waiting to see you, so I'll send him in now."

After Dr. Panas leaves the recovery room, he beckons to Mike Bloomburg and tells him, "Mark is doing about as well as possible, under the circumstances. Please be considerate in your remarks that might increase his blood pressure and heart rate. Please pass on my advice to Detective Donnelly too."

Bloomburg enters Mark's recovery room and promptly reassures him that this nightmare will soon be over, and sanity will prevail. He tells him, "The sooner we get to the bottom of the district attorney's accusations or suspicions against you, the better for everyone. So with your permission, I'd like to bring Detective Donnelly back into the room. He wants to resume his interrogation, but I'll be here at your side to make sure that his questions are brief and to the point. Think before you answer and tell the truth."

Donnelly resumes his questioning of Mark by explaining, "We found your Navy SEAL undershirt on the seat of Vera's car. Are you a Navy SEAL?"

He answers, "I was, recently honorably discharged."

Donnelly continues, "I've read that the Navy SEALS are taught and trained to kill, so that may place you in the position of being a "person of interest"...possibly a prime suspect here."

Bloomburg interrupts and says, "You're out of line, Donnelly. Confine your questioning here to questions that Mark can answer, without injecting your opinions, please."

Mark, still in shock, says, "I've nothing to hide. I have never killed anyone, including my combat days in Iraq. Furthermore, I have absolutely no knowledge of how I was found in the passenger seat of Vera's car, and now I'm considered a suspect in her murder. I want to cooperate with you as fully and honestly as I possibly can, but you're nuts to think that I would take Vera's life. I told you before that I liked her, and we would probably do some business together. The last thing I remember was leaving the dance floor of the saloon, then going to the Men's Room, and coming back to my seat to drink a beer. After that, I don't remember anything."

During Donnelly's questioning, Mark is interrupted periodically by hospital staff to check his vital signs and change the bottles of solutions being fed intravenously into his arm.

Doctor Steele returns and tells him, "I would expect you to have a giant hangover or headache, so here's something to ease that condition, and get you back on the path to a full recovery."

Mark beckons her to his bedside and whispers in her ear, "I love you. I mean, I love how well you're treating me. Would you like to get married?" He begins to laugh and tells her, "That's not an original line on my part. I borrowed it from our talking parrot in Betterton, except she says, 'Wanta get hitched, Doll!"

Dr. Steele laughs too and tells him, "Mark, you're on your way to a full recovery when you can kid someone about love!"

The police officer stationed outside the recovery room knocks on the door and enters the room just enough to hand Donnelly an envelope. Donnelly opens it quickly and reads the page, then hands it to Mike Bloomburg. The page is a report from the coroner's office which found traces of the same sedative given to Mark under the fingernails of Vera's right hand.

Bloomburg immediately asks Donnelly to contact the DA and change Mark's status from 'suspect' to 'witness'. He says "This young man was a Navy officer who distinguished himself bravely in Iraq. You and your superiors owe my client an apology. Murder, suicide, ridiculous, .beyond comprehension! He deserves an apology. You clearly jumped to the wrong conclusion."

Mark is relieved by this news and relaxes a little, albeit temporarily..

Four hours later, after the nurses have completed their routine of checking and recording his vital signs, all part of his recovery period, Doctor Steele enters his room again, picks up the clip board, studies it carefully, and tells Mark, "I think that we may release you soon, possibly later on this afternoon. All your vital signs are back in good order. How does your head feel?"

Mark tells her, "I still have a slight headache but no dizziness, thank God."

"Well, in that case, there are some important people all waiting patiently in the hall, wanting to see you. Can I begin to send them in? Gradually, of course."

"By all means, Doctor. Send them in."

After Doctor Steele leaves the room, Mark's mother and father enter and walk slowly over to his bedside. They separate and take a position on each side of his bed, then each leans over to give him a kiss.

His father suddenly shows a side of his character that Mark never knew existed. He confesses, "When I got Annette's telephone call in the middle of the night, and then your call in the morning, I was in shock and total disbelief, but never for a moment believed that you could have been involved in such a horrendous crime. Regardless of what has transpired between us before, I want to tell you this now: If you don't want us in your life, that's your business. But I want you to know that I want you in our life. That's our business." He pauses to sob, and continues, "We need you, son."

Mark's mother leans over and grabs even more tightly one of his hands, and confesses: "You know, Mark, I still remember when you were three years old, and your father and I were in the pool teaching you how to float on your back. You slipped away from your father's hands or maybe he just let go of you to see what you would do, sink or swim. You suddenly went under the water, and your father said…"

Mark's father interrupts, "I've heard this story before, so you better let me tell you what I said. I turned to your mother and said, 'Better not let him drown before we have a chance to see if he's any good'! Any good? Well, you certainly turned out better than expected. We were very proud of you that day. I could see early on that you were at home in the water, and very independent too. Of course, I had no idea that you would end up training to be a Navy SEAL, and a distinguished officer to boot."

Mark asks, "It's no surprise that I amounted to something, is there? Remember I always said, as far back as I can remember, 'Expect the Unexpected'."

Then Mark's mother, Sara, says, "We had a chance to talk to Sandy a few minutes ago. She's walking the hallway with your other new friends, waiting to see you. I must confess that I like her, even though I hardly know her. Perhaps when you have some time, you'll bring her to our home. In the meantime I thought you might like something from Baltimore."

She goes to the door of his room and is handed a case, then tells him, "I thought you might like to have your Martin guitar. Music will put your mind at rest, and certainly will help in your recovery."

Mark replies, "I thought you would bring me my favorite hot pastrami sandwich on rye from Attman's on Monument Street!"

Sara says, "Thinking about food at a time like this was the farthest from my mind. But a good appetite in times like this is a good sign too."

Mark asks his father to come closer to his bedside, and says, "I see a much more serious look on your face. What are things like at the steel mill? Having problems again with the unions?"

His father replies, "Your mother and I have had some serious talks, long into the night. There's a growing interest from two parties that are very interested in buying the plant lock, stock and barrel. We always thought of passing it on to you, but you made it perfectly clear that you want a different life. Right now we have two serious suitors who will give me carte blanche at the mill, but it's not easy letting go of something that has been our life for over 30 years. It's not only the years that your grandfather and I put into the mill, it's the tremendous strain and tension of those years."

His mother tells them, "I think it's time for Mark to see his friends waiting in the hall outside," then opens the door to invite Annette, Sandy, Reggie, Richard, Jesse James and his three track teammates, the seniors Manny, Mo, and Jack from the senior park, and finally Knute, who is the last to enter but the first to speak when he blurts out, "Gertie wanted to come too, but they don't allow no pets in the hospital here."

As they all parade into the recover room, each carries a big smile. They're eager to help him in any way they can on the road to recovery. Sandy is momentarily at a loss for words, but her loving smile is the best medicine that Mark could want at this moment.

Five minutes later, when there is a pause and everyone moves away from his bed, Mark beckons to Knute and waves him to his bedside. He motions for Knute to lean over so he can whisper into his ear. He tells him, "Listen Knute. I don't want to announce it in front of everybody here, but I've got to take a pee."

Knute pulls away from him and looks down into his face and says, "If you gotta go, you gotta go." Then he turns away from his bedside and raises his hands high in the air with a waving motion, and shouts, "Listen everybody. Everybody out of the room. Mark's gotta take a pee!"

Mark looks over at Knute and says, "I told you that I didn't want to announce it to everybody."

Knute says, "That's right. You didn't announce it. I did."

Laughter erupts in the room, so much so that the instruments and monitors begin to shake, and one scope begins to start beeping an alarm. Mark blushes and slides down into his bed and pulls the cover sheet almost up to his chin. Knute is the last to leave the room and gives Mark a big smile and thumbs-up sign just before he closes the door.

Finally, in the late afternoon, Mark is examined again by Dr. Steele and given permission to leave the hospital. Mike Bloomburg accompanies him to the lobby and along the way reminds him, "You'll remain an important witness in the on-going investigation of this homicide, and should write down anything that you remember about Vera, no matter how insignificant. Details about her life could lead to a break in the case, so keep an open mind. This case is not over until it's over, and I fear it will never be over for you. You'll have to cope with this experience for the rest of your life. But you have a loving family and plenty of friends to help you through this ordeal."

In the lobby, Sandy waits to drive Mark back to Betterton. On the drive home Sandy tries to engage him in conversation, but he asks her to wait until they get to Betterton. A few minutes later, however, he has a change of heart when things begin stirring around in my mind. He tells her, "I still can't believe what's happened in the last 24 hours. It's more than a nightmare. I don't know how in the world that I can look in the mirror, look other people in the face, especially all my friends who will soon learn about Vera's murder. What I really would like right now is to take a walk with you, down to the beach again where Reggie played that beautiful music in that cove."

Sandy asks, "It's a date, Mark. We'll do whatever you want to do. You're in good hands. Trust me. You're thinking about Vera, aren't you?"

Marks answers, "Yes, and it may surprise you to hear me say it, but I liked her. I hardly knew her, but found her aggressive for a woman, yet sensitive, full of life, perhaps mis-guided at times, but full of energy."

Sandy says, "Ambitious too."

Mark says, "I don't think Bud appreciated or respected her. He took her for granted like a piece of machinery in his marina. She tried to make the best out of her situation, with a gloomy husband who neglected her, perhaps even despised her ambition. I really feel sad that she was unfulfilled. She was reaching out, searching for something, always beyond her grasp."

Sandy mentions, "Lonely. I get the feeling that she could be with someone and still be lonely."

Mark answers, "That's an interesting perspective, Sandy. With her, loneliness was more than a psychological block. It was a brick wall that she couldn't find a way to go through."

Sandy continues, "I think also that she didn't know what was good for her and what was bad for her. Her choices for the ultimate man in her life seemed to depend on what was available in front of her eyes and not setting a goal to find the ultimate man. But I have a question about her that has been puzzling me, and it involves you."

Mark turns to her and asks, "Something puzzling that involves me?"

Reluctantly, she explains, "With Liz and me and almost all the women you have met, you eventually make a sort of declaration of numbers. I think you call it 'sizing up' someone. But you never did that with Vera. Why not?"

Mark leans back, sighs, and says, "That's an interesting question, Sandy. My brain must have short-circuited, like a relay or switch that prevented me from sizing her up. I was probably concentrating on more important things." He pauses and suggests, "How 'bout a walk on Betterton beach to clear the mind?"

An hour later, they're sitting side by side on beach towels on the sandy secluded cove at Betterton beach, looking out at the Chesapeake Bay.

Mark begins, "This is very restful, very peaceful, just the right medicine for me. While in the hospital last night, I must have been in and out of dreams or nightmares. I remember certain horrible episodes in Iraq, with one of my dead buddies rolling on top of me, and then suddenly my mind switches to images of Vera lying dead beside me in her car. Why am I still alive? The implications... Can you understand the shock, the disbelief, and then the grief?

I'm thinking about our business too. We're just starting to get lucky and make a name for ourselves, turn my discoveries into a big profit that will carry us through the winter when sales will be down, when this tragedy kicks us in the ass. When word gets out, it will hurt our reputation immensely. You know the way rumors fly around in a small town.

But while I was in the hospital, coming out of that drug, my first thoughts were about you. I never thought that I would see you again. Can you believe me? I felt lost, alone, and, maybe for the first time, without any power over my mind and body. Right now, my mind says that I need time alone, to work things out, but then I realize the best way out of it is to include you and your mother who have been so good to me, from the start of my life here in Betterton."

Sandy says, "The only way out of this quagmire is to find Vera's killer as soon as possible."

Mark says, "If we get out of this..."

Sandy interrupts him, "You mean, *when* we get out of this dilemma, don't you?"

Mark says, "Yes, Sandy, we will get out of this quagmire, trust me here."

Sandy says, "While you were in the hospital, I also realized how much I missed you and how much I love you. I know it probably doesn't make much sense to tell you, but that incident made me realize how important you are to me." They embrace.

Mark exhales a sigh of relief in getting his feelings about Sandy out in the open. Finally he concludes with, "I'll never rest until Vera's killer is brought to justice. And my suspicion here is that Bud had many reasons and motives for eliminating her from his life."

A few days later, Vera's funeral occurs precisely at noon, with a short service at the cemetery behind the Methodist Church in Rock Hall, attended by her husband Bud, their babysitter Bonnie, who's holding Jaime tightly in her arms, Bud's sisters Ruth and Jean, who are standing beside Mark and Sandy, and Steve 'Pretty Boy' Floyd, who is, conspicuously, several feet away from the casket. There are at least 50 other friends who gather in a circle around her coffin.

The expression on each face is one of despair and sadness. The bells begin to toll almost on cue to signify the official opening of the gravesite service. The bells toll exactly 30 times, one toll for each year of Vera's life on earth. There is an eerie silence at the gravesite: no wind, no sounds, no birds flying overhead, not even a whisper among the mourners.

The pastor, Dean Woods, begins the gravesite service by speaking each of his words in a slow and deliberate manner, so that they can register with every person gathered around the casket: "I believe Vera Wayne would be surprised to see all of you here his morning. She probably didn't realize that she had so many friends who cared about her. Today there are no answers, just questions about why a young lady like Vera Wayne was cut down in the prime of her life. Only the Good Lord can judge what each of us has done on earth. Only the Good Lord knows what's in our hearts. Vera's time on earth was short, too short for a woman full of energy and strength.

"But Vera left us with the joy of life in her baby, Jamie. So now I invite everyone here today to lift up your prayers to our loving God that his young woman, Vera Wayne, will find comfort in God's embrace. Let us all pray to God to extend his blessings and comfort to all her family, her relatives and friends, that everyone here will be strengthened with a new spirit of hope and reconciliation."

Pastor Woods takes a deep breath and motions for any family member who wishes to say something to come forward. No one moves an inch. He concludes the service by saying, "I will now read from the Book of Common Prayer. In sure and certain hope of the resurrection to eternal life through our Lord Jesus Christ, we commend to Almighty God our sister Vera Wayne, and we commit her body to the ground, earth to earth, ashes to ashes, dust to dust. The Lord bless her and keep her, the Lord make his face to shine upon her and be gracious unto her and give her peace. Amen."

The service concludes with each person taking a flower from a bouquet and gently placing it on top of the coffin. Mark and Sandy wait until last, because they want to see how Bud will perform this gesture. Bud looks at the flower with a sinister smirk, and studies it instead of looking at the casket. It's a strange behavior that forces Mark to pull Sandy closer to him. When Mark and Sandy finally place their flowers on the casket, they realize that they are alone. Each offers a prayer in silence.

Meanwhile, back at his office, Kent County district attorney, Winfrid Strong, despite the lack of a murder weapon, grows in confidence that the suspect, Bud Wayne, should be charged and tried for the murder of his wife.

A Grand Jury is convened and Bud appears before it to give testimony about his life leading up to the fatal night, then concentrating on his whereabouts on the night of Vera's murder and possible knowledge about the dagger missing from Mark's waist belt. Anger over his wife's behavior plus a $500,000 insurance policy all make for good motives. Because all details of Bud's appearance before the Grand Jury are sealed, everyone has to wait until the District Attorney issues a statement.

The day after Bud's appearance before the Grand Jury, DA Strong decides to file charges against Bud Wayne for murder in the first degree. He confides to an assistant, "We'll let the jury decide his guilt or innocence. It's easy to file these charges, but making them stick is another thing. This case is no slam dunk, but the preponderance of evidence and motive is certainly on Bud's shoulders."

The trial occurs in the Kent County Criminal Court in Chestertown. The courtroom holds a capacity crowd of about 80 people, all jammed into twelve rows. All the principal figures are present and scattered about the courtroom.

The Prosecutor's opening statement rings out clearly among the jurors: DA Strong says, "Murder starts in the heart. Only Bud Wayne had the motive here. On the surface he appears calm, cool and collected. Words don't come easily for him. But jealousy over his wife's adulterous behavior was stirring around in his mind and raging inside his body like a volcano about to erupt.

"Finally, there is the half million dollar life insurance policy on his wife, a big payday, wouldn't you say? And he will have to explain his whereabouts after he left the Saloon on that fateful night, right down to the hour, minute and second. He must be held accountable for his whereabouts after he left the Men's room an hour before midnight on the night in question. Did any see him after he left the Men's room or did he suddenly vaporize into thin air?"

The Public Defender, Basil Jablonski, representing Bud Wayne, weighs in and refutes every word and phrase of the DA's opening statement. He concludes his opening statement with: "You need facts here to convict someone of murder, don't you? You cannot convict someone without concrete evidence: a witness, the murder weapon, fingerprints, DNA. Motives for Bud Wayne are circumstantial figments of the District Attorney's imagination. It's that simple.

"And because Bud Wayne doesn't have a witness to testify that he was in bed at midnight is not a sufficient reason to convict him of murder. You have to have concrete evidence to link Bud with the subsequent murder of his wife, Vera. Show me the evidence. Show me the linkage!"

Mark is the first witness called by the DA to take the stand. Strong questions him in detail about his relations with Vera, starting with the first time he saw her. Mark begins by telling the court the first time he saw Vera was at Tommy Wells' funeral in Betterton, and later when he came to marina office to sell Vera and Bud the model ship *Gratitude*. He testifies that he showed them his dagger, the one used to repair it, even handing it to Bud and later cutting himself with the dagger that is now missing from his sheath. He recounts the occasions when he bumped into Vera at the Harvest Moon fest, and finally his invitation to join

Bud and Vera at the saloon on the fatal night. However, Mark concludes his testimony by saying, "About that fatal night, I remember dancing with Vera, but honestly can't remember anything after returning from the Men's room and drinking my beer."

The DA examines a list of witnesses that he has issued a subpoena to appear in court, especially those who were in or around the back booth of the saloon on that night, anyone who might shed some light on the case.

The second witness to testify is Gretta Howell, the hair stylist, who cries almost hysterically throughout the questioning. She reveals how long she has known Vera as a friend *and* a stylist who had fun doing her hair for a special event or a rendezvous. She says, "I can't characterize them as 'affairs' since I wasn't present before, during, or after her date." Her testimony will be limited only to what occurred between the two of them, and not hearsay or what encounters may or may not have occurred.

Then Ruth Wayne is called to give evidence about her knowledge, if any, of Vera's work schedule, time away from the office for liaisons, and general relationship. The DA asks, "Did you consider her part of your family? Can you think of anyone who would want to kill her?" Ruth says, "Vera was a complex woman who seemed to have demons lurking inside her mind. She was bright and hard working and really loved her child. I really didn't have the opportunity to spend a great deal of time with her outside the office. But, despite her drawbacks, and who doesn't have some drawbacks, I have to admit that I liked her immensely, but never told her so. I don't believe that she let anyone get too close to her.

She could be abrasive. She often rubbed people, including me, the wrong way. Her life was always in turmoil because, primarily, she was energetic, creative, occasionally even a little goofy, but in a likable way. She had a big heart, was a loving, caring, and perhaps lost soul, and as I intimated before, she loved her baby."

Then Jean Wayne is called and gives a completely different opinion of Vera by blasting her infidelities, neglecting of her child, illicit affairs that unexpectedly took her away from the office forcing Jean to cover for her. During cross-examination, Jean has to admit that she has no proof whatsoever of any illicit affairs.

The next witness called to the stand is Steve 'Pretty Boy' Floyd, who is crushed by her violent death. His former good looks, clean-shaven face, tanned skin and slick hair style are missing. His hair is unruly, he is unshaven, and his skin is dry and pale. All signs point to neglect. He is slumped forward as he walks to the witness stand. He is worried that he is under suspicion as a suspect in the murder as well, so he must be especially careful in his testimony.

When questioned by DA Strong, Floyd is asked specifically about his relations with Vera, and is portrayed as a coward who took advantage of people, including Vera, all his life. He is asked to account for his actions the night of the murder.

Before the DA can finish his question, Boyd shouts out, "Why would I want to murder the mother of…" He halts suddenly, realizing he was about to say, 'my' child Jamie. He gathers his thoughts and says, "Despite our differences in the soft crab business, no one in their right mind can suspect me of murdering Vera, can they?"

The DA continues, "That's what this trial will try to determine here. Do you know any reason why Bud might want to end his wife's life? Did Vera tell you anything about a crisis with her husband?"

The questioning does not go well for the prosecution, as the judge continues to throw out subsequent questions as 'irrelevant and immaterial', since they have no bearing on the case against Bud. Then Floyd is faced with the disclosure about his being fired as a partner in Vera's soft crab business. He lies about having an on-going affair with Vera over the years and denies the possibility of being the father of Vera's baby. He grows increasingly worried about being involved or implicated as a possible suspect in her murder, so halfway through his questioning on the witness stand, he takes the easy way out by responding to further questions with "I can't remember," and "I don't know what you're talking about."

Vera's baby sitter, Bonnie Bratcher, is called next to the witness stand. She stands up and unexpectedly turns around in her seat to see who might be available to hold Vera's baby, then hands the baby to Sandy, sitting directly behind her.

She asks Mark, "What do I say? What do I know?"

Mark says, "Just tell the truth, Bonnie."

When the DA asks her about her work routine and schedule, she explains, "I was on a salary and not paid by the hour. I got $125 a week, regardless of the number of hours I baby-sat. Since I lived nearby, Vera knew I was available at the last minute for emergencies."

DA Strong asks, "Would Vera having a last minute rendezvous with a man classify as an emergency?"

Bonnie says, "I know nothing about what she did away from the marina office. That was her own business. I think she called it, 'Don't ask. Don't tell'."

The DA continues, "Were you paid by check or cash?"

Bonnie answers, "Sometimes both ways."

The DA then asks her to remember as best she can precisely when Bud returned to the apartment above the marina office.

She says, "I never paid any attention to the time."

Strong continues, "What was his demeanor?"

She says, "I don't know the meaning of the word."

"Can you tell the court how he looked?" asks Strong. "And how he acted, what he said when he came back home?"

She says, "I thought he looked somewhat refreshed, relieved. I thought he must have had a good time at the saloon with his wife."

Strong asks, "Then what did you do or say?"

She says, "I checked on the baby in his crib, then started to walk towards the stairway when he pulled me back and led me into his bedroom."

Jablonski rises out of his seat and pounds the table with "Objection, Your Honor. That's irrelevant, immaterial, and has nothing to do with this case."

The judge says, "Overruled. Take your seat."

After order is restored in the courtroom, Strong tells Bonnie that he has no further questions for her and that she is excused from the witness stand.

Finally the DA asks Bud Wayne to take the stand. When questioned by the DA about his wife's behavior and illicit affairs, he carries the look of a depraved and remorseful soul, but is smart enough to keep his answers short and somewhat simple. For the most part, he "clams up."

When the DA asks him about his wife's behavior and time away from the office, he says, "You'll have to be more specific."

The DA asks, "O.K. Tell us if you have any knowledge of your wife's encounters with other men?"

Bud answers, "I don't know nothin' about any encounters. I know nothin' about any such behavior, and saw nothin' about any such behavior. I was busy with my work in the marina. Whatever my wife did on her own time was her own thing. I trusted her. I had a marina to take care of."

During further questioning, Bud blurts out, "If you're looking for the murderer with a motive here, why don't you ask Steve Floyd. They don't call him 'Pretty Boy' for nothing? Everyone knows he was fired a few days before Vera's killing. Ask him to tell you more about what caused him to get fired. He's the one with a motive."

Both prosecutor and defense attorney jump to their feet and voice "objections" which are drowned out by the judge who beats his gavel repeatedly in an attempt to regain order in the court. During further questioning, Bud is asked directly in cross examination by the DA about his knowledge of the Baghdad dagger. He tells the jury, "I never saw the dagger, and don't know what you're talking about."

"Are you telling this court that you never saw the dagger, the one that Mark Hopkins showed you in the marina when you bought the *Gratitude* model?

"As I said before. I don't know what you're talking about. I know nothin' about any dagger." When Bud finishes with this statement, he crosses both arms in front of his body and grabs tightly onto his wrists, in a fit of strength. It's clearly a sign of his holding in or holding back something.

Mark, sitting next to Sandy in the middle of the courtroom, leans over and whispers in her ear, "He's lying here. I showed it to him and Vera in the marina office when they bought the model ship."

Sandy whispers back, "Yes, but Vera is dead, and now it's your word against his."

The DA ends his cross-examination by asking Bud, "Do you know what perjury is?"

"I know it's a crime."

"A serious crime."

"I wouldn't do it. I wouldn't lie. I've told you the truth as best I can."

The DA completes his examination and shakes his head from side to side, realizing he was unable to budge him from his seemingly innocent behavior in the last days of Vera's life. Bud walks dejectedly away from the witness stand, passes the jury with his head bowed down, and slumps into his seat beside his attorney at the defendant's table.

After two days of trial, the jury brings in a verdict of "Not Guilty." The judge pounds his gavel and declares, "The jury, after due diligence and deliberation, has found the defendant not guilty of the murder of Vera Wayne, and is now free to leave the court."

Bud is unfazed and shows no outward emotion whatsoever. Mark, Sandy and Annette huddle together in their narrow aisle between rows of seats and clearly are dejected by the jury's decision. Mark says to them, "If it wasn't Bud, then who did it and why? For my money, Bud's the killer and escaped the jaws of justice, at least for the moment."

As Bud Wayne walks down the center aisle on his way out of the courtroom, Mark loses control of himself. "You bastard! You set me up! I'm sure you killed her," he shouts. The rage and fury in Mark's heart are unleashed as Sandy and Annette pull him away and back into their huddle

Mark tells them, "This is not the end. It's just the beginning. It will be almost impossible not to think about revenge here, but I have to find a way to stop thinking about myself and continue the search for Vera's killer. Until we find the killer, if for some reason it's not Bud, there will be problems with my credibility as an antiques dealer, especially in a small town like Betterton."

When Bud Wayne slowly walks down the hall and out of the courthouse in Chestertown, there is no one to meet him, except for Bonnie Bratcher who holds Jaime tightly in her arms. She hands him the keys to Vera's red Cadillac and climbs into the back seat. He pauses momentarily to catch his breath, turns the ignition key, and let's the motor hum for several minutes. Only Bud knows what's lurking, if anything, in his mind at this moment.

Bonnie asks, "Are you all right, Bud?"

He turns around in his seat and tells her, "Not to worry about me anymore. From here on out, we're going to build a new life for ourselves together. I'd like you to stay with me for awhile, at least until I can get things back into gear at the marina." He slowly drives his car out of the parking lot of the courthouse and into the traffic of Chestertown.

CHAPTER 13

Every night for the next week Mark experiences a repetition of those nightmares, from episodes of explosions in Iraq to frightening images of how Vera was murdered. His imagination is having a field day, with all sorts of images that flash through his mind. Being implicated in this homicide also unleashes an anger and fury. If someone talks the wrong way or says something peculiar, he becomes touchy and sullen. His lack of concentration on work in the shop is noticed by Sandy and Annette, who are sympathetic and patient with him. Their partnership in the antiques business doesn't seem to be important, interesting, or as much fun as it used to be.

He tells Sandy, "You cannot begin to imagine how I feel. No one can. To go from a respected, educated military officer who served his country well to being implicated in a horrible crime is beyond anyone's imagination. But it is real, not imagined."

Sandy tries to console him by reminding him of all the good things that have happened, from her rescue, to meeting new friends Richard and Reggie, the success at the Dixon auctions, meeting Lois, Clowie, and Knute. She tells him, "You can't forget the past, but you should consider everything you've accomplished in Betterton."

During a weekend inside the antiques shop while tourists browse, Annette engages Mark and tells him, "I cannot imagine what is stirring inside your mind, but whatever you're feeling, we are feeling it too. You are still part of us, part of our family. You know, the French have an expression, 'Joie de Vive', meaning 'Joy of Life'. What you and I and all your friends have to do is put that "Joy of Life" back into you. It won't be easy, but we have to get back into the days when you first arrived in Betterton, full of energy and ideas. The old adage, 'work heals things' should apply for all of us. Maybe some time off will help clear your mind a bit too. Maybe take a trip to New York with Sandy or Liz or Reggie. Attend one of his recording sessions. What do you think?

Mark says, "I'll take it under consideration."

Meanwhile, Bud is back at the marina, running it again as if nothing happened, except now he has to take care of the bills and all the accounting services that his wife handled. It doesn't take long for mail and paper work to pile up, but he thinks, "If it's something important, people will telephone me. Otherwise, I must try to behave and run things like nothing happened here."

For now, he has escaped from the jaws of justice. He depends more and more each day on Bonnie, to baby-sit, watch the office and take messages over the telephone. He goes about his work, but clams up when anyone tries to engage him in a conversation, regardless of the subject. It doesn't seem possible, but he is even more distant than ever before. He retreats into his own sanctuary, his own private world in the sanctuary called Swan Point Marina.

But there is something artificial on the surface, lurking below his skin. Someone who could resort to such violence in cutting the throat of his spouse is likely to relish and relive the memories. Who knows what evil lurks in the heart of such a man. Is there anyone to stop him or catch him and make the crime punishable? In the back of his mind, Bud thinks about that life insurance payout, that big payday. .

Two days later, Bud receives a telephone call from the insurance agency requesting a meeting to discuss the payment of his wife's policy. The next day, Bud and the agent, Guy Calibey, meet at the marina office, whereupon Bud is informed that the payment of $500,000 will not go to him, but instead will be deposited in a trust for their one-year old son.

Shocked and stunned, Bud is unable to speak. Calibey informs him that his wife made a significant change months ago by removing her husband as co-beneficiary. In other words, upon her death, all proceeds from her life insurance, on which she paid all the required premiums herself, pass solely and entirely to her sole beneficiary, her child, Jaime. Calibey remembers Vera telling him, "I pay the premiums, therefore, I can decide on the beneficiary too, can't I?"

When Bud regains his senses, he mutters to himself, "She's still provoking me, even now, from the grave."

About two weeks later, Abigail Woods, a 55 year old retired museum curator now living again in Baltimore, visits Betterton by ferry, for a day cruise and walk around the town. She walks up Main Street, notices the sign Annette's Antiques, and says to herself, "Maybe I'll find a nice model ship for my nephew for his upcoming birthday."

She browses alone inside until Mark spies her and greets her with, "Nice to have you here today. Did you come in on the ferry from Baltimore?"

Abigal confesses, "Yes, I love that ferry ride up the Chesapeake Bay. I've been coming here since I was…" She laughs and asks, "You're not trying to figure out my age, are you?"

He says, "Someone's age to me is only a number. It's what you do with your life that counts, don't you think?"

Abigail continues, "How kind of you. My name is Abigail Woods of Homewood in Baltimore."

"I don't believe you. I used to live in Homewood too."

"Don't tell me you went to Hopkins as well?"

"Don't squib me. I don't believe it. You're putting me on. Who sent you to tease me this morning? By the way my name is Mark Hopkins.".

"This is no trick. I'm interested in buying a model ship for my nephew who has a birthday coming up in a few weeks. I thought I'd look for something that he could enjoy for the rest of his days and remember something about the Chesapeake Bay. What in the world is a Johns Hopkins grad doing in a small town like Betterton?"

"That's a long story. Maybe you'd like a nice cup of freshly-brewed coffee?

"That sounds like a winner. I'll continue browsing if you don't mind while you brew the coffee, Mister Hopkins or is it Mister Coffee?"

In less than a minute, he hands her a large cup of coffee with 'Annette's Antiques' emblazoned around the body. As Mark raises his cup, she brings hers close to his, gives it a gently tap, and says, "Here's to the start of a beautiful friendship."

"That expression sounds familiar."

"It's from Casablanca. When you're retired like I am, you have lots of time to watch the old classic movies, and I try to remember all the great lines."

"Retired? From what, may I ask?"

"Director of the Washington County Museum of Fine Arts in Hagerstown. When my parents died a few years ago, I decided to take early retirement and use the contacts I'd built up over 25 years to become a private consultant and agent in the fine arts field. That's something nice to do from the confines of my second home in Mercersburg. I have my reference books, universities and museums close by for research, libraries everywhere, and, most importantly, people that I can see on a regular basis, cultured people interested in fine arts. Oh, I love having the time to go to auctions and buy some things for my own collection."

"Whew! You're like a fresh breeze blowing in off the bay. I hope that we'll be friends and maybe find something to work on together. Right now, my real joy comes from the Wednesday auctions in Crumpton. Do you know about them?"

"Mark, I'm way ahead of you there. I've been a client of Dixon's Auction for over 20 years, and always managed to find a nice painting whenever I went there on Wednesday. Do they still drop everything in the mud and puddles outside in that field?"

"Yes, in the mud, puddles, on the gravel, whatever, but as you know, the best stuff is sold inside."

"Well, Mark, what do you have today in the way of a model ship?"

"I'm afraid that I have nothing at the moment. I sold a nice model ship called the *Gratitude* recently, but nothing has crossed my eyes since."

"I'm curious about the *Gratitude*. By any chance, do you have a photo of it?"

He admits, "As a matter of fact, I have a photo of it in my files." He turns to a small file cabinet nearby, quickly finds the folder marked "Model Ships" and hands it to her. He continues, "I don't know much about the history of the *Gratitude,* but here's the file. There should be some photos of the model here."

Mark hands her the file containing a stack of photos taken by Sandy during the stages of restoration as a record of repair. Abigail scans the folio of photos showing the repair process, gasps, and holds her breath when her eyes focus on one particular photo. She sees the model ship in the center of this photo, but also focuses on an image of the jeweled dagger with the Arabic writing.

She asks, "Would you mind terribly if I borrowed several of these photos? I can't tell you anything more at this time, but something has aroused my curiosity about the dagger in these photos."

Mark says, "That dagger has always fascinated me too. Richard Wagner, my friend and retired professor of music at Washington College, told me an incredible story that I'll tell you about later. Your curiosity has aroused my curiosity."

They exchange cards. Before Abigail hurriedly leaves the store, clutching her handbag with a large manila envelope sticking out, she pauses at the door and asks, "I take it that you have no objections if I show this to a colleague, do you?"

Mark says, "You have my permission to show it to whomever you please, for whatever purpose you please!"

A few weeks later, Abigail returns to Betterton to see Mark and gives him the results of her research. She laughs and says, "I'm referring to that dagger in the photo. I think you'd better take a seat, because what I'm about to tell you may be a bit shocking."

Mark finds a heavy maple captain's chair and plops down into it, and tells her, "Please continue, professor."

Abigail confesses, "How's $500,000 sound to you? I certainly don't want you to faint on me here and now, but that's what the dagger is worth today!"

She shows him photographs of museum collections in the Middle East where a Sultan in the 19th century is wearing a belt around his waist with a similar dagger, the handle encrusted with jewels and Arabic writing. She mentions, "There's also a new museum about to open in New York that will specialize in Middle Eastern relics of historical importance. If you still have that dagger, I would like to be the agent for a possible sale."

Mark then explains how he acquired it and how it disappeared during the murder of Vera Wayne.

Unbeknownst to them, Sandy has been eavesdropping and overhears their conversation. She introduces herself and suggests that

Mark should place an advertisement in the newspapers, offering a huge reward for the safe return, with no questions asked.

Abigail offers to be their consultant and tells them, "When news leaks out about the value of this dagger, other magazines and newspapers will pick up and publicize it all over the world, and you don't have to pay a cent for all that free publicity."

Mark asks Abigail to prepare the ad and insists on paying for it personally since the dagger is his personal property, and Annette has no right of involvement here.

Two days later, the ad is published in the Kent News, with a photo of the dagger, an unlisted telephone number for anyone to call with news relating to its recovery, and a reward of $50,000 for information leading to the recovery of the dagger. 'All inquiries are treated with confidentiality' appears in bold type at the bottom of the ad.

The day the ad is published, Sandy, Mark and Abigail are huddled in Annette's Antiques, buoyed up with enthusiasm and the hope that maybe, just maybe, someone will come forth with a lead.

"The money or reward is one thing," says Mark. "But I'd like to know for certain if that dagger was the murder weapon used to kill Vera Wayne. I'd love to know if Bud Wayne is involved somehow, and what he's thinking."

When Bud reads the information in the Kent News, his first thoughts are about a possible big payday. A reward of $50,000 sounds like music to his ears, but he's no musician. He's doing the math, calculating and counting the numbers. After some contemplation, he makes a telephone call to his attorney Jablonski. "If someone stumbled across that dagger, would the discovery affect me?" asks Bud. "And what if that someone happened to be me? What are my liabilities here? Would I be stepping into a trap? Can they try me again for Vera's murder after I've already been acquitted?"

Bud is informed by Jablonski that he can no longer be tried for the murder of his wife, after having already been acquitted in court. He tells him, "It's the double-jeopardy law that will protect you. Let me repeat it, Bud. You cannot be tried twice for the murder of your wife."

Bud will have to think long and hard about this opportunity to take the reward of $50,000 cash.

Back in Betterton, a few days later, around sunset and after dinner, Sandy has a quarrel with Mark over his thoughts of starting anew, possibly moving away from Betterton, and not wanting to be a burden to them or damaging their reputation in their business partnership. She is hurt that he fails to grasp his importance to their family.

Mark surprises her by giving the impression that he wants to turn everything upside down and start over in another town. He blurts out, "Perhaps Betterton is just too quiet for me."

She tries to explain how Richard has entered her mother's life and how Mark has now entered and occupied her every waking moment from this time forward. She finally tells him that she is ready to settle down with him if that is still his goal.

But now it's Mark who is reluctant to repeat his proposal of marriage. He tells her, "Until Vera's killer is apprehended, my mind and heart are not at peace."

In a fit of anger and disappointment, Sandy loses her temper, bolts away from his arms and, within a few minutes, drives to the Saloon in Rock Hall. She rarely would ever be seen at the saloon but says to herself, "The hell with it, the hell with Mark. If he wants to start over, then I can start over, too."

Once inside the dark and dingy joint, Sandy notices one of her high school classmates calling her name and beckoning for her to join their booth almost near the back of the saloon. Sandy squeezes into a seat and, when a stein of beer is passed to her, quickly downs it. A waitress, slightly tipsy, comes over and dares them to chug-a-lug down a stein of beer, just like Sandy did, for a freebie on the house.

She quickly brings them another round of beer and loses the bet when they all down it in a few seconds. A recording of Patti Paige's 'Tennessee Waltz' blares out from the jukebox, over the saloon. Everyone in Sandy's booth gets up to dance. They are all tipsy too at this point, but who cares? It's a slow tune and it looks like each partner in each couple is holding the other closely to keep one from falling to the floor. It's pathetic and funny at the same time.

Sandy, tired and frustrated, leans back with her head resting on the top curve of her booth, her eyes focused on the ceiling. By sheer coincidence, Bud is plastered in the next booth, his head resting adjacent to Sandy's head.

He is unaware of anyone around him and words begin to flow from his mouth like the slobber of a drunk. Nevertheless, they are clearly audible for anyone nearby to overhear. He holds up an empty glass of beer and sees his face reflected in the mirror-like finish. In a chilling voice, he begins to brag about killing his wife. He mutters, "I should have made her suffer more, like she made me suffer. Watching her throw herself after any man able to satisfy her sexual needs, it was never enough. Cutting her throat with that dagger was too easy, too quick. I should have made her suffer more, and what about the insurance money that should've come to me, blood money? Perhaps the dagger will give me the money I should have gotten in the first place!"

Sandy sobers up instantly. She is horrified but manages to concentrate enough to remember his words. That same night, she speeds back to Betterton and drives right up onto the lawn beside the garage. She blows the horn frantically to awaken Mark. Seconds later he comes running down the steps, and they rush into her studio, where she tells him about Bud's admissions at the saloon. Although it is after midnight, he wastes no time and telephones his lawyer, Mike Bloomburg in Baltimore, who asks them to write down everything on paper.

Mike tells Mark, "I'll get Virgil Tubbs, one of the best private eyes in the state, on this case. He looks like one of those big St. Bernard rescue dogs they use to find buried skiers in the snow. But Virgil has a bulldog tenacity and mentality, and he never lets go when he's on a case until justice is served. I'll contact the sheriff in Kent County to get his advice about bringing in the local police from Rock Hall."

The next morning a meeting occurs in a small room on the second floor of the old fire house in Betterton. It's a quiet and peaceful autumn day, at least outside. Present in the room with just a fan circulating hot air are Virgil Tubbs, a handsome and athletic looking African-American private eye; Steve Morehouse, the local police lieutenant sporting a short crew cut like an ex-marine; Mike Bloomburg, muscular six foot six inch, longtime attorney for the Hopkins family in Baltimore; and finally Abigail Woods, Mark, and Sandy.

Virgil chairs the meeting and announces, "The murder weapon, assuming it is the dagger taken from Mark on that fateful night, is the key to this case." "Its disappearance leads me to suspect that Bud used it to kill his wife and hide it close to his marina, perhaps buried along the shoreline or on one of those million dollar yachts tied up at Swan Point Marina. Everyone here should follow their instincts, trust their hunches, leave no stone unturned. Remember there's a killer out there, so be smart, be cautious. Also remember this is a team effort. I'll be managing this investigation and available day and night, waiting to take your telephone calls. Everyone write your name and number where you can be reached, on this clipboard, and I'll get copies for each of you.

"Furthermore, we, and I mean everyone in this room, will do everything according to the law. We don't want to screw up this case by doing something stupid and jeopardize our investigation and have the judge throw out the case on a technicality, like not reading Bud his legal rights, right?"

Moorehaus says, "We will begin a surveillance of Bud's activities, especially any movement away from his marina office. You never know when he will go away, for whatever reason. Our experience here tells us that a murder weapon, if it is hidden by a killer, will always be hidden close by."

Mark says, "I've read somewhere that a killer always keeps his weapon hidden, but still within his grasp so to speak. He may even decide to revisit the murder scene, in the daytime, to recollect the killing, take delight in reliving the incident. And if he has hidden the murder weapon, he'll want to see and hold it again. In a way the weapon now possesses him, instead of vice versa. Finally the only way he will give up or surrender that weapon will be for a ton of money, with no strings attached. It's strictly a money deal. Bud already gave me the impression that he likes the exotic. He told me about his reading 'Arabian Nights' as he called it. He admired the jewels in the handle and workmanship, when I showed it to him at the marina, which surprises me every time I think about him saying it."

Sandy says, "We're dealing with a killer who might turn against his best friend to hide his crime. Isn't each of us at risk? Do we have any protection here?"

Morehouse interrupts, "It's best to stay calm, keep a low profile, and be aware of everything around you. Don't expose yourself needlessly. Think first, and act accordingly."

"If Bud is the killer," Mark declares, "and we all know that he is still the main suspect, my classes in psychology at Hopkins remind me of something else that I should tell you. In the subconscious of a killer's mind, there's always the truth that is struggling to be heard, wanting to get out. Bud might slip up if he is pushed or nudged properly."

There is a long pause as everyone contemplates their next step. Mark continues, "In this situation, nothing's for certain until it's for certain, until it actually happens. As I said before, we have to find a way to push him without him knowing it, into an act of desperation. He isn't quite a desperate man right now, but perhaps with a little coaxing, he might be forced over the edge. Do you all get the point here?"

They all nod their heads..

Morehouse excitedly says, "I just remembered something, something very suspicious."

Sandy asks, "What was that?"

Morehouse scratches his crew cut and answers, "When I went to Bud's house to inform him of his wife's murder, I remember a pair of watermen's boots on the lower landing."

Mark asks, "And what was so suspicious about a pair of watermen's boots?"

Moorehaus answers, "They were bright yellow and" He suddenly hesitates.

"And what?" Mark frantically asks.

"They were wet, very wet, and covered with sea grass and mud. I didn't think much about it at the time, but now, it seems possible that these boots were worn shortly before I discovered them on the lower landing that terrible night."

Mark asks, "Well, what's the next step?"

"Surveillance, 24 hours," says Bloomburg. "I've been instructed to tell you that the Hopkins family will foot the bill, no matter how costly it will be, until we find Vera's killer. We will leave no stone unturned, no lead dangling in the wind."

Morehouse squirms in his captain's chair and says, "I would like Abigail to begin closing the net over Bud."

Abigail asks, "And what would you like me to do?"

"You're now the key to our plan," answers Moorehaus. "Make a telephone call to Bud and tell him that you're researching a lost dagger that Mark Hopkins brought back from Baghdad, the same dagger that Mark showed him when he repaired the model ship. Ask him if he read about the reward offered...explain the importance and value of this dagger...tell him anything that might get a response from him, feel him out...try to entice him a little... arouse his interest in possibly retrieving it if he knows where it is."

She asks, "Including a statement about not being implicated in Vera's death? Remember he cannot be tried a second time for the same crime."

He answers, "You've got it."

She opens her purse, takes out her cell phone and telephones Swan Point Marina. After a tense 10 seconds, Bud answers his cell phone while walking slowly along a dock of his marina. "This is Abigail Woods," she tells him. I'm a consultant and broker in lost works of art. I've been researching a valuable dagger of great historical importance. This dagger was brought innocently to this country by a military man serving in Baghdad. Do you follow me so far?"

Bud asks, "What's this all have to do with me? I don't know nothing' about any dagger."

She continues, "It seems that an antiques dealer named Mark Hopkins does know something about that dagger. He used it to repair a guitar in Betterton when he was working for Annette's Antiques. According to him, he showed you the dagger when he sold you the model ship. In fact he told me he accidentally cut himself in your office. That dagger disappeared when he was involved in your wife's death. Now, I'm not concerned and neither should you be concerned about whether or not it was used in your wife's murder. I just want to let you know that the reward is $50,000, but the dagger is worth $500,000, if it can be retrieved and sold to a museum. But I, for all my work, would be the agent and take a fee of ten percent for arranging the sale. Do I make myself clear here?"

Bud answers, "I follow you, but you're barking up the wrong tree. I don't know why you're calling me, out of the blue."

"Well, Bud, I'm trying to follow up all leads," she continues. "I just want to advise you to be on the lookout for the dagger, if you should stumble across it. I'll be placing another ad in the newspapers for information leading to the recovery of the dagger. Your trial is over now, buried, gone, and forgotten. What I want here is simply to let you know of its importance money-wise, and be your agent. I'm only interested in the money that would come in handy for me right now. I'll let other people worry about seeing it eventually in a museum."

Bud wanders further towards the far end of the dock where no one can hear him talking over the telephone, and gazes up at some sea gulls flying overhead. As always he is quiet and patient. Words never come easy for him, especially at this tense moment. He is clearly reluctant to admit anything, especially over the telephone, where it might be recorded. "Caution and care" are words running through his mind. Certainly he could use the reward money, money that would offset the loss of money from his wife's life insurance policy.

Abigail continues, "A check for the reward of $50,000 can go a long way to prosperity."

Bud says, "Why not a million, a million dollars for a rare dagger? I like the sound of it, a nice round number."

There is silence, followed by a click as Bud closes his cell phone.

Although a deal is not confirmed at this point, everyone in the meeting agrees with the feeling that 'the cheese is in the rat trap'. Something just might be brewing inside Bud's mind. Mark says, "Time will tell. Now we just have to be patient and wait it out."

From this moment forward, Bud's actions at the marina are secretly monitored. Bloomburg in Baltimore telephones Lieutenant Moorehaus and explains that the Hopkins family in Baltimore can hire more private investigators to support him whenever he feels it's necessary. He reminds him, that Mark's father has declared that he will never rest until he brings Vera's killer to justice. He wants every step, every second, minute, and hour of Bud's life now under surveillance. He tells Morehouse, "Mr. Hopkins last orders to me were to tell you to do whatever it takes, to see this case solved."

CHAPTER 14

For the next two days, Bud's activities at the marina are completely normal. On the third day, Bud leaves his apartment above the marina office at dusk. Unbeknownst to him, Moorehaus sits in his vehicle, nursing a cold cup of coffee, hidden in a driveway of a vacant neighbor's house. Bud drives his pickup truck a half mile along Route 20 to a blinking yellow light at Main Street, then makes a right turn and drives about six miles down Eastern Neck Island Road towards the wildlife refuge.

Moorehaus follows Bud by about one-half mile. Within a few minutes, Bud's truck crosses over the wooden bridge to the island. The wooden planks rattle from age and disrepair. Bud abruptly parks on the right shoulder. He changes his work shoes for the waterman's boots laying on the floor in front of the passenger seat. He opens his door slowly, quietly. A rusty spring in the door hinge squeaks as Bud pushes the door away from his seat. There's another pause as Bud seems to listen for any sound in the air. There's a complete and eerie silence. He turns his body to his left and both yellow watermen's boots slide to the ground. He quietly closes the door and pauses again to survey everything around him.

Before making another move, he wants to be certain that he is alone, not even a deer around to watch his next steps. Feeling confident, he walks carefully into the marshy wetlands with phragmites and high grass, leading to the shoreline. He tries to feel his way with each step in this special habitat normally used for geese and crabs. .

Meanwhile, Moorehaus stops and parks his vehicle on a curve several hundred yards away. When he sees Bud park his vehicle on the right shoulder, he uses his binoculars to watch Bud carefully look around and then disappear in the high grass. Moorehaus drives his vehicle over the wooden bridge and parks on the left shoulder, facing the direction of on-coming traffic. The tension and pounding in his heart elevates into his mouth as he begins to bite his lip. He can't sit still any longer. He exits his car.

Bud walks another 40 feet along the shoreline and spots a mound of rocks. He removes the top one and picks out a plastic pouch just as the first light of dawn appears. The Bay Bridge lights appear on the far horizon. He grips the pouch tightly in his right hand and retraces his footsteps back to his truck.

When he reaches the door to his truck, Moorehaus suddenly bursts through the high weeds and says, "Been crabbing, Mr. Wayne, without a net?"...

Bud freezes in his tracks until Moorehaus orders him to raise his hands high over his head. Bud drops the pouch behind his head onto the shoulder of the road. Moorehaus pulls one of his hands down and slaps a handcuff on it, followed by the other hand.

He bends over and picks up the pouch from the dirt on the shoulder, then reads Bud his rights, especially the part about 'anything you say may be taken down and used against you in a court of law'."

"You're under arrest for suspicion of withholding evidence in the murder of your wife," he declares. He orders him to walk in front of him as they cross the road to his vehicle. Moorehaus forces him into the back seat, where he applies another set of handcuffs attached to a chain on the floor. He telephones the sheriff's office in Chestertown and gives the dispatch officer a quick rundown of events and requests back up. .

Within 20 minutes, another patrol car is on the scene. The other officer removes Bud's waterman's boots, to be sealed as evidence, and retrieves the pair Bud left in his truck. While Bud puts on his everyday shoes, Moorehaus places the waterman's boots and plastic pouch in separate security bags for identification labeling and eventual transport to the state forensic lab.

He then telephones Virgil Tubbs and gives him a blow-by-blow description of his actions with Bud.

Virgil tells him, "Well done, Lieutenant. Now, let justice take over. And remember to handle those evidence bags like your life depends on it, and get them to the forensic lab as soon as possible."

Once the state lab takes possession of both evidence bags, they will examine the dagger for the presence of fingerprints, blood, or other elements important to the case.

Two days later the District Attorney receives the state lab report, which indicates the presence of traces of Vera's blood still present in the cracks and crevices of the jeweled handle of the dagger. Although Bud had wiped the blade clean after the murder, he had not completely wiped away all evidence of Vera's blood on the handle. Fingerprints belonging to Bud and Mark are also found on the handle.

Morehouse telephones Bloomburg and Mark on a conference call and tells them about the results of the state lab's analysis.

Bloomburg asks about the fingerprints, and is told that they do not have any significance here, since both men handled the dagger at some point before the killing.

Morehouse tells them to be patient a little longer while the District Attorney reconvenes the Grand Jury.

Within the next two weeks, a new criminal case is filed against Bud Wayne, who is placed on trial for perjury. Bud neglected to consider this element: Although he could not be tried a second time for the murder of his wife, he could be tried for lying under oath and denying any knowledge of the Baghdad dagger used to kill his wife.

Public Defender Basil Jablonski consults with Bud in a small prison room and suggests he plead guilty to perjury as a sign of reconciliation and repentance, which would demonstrate his willingness to cooperate with authorities and show a feeling of remorse, anything that might lead the judge to give him a more lenient sentence. It would also save the county the expense of another trial

He tells him, "They have you in a corner, Bud, with no way out that I can see. It's your own doing. You took the bait and retrieved the murder weapon, after telling the Grand Jury that you knew nothing about the dagger."

Bud sighs and shakes his head dejectedly, unable to utter anything intelligible. Jablonski tells him, "Think it over, but you really don't have many choices here, do you? You know where to find me if you need me. One more thing. The DA did not bring up the element of theft here. You could face that charge when you stole the dagger from Mark. So far, the district attorney has not mentioned anything about theft in this case. I just thought you should be aware of this element when you make your decision."

At the courthouse a few days later, Mark walks with Sandy towards the courtroom. He excuses himself, saying, "I'll be with you in a minute. Nature is calling."

She says, "While you're in the Men's Room, I want to see Vera's baby over there." Sandy walks over to Bonnie Bratcher, who hands Vera's baby to her and says, "He's getting heavier every day. I can feel it when I lift him up, or maybe it's the morning sickness that has been draining my energy lately."

Sandy asks, "Bonnie, are you telling me that you're pregnant?"

Bonnie nods her head and says, "It looks that way. I missed my period and the doctor told me to prepare myself for motherhood. The only problem I have now is guessing who the father might be."

Sandy sighs and says, "That's no guessing matter, kid," and returns Vera's baby to the outstretched arms of Bonnie. .She walks towards Mark, who is waiting near the courtroom entrance doors.

The courtroom is filled to capacity. In the third row, sitting side by side are Mark, Sandy, Annette, Reggie, Ruth, and Jean. The bailiff calls the courtroom to order as Judge Bates takes his seat as presiding judge.

He orders, "Bring in the defendant."

Flashbulbs go off as two newsmen take pictures of Bud Wayne entering the courtroom from a side door. Bud is dressed in an orange prison jumpsuit with handcuffs and leg chains.

The judge pounds his gavel and yells out, "There'll be no more picture-taking inside the courtroom." He opens a folder placed squarely on the desktop before him and begins to read the perjury charges against Bud Wayne.

Afterwards, DA Strong rises and declares that an agreement has been reached with the defendant who will plead guilty to the charges of perjury, and rely on the judgment and mercy of the court.

The judge says, "Will the defendant Bud Wayne rise? Do you understand the nature and significance of your plea?"

Bud stands with a hunched back, his body sloping downward in a dejected pose. He nods his head, and mutters, "Yes."

The judge glances down at a document and reads, "Before I pronounce the sentence prescribed by law, I must advise the court that

Bud Wayne has been fully advised of the charges for perjury, to which he is pleading guilty today. The penalty for perjury is very serious, and the sentence must match the severity involved."

The judge adjusts his glasses, blows into a handkerchief to clear his nasal passages, and continues in a louder voice, "Bud Wayne, your guilty plea is noted by the court, by the court, but your conscious and deliberate act to murder your wife in cold blood, is heinous and unforgivable. Frankly, the penalty about to be imposed on you is insufficient to match the severity of your crime. Therefore, Bud Wayne, I hereby impose, as the penalty for perjury, for lying to the Grand Jury and denying any knowledge of the murder weapon used to kill Vera Wayne, a sentence of 22 years in prison without the possibility of parole. Case closed."

The crowd in the courtroom erupts in a thunderous outburst of applause.

The Judge pounds his gavel to restore order and continues, "For you newsmen and women here today, this penalty is the longest sentence ever handed down in the criminal justice system in Kent County of Maryland."

After the Judge finishes his comments to the press, Bud is lifted from his seat by the bailiff, and led away from the courtroom.

"I want to get a closer look at him again," Mark tells Sandy. "I've got to see his face close-up." Mark walks towards the front of the courtroom. When he catches a glimpse of Bud's eyes, he can no longer control his emotions. "You bastard!" he shouts. "You should've gotten life. I hope you rot in hell. No one deserves to die like Vera did."

Without realizing it, Mark gradually pulls Sandy closer to him and begins to weep silently into her shoulder. "It's a tremendous relief from your subconscious mind," Sandy whispers. "Perhaps now you can breathe freely again, Mark." Tears begin to flow from her eyes too. "Perhaps now the fury over being implicated in Vera's murder and all those nightmares will go away, and we can move toward our future."

Within a few minutes the courtroom is empty of everyone, except for Sandy and Mark. Both listen to the haunting, muffled words from the judge that echo off the walls, especially words like 'guilty of perjury', 22 years in prison without the possibility of parole'. They walk slowly over to a window overlooking the courtyard parking lot, and gaze outward.

Mark pulls Sandy closer to him and puts his arm around her shoulder and says, "Isn't that Ruth and her sister Jean talking in the center of the parking lot? I feel sorry for Ruth, who may have to resign from American Airlines and take over, at least temporarily, the management of the family marina, perhaps with a little help from her sister Jean. There will probably be repercussions, a stain on the family's reputation."

Sandy says, "And look down below us at the red Cadillac. Isn't that Vera's car? Do you see Bonnie, carrying Vera's baby, about to enter her Cadillac? Look who's behind the steering wheel. Isn't that Pretty Boy Floyd? .Now isn't that a pretty sight! Vera would be turning in her grave,"

Mark says, "If Bud could see this, he'd be turning in his prison cell."

Floyd starts the engine and begins to drive away from the courthouse parking lot.

Suddenly a Persian cat comes from out of nowhere and jumps up onto the courtroom window ledge. It sits upright, looking out through the window in front of Mark and Sandy, and waves with one paw at its reflection in the window pane.

Mark looks down at the cat, noticing its coat of autumn colors, then peers again through the window and says, "Could this cat be waving to them, seeing Pretty Boy Floyd with Bonnie holding Vera's baby? Doesn't a cat have nine lives, Sandy? Too bad, Vera couldn't have had one of them."

The cat lifts his head upward and yawns with a slight meow, then turns its head 45 degrees and meows again, this time twice as loudly. With steroids, this cat could one day replace *Leo, the MGM lion!*

But what about the dagger worth $500,000? As Billy Wilder said, "But that's another story!"

THE END

GLOSSARY AND PRONUNCIATION GUIDE

(Credit to Gordon Beard who published "Basic Baltimorese" in 1979, '90, '99)

SPELLING	PRONUNCIATION
Aquarium	Quairyum
ambulance	amblanz
Annapolis	Naplis
Anne Arundel	Anne-arunnel
Arab	Ay-rabb
author	arthur
awning	orning
Baltimore	Bawlmer or Balamer
bathroom	baffroom
beautiful	bootiful
bobbed wire	bobwar
bureau	beero
Belair	Blair
Bethlehem Steel	Bethum Steel
careful	keerful
choir	quarr
Columbia	Clumya
complexioned	complected
corrupt	curupt
Curtis Bay	Curt's Bay
dial	doll
Druid-Hill	Droodle
Dundalk	Dundock
eager	igger
eagle	iggle
eat	eht
Elite	Ee-light
escape	excape
Europe	Yurp

Exactly	zackly
film	fillum
fire	far
flu	faloo
for	fur
Fort McHenry	Fert MiKenny
Geography	jografee
Golf	goff
Glyndon	Glenin
goalie	goldie
governor	guvner
Greenmount	Greenmont
hire	har
hired	harred
Howard Street	Harrid Street
horse	hoss
horrible	harble
hospital	hosbiddle
Howard	Harrid
Humid	yewmid
Humidity	yewmidity
idea	i-deer
ignorant	ig-nert
interested	inner-rested
iron	arn
jagged	jaggered
jewels	jools
karate	kroddy
kindergarten	kidneygarden
league	lig
library	lie-berry
Little Italy	Liddleitly
Locust Point	Luck's Point
Lombard Street	Lumbered Street
meringue pie	moran pie
mezzanine	mezz-aline
Maryland	Murlin
Mayor	Mare

next door	neck store
nothing	nothink
awning	orning
Orioles	Oryuls
oyster	urshter
Patapsco River	Patapsico
pavement	payment
please	pa-lease
police	po-leece
Potomac River	Patomac River
pollution	plooshin
portrait	pawtrit
Pulaski	Plaski
quarter	corter
Reisterstown	Ricerstown
rollerskates	rowerskates
royalty	roolty
Sagamore	Sagmor
secretary	sec-er-terry
sewer	sore
Sinai Hospital	Sigh-a-neye Hospital
sink	zinc
soliloquy	sil-lo-kwee
spigot	spicket
Sparrows Point	Sparris Point
tarpaulin	tarpoleon
tomorrow	tuhmar
Towson	Talzin
twenty	twunny
umpire	umpar
up there	uhpair
Vanderbilt	Vandabill
viaduct	vydock
violence	vollince
W	dubya
warder	water
Washington	Warshtin
Westminster	Wessminister

window	winder
Wolf Street	Wuff Street
worse	varse
wrince	wrench
excellent	x-lint
x-rated	x-raided
yellow	yella
you	ya